MISCHIEVOUS

Lies

Warning

This book contains sexually explicit scenes and adult language and may be considered offensive to some readers. This book is intended for adults ONLY. Please store your books wisely, where they cannot be accessed by under-aged readers.

Blurb

Hawke Ivanov is known to excel at two things. Sex and violence. It's why I never took our fling seriously, accepting it with no strings attached.

Except now, his mischievous ways have become all-consuming, and I'm his new obsession, especially after one night that changed everything between us.

Hawke is using me to run away from his own demons, and when I realize it's not only matters of our bodies but hearts as well, I tell him sweet little lies to keep him away.

All I wanted was a good boy in my bed. The last thing I needed was a dangerous man carving his way into my heart, especially when he was the one to be feared the most.

CHAPTER 1

Ivy

"I reckon they're a handful," the guy across from me says as he stares down at my tits. Raising a brow at him, I wonder if I should lean across the table and punch him. Because, let's be honest, his face might look better after a reconfiguration. Or maybe I should let it go. "You have curves—beautiful ones—and I reckon they're a handful," he reiterates as if my delayed response has something to do with a lack of understanding. I try not to laugh as I tuck a piece of my short blonde hair behind my ear.

This is what happens when you decide to go on a spontaneous date with someone off a fucking dating app.

You end up with dickheads.

Some have been enough to entertain me and a few to take the edge off in the bedroom, but none of them are mind-blowing. I like sex. No, I *love* sex. But finding someone who can keep up with my appetite for it–with my demands and not be emasculated by them? Well, that's difficult to find here in Manhattan.

Maybe I need to take another trip to Europe. I ponder the thought as he keeps talking about God knows what.

This guy seems the type to have a pole up his ass and a tiny dick. The moment I let him down, he'll probably call me a slut or a whore because his little man ego can't handle rejection. But in truth, he's fucking punching anyway. Meaning I refuse to lower my standards for any man, and I understand my sex drive is frowned upon comparatively to that of men, but I don't even know why they have such a high level of need when they're predominantly shit at the act. It just always feels like it's missing something.

Despite that, I like to fuck and be fucked.

So fuck them all and society's opinions about a woman getting her fix.

"My place or yours?" he asks, and that brings me back into the conversation. Wow. He really likes the sound of his own voice. Usually, when it gets to this part of the night, I go back to theirs, praying I might at least learn a new trick. I don't need flowery shit. I just need hard fucking.

Except tonight.

It's not happening tonight. No, this one is giving me the ick. No matter how horny I might be right now, I'd much rather use my magical little toy that I know is going to be far more effective. It's not worth letting this guy put his hands on my body, and that speaks volumes as to how much I can't stand him since we've only been sitting here for thirty minutes in a less-than-cute bar, whose drinks are limited to any spirit mixed with soda.

I want to scream. If the date's shit, at least give me a cute cocktail.

"Aww, look, she's on a date," someone interrupts over my shoulder. I recognize the voice, not even tempted to face him.

Sometimes, Manhattan really is too small. My date, who had no issues telling me how amazing he would be in bed or how much of a handful my tits are, goes quiet. And I know why.

I can feel his six-foot-two, built-like-a-truck, lethal presence looming behind me.

Hawke Ivanov.

"Hi," my date, whose name I can't seem to remember, says, licking his lips. His gaze slides from Hawke to me only for a second, as if the moment he breaks eye contact, Hawke might pummel his ass. Which, to be fair, might be accurate, depending on his mood. "Do you know him?"

"No, ignore him," I say, bringing the drink to my lips because handling Hawke can, at times, be far more troublesome than this shit date.

Why is he even here? Trust this asshole to appear out

of nowhere. Shouldn't he be focusing on his own conquests?

"Come on now, lover, you ignoring me?" I bite the inside of my cheek, keeping my eyes glued to my date. And that's when I feel Hawke getting closer, his breath tickling my ear as he leans down and says, "You look real good tonight. Good enough to eat. But I don't know if your date has the appetite for a woman like you."

This cocky, insufferable asshole.

Turning to face him is a mistake because he didn't pull away. Instead, I find his lips hovering against mine. His dark, almost-black eyes take me in. His black hair is messy, and tattoos peek out from the casual shirt he's paired with well-worn jeans.

"You smell even better," he adds, and I open my mouth to unleash hell when his lips suddenly land on mine. His tongue twines with mine, provoking my most primal needs, and it's an immediate dance as he devours me like we're lovers who haven't seen one another for several days. Tingles rush over my skin, and the moment my body wants to pull him in closer is when my senses snap back to reality, and I jerk away.

Hawke smirks. And that deadly and arrogant but utterly gorgeous smile makes me want to kiss him again as much as I want to punch him in the face. And this fucker is definitely someone who deserves it. In fact, I think if it were part of foreplay, I believe he'd get off on it. This guy gives no shits in the world as to who he pisses off. It's part of his charm and also why no one takes him seriously. Until, of course, it's too late. The fucker is a second to the Italian mafia boss, Eli Monti, after all.

Averting my gaze, I see his twin brother, Ford, waiting for him with his hands stuffed into the pockets of his jeans, shaking his head.

I wipe my lips and turn back to my date. Not that this date was going well, but Hawke's nothing but a shit-stirrer, and I adamantly refuse to let him think he's won right now.

"I'm sorry, you'll have to excuse him." I lean across the table, giving my date a cleavage shot, purposely playing into Hawke's games. "Don't worry about him. He prefers penis over vagina, if you know what I mean." I wink at him.

"Oh, he's gay," my date says with a smile, and I can't help but roll my eyes because this guy isn't any fun. He witnessed the way Hawke kissed me, and yet he still believes the jerk is anything but a womanizer. This guy has screws loose, and I can't even pretend to be interested in him anymore. I grab my handbag and stand, but Hawke is blocking my path with that cocky smile.

"You can fuck off," I snap, no longer amused by his antics as I glare at him.

Tonight was meant to be fun, and I'm not going to get that here, so I'll create my own somewhere else. I shove past Hawke, who is laughing. He loves riling me up, and I often throw it back just as much, but tonight, I can't be bothered. I don't even want to know why they're here at this run-down bar, but it probably means they're up to no good.

"Evie!" my date calls out, but I couldn't care less.

"Her name's Ivy, fuckface. Not that I give you permission to use it," Hawke says. Ford simply nods at me as I pass him, an apologetic gleam in his gaze. I like Ford; he's the more stable of the two—in demeanor, at least—and is dating my best friend, Billie, so I'm a bit biased.

His brother, however, can indeed fuck right off. It's been a long time since I've slept with Hawke, and no one within our friends' group knows it. We both know how good it was, and that keeps us in an endless cycle of not wanting one another but interfering when the other tries to hook up with someone else. It's kind of fun, but only when I'm messing with him.

Tonight is his win, but it certainly doesn't end here because Hawke and I are forever in a little war of our own.

The guy might be able to fuck like a god, not that I'd ever admit it to him, but he's also a total ass.

CHAPTER 2

Hawke

Watching her hips sway as she walks out of the room has me fucking hypnotized like always. I can't help the smug smile that pulls at my mouth, knowing I got under her skin yet again, though I'd much rather be under her body or her under me. Either way would be fine with me.

What I like about Ivy the most is she knows exactly the power she holds over men, how they'd almost do anything to spend a night with her. And I'm no exception. I've been caught in her web before, and although I want to fuck her again, I quite like the games we play.

Out of our group of friends, I feel like she's the only one who actually gets me and matches my energy. Right now, she's just sulking because I one-upped her, but I know my girl will come back swinging.

"Think she's coming back?" Her date asks as I turn to look at him and rap the table with my knuckles.

"Sure," I reply. But I know she isn't. A run-down place like this, an unfinished drink, and a guy who looks as boring as watching paint dry will never keep someone like Ivy entertained.

I've fucked a lot of women. I love women. Women are fucking amazing. From their soft skin to the curves of their hips to their puckered lips. To the sweet taste of pussy. Yeah, I fucking love women. And Ivy Walker is probably my favorite woman.

After our one night together, I knew I couldn't be with her again, even though I desperately wanted to. She's addictive, and I get addicted very easily. So, for our families' sake, and ours, I just play with her because seeing her lips pucker and her little nose scrunch is one of my favorite things, apart from what's between her legs.

My twin brother, Ford, joins me as I walk toward the back of the restaurant.

"Kissing her was too much, don't you think?" he asks. "Billie might chop your balls off for doing that. Ivy isn't one of your party girls."

I smirk because Ivy certainly isn't. But he doesn't know we've already been together. It's the great thing about being known as the clown of the group—no one takes me seriously, and they're not surprised by any of the things I do.

"It was just a friendly greeting. I kiss Billie the same

way." He stops dead in his tracks, and I'm quick to say, "You know it's a joke, bro." I laugh, but he's anything but amused. I roll my eyes. Fuck, everyone around us is getting all in their feelings and stepping into relationships and are possessive assholes.

"Let's get this over with," he grits. "We don't want to be late for Mother's dinner." I internally grimace because our mother, Anya Ivanov, can't cook for shit. But if we're late, she legitimately might remove one of our fingers as a consequence. It's what I find so charming about our crazy adoptive mother, who runs the underworld auctions. And our adoptive father, River, who's a gun dealer, will most likely laugh and say he warned us.

I don't bother knocking as I open the door to the office. The man behind the desk pales as he looks up at us.

"I-I have the m-money!" he splutters, and I hear my brother close the door behind us. I crack my knuckles with the same beaming smile I gave Ivy only minutes ago. The truth of the matter is, there's one thing I like just as much as women. And that's blood.

"But we should've received the money yesterday. See where the problem lies?" I ask rhetorically, my smile never dimming.

My brother and I were nothing but street rats when we were kids. We were fortunately stupid enough to break into our adoptive parents' home, and instead of killing us, they took us in. Then we hit the jackpot when we caught the attention of Eli Monti as teenagers. He's around the same age as we are, and our fangs were sharpened to work for the now Italian mafia boss in Manhattan. As his seconds, we get all the fun jobs. And although Ivy's night might've turned to shit, mine's just getting started.

CHAPTER 3

Ivy

Because I go out on a lot of dates, I've become very good at hacking into guys' phones and deleting my number as well as any trace of our meeting. I used to change my number until I realized this way was much more efficient. The men I go out with seem to get attached way too quickly. Even though I explain very clearly that I'm not looking for anything other than one night together, they always try to pursue it further, and I wonder if it's the old saying of wanting what you can't have.

I tried having a boyfriend once. It only lasted a few weeks before I became so bored with the back-and-forth texting and his need to call every night that I had to end it. Talking about the weather, his job, and what I was up to put my brain into snooze mode. So I've decided one night is all a guy gets. Sometimes, if they're decent in bed,

I might see them a few times, but that rarely happens because they only care about their needs, and Lord forbid I use them for my own.

Having the apartment to myself today gives me the opportunity to laze about with only my underwear on. Billie, my best friend and roommate, is at work and will most likely go to Ford's house tonight. She seems to go over there more than he comes here since she picked up a stray cat and made him keep it to make her happy. I'm allergic to cats, so that little fucker wasn't coming anywhere near here. No, thank you to a leaky nose and watery eyeballs.

I grab a bowl, shake some Super Crunch cereal into it, and then pour some milk over it before I sit on the couch, kick my feet up, and watch television—the perfect type of lunch.

My friends call me a serial dater. And while I agree with them, I look at it as exploring all of my options. Why would I settle for one bad lay when I could find multiple, hoping I'll discover a few who know how to use what they have? Who knows how to please and pleasure?

I remember one of my best friends, Hope Ivanov, asking me once who was the best I've ever had in bed. And while I tend to tell my friends everything, I didn't tell her it was her cousin, Hawke.

My grip tightens on my spoon as I think about the audacious asshole from last night and how he's always been one.

The thing about our families is that we're all connected by our parents' underworld dealings and long-term friendships. I've known almost all of them since I was a child. Hawke and Ford were later additions to the gang, coming into our lives when I was thirteen. Anya Ivanov adopted them when they were fifteen, and not much is known about them prior to that. I've always been curious, though, and was even tempted to dive into their history since my father taught me how to dig for information on anyone, but I respect my friends' privacy, so I haven't done it.

When I was first introduced to the twins, I thought they were a little quirky. Not much has changed, but I suppose I also grew into my weird self. Anyone made for this world—the underworld—is bound to have a screw or two loose.

My father, one of the best trackers in the world, is no exception. He's highly intelligent and has the incredible ability to piss everyone off. Contrary to the belief that he's where I get my pranking and carefree nature from, I think I equally get it from my mother, a highly sought-after interior designer who can give it back just as much as my father.

As we grew up, I began to understand the twins a little better, and they couldn't be more opposite from each other. While Ford is seemingly quiet and reserved, Hawke is loud and obnoxious. It's a part of him that I actually love, along with his unwavering confidence. I don't know many men who have the confidence that he has, and I find it very attractive.

Not like that guy I went on a date with the other night, the date Hawke interrupted. Telling me he wanted to grab my tits wasn't confidence, it was stupidity and lacked tact. I had no issue walking out on that date. I did have to erase any trace of myself from his phone, though, because he tried calling me several times and even sent me delusional messages asking if we could meet up again for a "movie" at his place, which happened to be a hostel.

It turns out one has to be more direct because walking out on a date isn't obvious enough to show one isn't interested. But the positive of him casually contacting me so much is that it means that Hawke and Ford didn't go overboard in whatever their business dealings at that restaurant were. I never know what to expect from those two, but often, if they're on the job, it's not good. I suppose that's part of Hawke's charm. I don't go for the bad boys, per se, but that unwavering confidence, even in his job, draws my attention.

I'm mid-bite when the apartment door opens. I turn my head to find my other best friend, Hope, standing there. She doesn't even seem surprised to see me almost naked.

"Welcome home!" I say around a mouthful. I knew she was arriving sometime this week, but wasn't sure when we'd see her. Hope doesn't live with us but often pops in when she's back in Manhattan and not traveling the world for her sculptures. The babe's practically a celebrity in the art world, and for those who truly know her, she's also a socially awkward serial killer. For real.

"Where is your detective?" I ask as she walks in. Not everyone in our circle knows about her fascination for killing people, and honestly, I'm not too fazed by the knowledge. The girl has a type she chooses as her victim —men who try to hurt women, although she did kill a colleague once. Apparently, it was because she was jealous of the woman touching her new beau. Each to their own, I guess. I learned not to judge after half the shit I've seen in my side gig jobs in the underworld. And besides, she's still Hope. But her name's ironic considering her bloody hobby.

This is why it's a big deal that she's dating a detective, especially considering who her family is. Her father is a renowned killer and the twin of Hawke's adoptive mother. They run the underworld auctions, and he's known to be ruthless. The guy's got a screw loose, which is most likely why my father somehow became best friends with him.

"He's at work. I'll see him later," she says as she places her handbag on the table and glances at my bowl of cereal. She shakes her head before I can offer her any. I'm not exactly someone who cares about cooties and back-wash, and besides, I'm of the mentality that sharing is caring, especially of the sexual partners kind. She takes a seat beside me and tucks her feet under her ass.

"I'm surprised he's still alive, to be honest," I reply as I mute the television, far more entertained by our little Hope's love life. She's only two years younger than me, at twenty-two and far more mature, but I certainly didn't expect her to get into anything serious so soon. The two are as grossly loved up as the rest of the fuckers around us lately.

"My parents like him," she says, tucking a piece of her vibrant red hair behind her ear before removing her glasses to wipe them.

I gasp dramatically. "And here I didn't think your papa could like anyone."

She covers her smile with her hand as she looks away, a slight blush streaking her cheeks. It's cute.

"So when's the wedding?" I joke, and her face goes bright red.

"I don't think he likes him *that* much." It goes without saying that I still don't think Alek likes him at all, but probably tolerates him. I don't think that's because of who he is or what he does for work, but simply because it's his little girl. It's the same way I imagine my father would react. The care-free, happy-go-lucky man turns into a prude if he hears about me seeing anyone. Luckily for him, I see a lot of people, so by the time he's tracked and compiled information on the man of the hour, I'm already on to the next. I'm certain he gave up on threatening them when I was a teenager.

"Any new dates you want to tell me about?" Hope

questions curiously. I slurp on the remains of the flavored milk and look at her.

"What do you mean?" I ask. I'm always on a new date, so that shouldn't be such a surprise.

"Hawke mentioned he saw you on a date," she says. I roll my eyes, that little gossip.

"He interrupted my date," I correct as I stand and take my bowl and spoon to the sink. She eyes me and puts her glasses back on. "What?"

"Nothing. It's just..." She thinks about how to word whatever she wants to say. "I think there's something between you and my cousin that neither of you is telling me. You two always have a weird challenge thing going on. And he seemed rather smug about ruining your date."

"Ha! He didn't ruin my date. I was already planning on leaving. Anyway, he can only wish he had that much control over my actions. There's nothing between us, either. You know what Hawke's like; he gets on everyone's nerves."

"And yet everyone loves him," she points out.

"As much as they want to strangle him. Listen, it's just a little game we play with one another, that's all. And, besides, he's your *cousin*."

"That doesn't mean he's off-limits to you. And I have eyes; I can see how he looks at you."

I smirk and glance down at my perfect tits. "I can't

blame him. He is but only a man and one who thinks mostly with his dick."

She smiles. I'm bigger than most girls, with curves, tits, and an ass, and I fucking love my body. Not that I'd ever admit it to Hawke, but I love his body, too. It would appear I'm just better at hiding it than he is.

"If you say so," she says, still smiling, and I dislike the way she looks all-knowing or as if she's clued into something I'm not.

Yes, there's sexual tension between me and Hawke, but it's not that deep. And she should be so loved up that she can't focus on anything else. It seems like that's how everyone else is.

"What do you plan to wear to Dutton's birthday this weekend?" she asks.

I grin because I'm known for my outfits. My wardrobe is one thing I take great pride in, and if I get the chance to dress either Billie or Hope, I do. Not that there's anything wrong with their clothes or style. I just always wanted a little sister, and so they humor me. None of us has sisters, so we've become sisters for each other, especially growing up together.

"Who said I'm going?" I ask mischievously.

She raises a perfectly manicured brow. "Since when have you ever not gone to a party? And, besides, Dutton might've invited some interesting men."

I try to hide the smile as I walk back over to her. She

does know me well enough, and these last few weeks, I've been striking out on the men front.

"I'll consider it. Are you bringing your detective?" I'm asking for selfish reasons. If no men grab my attention, then the potential tension of having a dirty cop in a room full of criminals interests me greatly.

"No, he's working."

"And he can't take time off for this?"

"He said he would, but I'm still not comfortable with it all," she admits, and my bubbling anticipation of the drama recedes because I see how anxious she is. She might've found her man and is enjoying their love bubble, but outside of that, in the real world, relationships look complicated.

I rest my arm over her shoulders and give her a reassuring smile. "Your family accepts him, and you know that says a lot," I remind her. She lets out a shaky breath and gives me a half smile, putting me at ease that I reassured her slightly. Hope, despite being a serial killer, is a good girl. A little morbid, maybe, but her heart is in the right place when it comes to her family. However, her social awkwardness and introverted ways, get the best of her, which is why we balance each other because I am the party, no matter where I go.

"Thank you, Ivy," she says, but is quick to put up her hand. "But please don't hug me; it's awkward enough when you have clothes on."

I click my tongue and throw myself back against the

couch cushion as I grab the remote. "Ah, come on, I'll let you have a tit squeeze for free," I joke. "But seriously, I'll go to the party, so you don't have to stand around by yourself."

She lets out an easy breath, and I can't help but smile as I add, "Who knows, I might even bring a date to stir some things up. Daddy Walker would totally be pissed."

Sometimes I bring bottom-of-the-barrel dates if I know my parents are attending, just to fuck with my father. My mother clued in on it years ago, and now she challenges me to find specific types of guys to push my father's buttons further. I love it.

Hope laughs, cozying up to watch television with me. "Of course you would."

CHAPTER 4

Hawke

The hands of the two women I'm currently with touch me everywhere. My mother likes to say I have ADHD, but I like to say I have charisma. We agree to disagree on many things, but my stamina is not one of them. Not that I discuss that with my mother, of course.

"Hawke," one of them says before her lips wrap around my cock.

Fuck.

She takes me as far as she can as the other one grabs my hand and places it on her tit. I can't help myself as I reach forward and pull her closer so I can play with her cunt. The one on my cock gags as I thrust my hips up.

"Hawke." I look to the redhead, whose pussy is currently taking my fingers very well, just as the door bursts open.

Eli comes to an immediate stop and gives me an unimpressed look, and my brother almost crashes into him from behind. Neither of them appears surprised at what they see.

"Fucking hell, Hawke. Really? Here?" Eli grumbles as he enters his office. But I'm so close. I fixate on the blonde positioned on her knees in front of me as I slide my fingers out of the redhead's pussy and put them in my mouth. We've been at it for thirty minutes now, and I need to blow.

She scrapes her teeth lightly over my cock. It's not how I told her I like it, but it's enough to get me over the edge as I slam my cock into the back of her throat and come. I grunt as I jerk into her. *Finally*, I thought I was never going to come.

That's when I look back up at Eli and Ford, who are looking elsewhere, and I smirk. It's not the first time they've walked in on me having sex, and it won't be the last. I don't know why everyone gets weird around fucking. It's literally one of our most instinctual acts. And my personal favorite.

"You were late, and I was bored," I say, smiling as I look over at the woman who is putting her dress back on and trying not to smile. As for Eli's newest employee, I look down on her, stroking her cheek as she swallows like a good girl. When she pulls away, she wipes her mouth. She has the same look that most women I fuck have— one of disbelief that they just did that. The question is whether she should be coy or impressed. Perhaps her boss walking in on her isn't ideal, so I say, "Don't worry about him, he's usually a grumpy ass anyway."

She tries to hide the smile as she gets up from her knees.

"Get back to work," Eli growls as he sits at his desk where I was leaning while getting sucked off. He doesn't even look at the women. Lord forbid this pussy-whipped fucker looks at anyone but his wife. Ford follows him like a shadow, which is not that surprising, and he also ignores the women who are quick to vacate the room.

I tuck my cock back into my pants. These two are all loved up, and they reprimand me for still getting mine where I can just because I'm not a love-sick fool and prefer variety.

Eli pours himself a whiskey on ice. He doesn't offer Ford one because Ford doesn't drink, but I accept the fine whiskey, having acquired an expensive taste since working for Eli. With that said, I'll just as easily drink from a cheap bottle, too. Ford and I practically raised ourselves on the streets, so I'm still in the habit of being able to stomach anything.

"Have the preparations been finalized for Dutton's party?" Eli asks, looking over some paperwork.

Ford and I stand across from him.

"Yes," I reply.

Throwing a party in his club isn't exactly hard for someone like me. However, I would've much preferred it if we'd thrown it at Dutton's gentlemen's club. It's been one of my favorite spots since he took over.

Lucy's, which is the club Eli owns and where his main office is, is where we'll be hosting this year. It was a wonderful surprise when I showed up today to find a new employee among the staff. And, of course, I had to approve them.

"Do we even want to look at the guest list?" Ford asks me.

I smirk. "You put me in charge of it for a reason, right? Party, party," I say, and he rolls his eyes. The thing with Dutton is he prefers lowkey, which is precisely why the entire club will be packed. Yes, the public can line up to come in, but I've sent an invite to everyone and anyone we know. It's going to be a good fucking night.

The club has been staged differently, with decorations, extra security, and the booths completely blocked for our more intimate group only.

Eli takes another sip of his drink. "Everything seems to be going smoothly this month," he says, almost bored. When Eli first officially took over from his father, Crue Monti, a dull day was rare.

People initially tested boundaries with Eli, and met with him directly or us in his stead. Either way, it was never pleasant. Hits were made, even from his wife, Jewel, and we'd dealt with multiple shifts in our dealings and new contracts, so with all that happening, it's fair to say we were more on edge during that time.

In our line of work, a quiet day is like the calm before a storm. I credit Eli, though, for how quickly he resolves issues, often by torture and death. He's lethal. If someone's caught in his web, they don't usually walk away alive. He's also spending more time with Jewel, which means, by default, we're not with him as much, and I'm becoming bored. No one to hunt, to kill, to even intimidate a tiny bit. My only outlets are the gym, partying, and sex.

As for tonight... I've already gone to the gym today, so it's time to do my two other favorite things. And, yes, I realize I've already blown my load once today, but you can never have too much sex, right?

CHAPTER 5

Ivy

Do I want to go to the party?

Yes, of course.

Am I disappointed my parents are out of town on a random Europe trip they didn't tell me about?

That answer is also yes.

So I didn't bring a date because, frankly, the only reason I was going to was to piss off my dad. I even had a bird watcher lined up as my plus one. I don't care so much what people's hobbies are, but I know my father won't tolerate much, let alone a bird watcher. My father is far from being at one with nature, which is why the guy would've been the perfect date.

I'm running late, but that's probably no surprise to anyone. I considered inviting a handful of dates all at the same time, just to see how that situation played out, but as I went through the app and came across the profile of the dickhead I went on a date with last week, I ended up removing the app from my phone entirely.

Maybe I'm turning a new leaf, you know? Maybe I plan to start fresh and not date and fuck so many people.

I try not to snort at that thought. I'm just going to catch them the old-fashioned way. I've been using dating apps for almost a year, and I'm honestly not a fan, even if it is easy to get dick from them.

I receive another text message from Hope as I approach the entrance to Lucy's, I feel almost smug as I see the line of people who look irritated when I walk straight in.

"Good to see you, Ivy," the bouncer says with a smile. I squeeze his shoulder.

"You too. Promise me it'll be a fun night." I laugh.

"Always when you're around," he jokes, and I stride inside like I own the place. Most bouncers know me because of my family. And because—let's be real—I'm a good time. I'm trouble only in the number of hearts I break. But that doesn't pay their salary.

My phone buzzes again, reminding me of the text from Hope, and I check it.

Hope: Where are you? You're late.

I adjust my short, blonde hair, making sure it's slicked back. I'm wearing a light pink dress that fits like a glove and stops just below my ass. I paired it with my favorite silver heels that sparkle under the fluorescent lights.

My soul purrs with satisfaction as soon as the music pours into my ears, and I sweep my gaze over the crowd. Tonight is going to be fun.

I look up to my left, where I see the designated spot for Dutton's party. It's the usual section we claim when we're here. I head toward the familiar group, spotting Hope first. It seems like a sigh escapes her as she sees me walking up the stairs. Bouncers guard both the top and bottom of the stairway.

The one at the top smirks and says, "No breaking hearts tonight?"

"Me? I would never," I lie. I like going to these places; they make me feel comfortable, and I know no matter what happens, I'm safe. I'm a party girl through and through, but the reality is, I'm still a woman, so it never hurts to be extra safe.

Hope pulls me in straight away, holding a drink in her hand that barely looks touched.

"You're late," she grumbles, and I know it's most likely because her social battery is already dying. Even around just family and friends, she flickers out quickly.

"Fashionably late, right?" I ask, waving a hand down my new dress.

She shakes her head, trying not to smile. "Always.

Billie ran off with Ford ten minutes ago, leaving me here by myself." Pretty sure they're fucking in some dark nook somewhere, or maybe his car. They seem to do that a lot.

"I'm going to miss her when she moves out," I say wistfully. We've already started packing her things. And although I don't see her that much with her job, and now that she's with Ford, it'll be different having the apartment entirely to myself. "Want to move in yet?" I ask Hope with a nudge.

She rolls her eyes. "I won't be a consolation prize. Besides, I told you I'm looking for my own apartment."

Which translates to she's also fucking her detective nonstop and most likely going to move in with him soon. Everyone's become a buzzkill. I'm happy for them, but I just don't get it. I thought I was a ho, but it turns out that when they've got someone specifically for them, they're at it all the time. I ponder the idea of having only one person, and the image in my mind becomes blurry. I can't imagine it or what that person would look like to keep me hooked for long enough.

"Where's Posie?" I ask, glancing over her shoulder at the others seated around and spotting her straight away.

She gives me an eye roll. "With Dutton."

"I should've expected that since we're technically here for *his* birthday." All I care about is that it's an excuse to hang with my girls.

When she steps to the side, Dutton and Eli stand

from the leather booth in the corner. I see multiple bottles on the table and lick my lips with anticipation. Posie and Jewel are in a deep discussion in the back of the booth the guys just got up from.

"Happy birthday," I say to Dutton, who offers me one of his charismatic smiles. They've always given me chills. Although he's the older brother of one of my best friends, there's always been something unsettling about Dutton. I know he'll never hurt me, but his cold demeanor beneath those smiles is terrifying. For the life of me, I don't know how Posie wore him down.

"Thank you. Now, I'm depending on you to get my wife very drunk tonight while my parents babysit," he says, keeping that smile.

I angle my head, looking at Posie and Jewel, who each take a shot. "I don't think she needs my help, but I can promise a good time nonetheless." I salute him.

He joins Eli at the edge of the railing, overlooking the crowd. I hear him say to Eli, "I don't even know half of these people. You put Hawke in charge, didn't you?"

I smirk at that because although Dutton knows a lot of people, I imagine half of the business people he's acquainted with have a pole up their asses. If they wanted a party, then Hawke is the person to go to.

Posie and Jewel finally spot us as we get closer to the booth. "You came," Posie cheers, pulling me into a hug while Jewel nods her head and pours me a drink. Jewel is probably one of the deadliest women I have ever met. She is fucking great with a gun, and that's saying something, considering I know Anya Ivanov. Jewel and Posie are the newest to the crew, and I like them both, but it still baffles me how they were able to leash their murderous men.

"Wouldn't miss it," I say and accept the drink Jewel offers me.

"Still no Billie?" Jewel asks, trying to hide her smirk.

Hope shakes her head.

"Fifty bucks says they're in his car. That's where I first caught Ford and Billie in their 'trying to keep the relationship a secret' phase."

"I found them coming out of my pantry," Jewel adds with a smirk, and we all laugh as we take a sip of our drinks. I sigh as I let the music take over my body, acting as a natural relaxant. I can't wait to dance the night away.

That is, until a loud laugh booms from behind me, grating on my nerves. Hawke walks up the stairs with a woman. Of course, he has a woman with him. Does that man ever not have a woman with him?

I doubt it.

Instead of going to his usual booth farther back in the open room that looks over the rest of the club, he heads straight over to us.

"No fucking in front of my wife," Eli growls as he walks past.

Hawke simply laughs as he throws an arm around the woman he's with. I can't hear his smart-ass reply as he scans the booth, but before he looks at anyone else, his gaze stops on me. I haven't seen him since his assholery interrupted my date.

I straighten my back and offer him a smile, even though we both know it's anything but friendly. He always sees it as a game; I enjoy it just as much. I don't like it when he has one up on me. His arrogant smile kicks up as if reading my thoughts, and his hand drops from the woman he's with as he stops in front of me. I maintain eye contact because I refuse to show any type of submission to this asshole. It's the song and dance we play.

He might be intimidating to a lot of people, but he's not to me, and I think that irks him the most. Not that he tries to intimidate women, but he's used to them falling into submission in other ways.

"Lover," he says to me in greeting, and I give him my best eye roll. He takes the seat next to me, angling himself in my direction. His whole body facing me makes it awkward for his date to try and sit beside him, so instead, she sits across from us and uncomfortably looks away from Jewel, who's intimidating as all shit to anyone who doesn't know her.

"Hawke," I reply before looking away and shaking my head. This guy's such an asshole.

"I've missed you," he says, and I sigh, staring up at the ceiling and asking for strength to deal with this jackass tonight. Hope is observing us both carefully. But I realize the others are too.

"You can leave now." I wave him off and then turn to the others again as if to pick up where we left off.

"Good luck, Hawke," Jewel says with a smug expression as she stands, and I can't help but replicate her look. I really like her. She saunters over to Eli, who makes room for her at his side.

"Want to explain why Hawke's calling you lover?" Posie asks as she leans back as if enjoying the show.

I expel a sigh. Hawke's shit-stirring doesn't come as a surprise.

This fucker isn't going to leave.

I roll my eyes. He's had it as my name in his phone since we fucked years ago, but he's most likely using it openly to rub in the fact he thinks he ruined my last date. Which is far from the truth. I don't really care if they find out about Hawke and me, but it always seemed easier to keep it between us. We had sex to see if we were compatible in that way. We are. That's that. Check it off the list.

"I saved her from an awful date the other night," Hawke begins, but I cut in.

"This asshole here thought he'd be funny and try to ruin my date, but I was already planning on leaving," I say, correcting his version of the story. Then I address his date, who is awkwardly sitting by herself. "Hi, you fucking Hawke?" I ask her, bringing her into the conversation. Her cheeks go red at my question, and she looks to him for help. Oh, fuck me, he's caught himself a little lamb.

"Not yet, but we will be. Isn't that right, sweetheart?" he croons with an arrogant smirk. I can't help but bite my bottom lip. He calls them all sweetheart when he doesn't remember their name. Payback can be so sweet.

"What's her name?" I ask him, and he glares at me, his smug expression dropping. She goes to speak, but I lift a finger and hold it up to her. "What's your date's name, Hawke?" I ask again.

"Why are you so mean to me today, lover? You know, I don't know her name." I drop my hand as his date gapes at him in shock. I'd like to think I'm doing her a favor by showing her what an ass he is, but I know he can charm himself out of almost anything. "I'm sorry, it was loud when you told me your name down there."

I laugh as I stand and tap him on the shoulder, saying, "Let me pass." Then I turn to Posie and Hope and ask, "Should we dance?" They both nod, and I grab my drink.

Hawke is staring up at me, that mischievous glint in his eye. "You'll have to climb over me, lover."

I smile sweetly and lean into him. He thinks I'm doing it to shuffle over him, but instead, I whisper into his ear as I press my knee close to his balls, forcing him to move back. "The only thing I'll be climbing over is your dead body, *lover*."

He chuckles as he lets me through, and I feel rather smug as I sashay toward the stairs.

"I never understand you two," Hope comments from behind me.

Posie laughs and says, "Can't blame him for trying; you're hot as fuck."

"I couldn't agree more," I reply with an appreciative smile.

I throw back my drink, more than ready to enjoy the slight buzz it's sure to give me. After ridding myself of my glass, I notice a lot of familiar faces, both family and friends. There are also a lot of people here that I don't know, which is a good thing, especially while I'm on the dance floor. I love to dance, and I especially love enticing men with my dancing. Don't get me wrong, I do it for myself, but dancing is an easy way for me to see which men are ballsy enough to approach me and which one I might be inclined to go home with. I think when two people dance, it's so fucking sensual, it's almost a form of fucking.

"Damn girl, get it. I'm surprised you never tried to get a job at Pearl," Posie shouts over the music. I offer her a devilish smirk. Pearl is the Gentlemen's Club that Dutton owns, where he first met Posie as a dancer. She's since changed roles, as Dutton doesn't let her dance for anyone but him now.

"I suggested it once, but Billie was against me working at one of her brother's clubs. Besides, I think the 'don't fuck the clients' rule would get in my way of having fun." I laugh. Hope awkwardly bops, nowhere near drunk enough for the dance floor. *Yet.*

Posie laughs as she not-so-subtly points at some guy. "He looks *very interested,*" she says. I recognize the guy, though I can't remember if I've hooked up with him before, with or without sex. Some nights get blurry. His gaze is glued to my hips as I sway them, feeding my feminine ego.

I approach him, letting his bold hands pull me in when I'm close enough. I wrap them around me and place them on my ass and hips, giving him full rein. The contact right now is everything I need, and I hope he doesn't speak much so he doesn't ruin the attractive face and sizeable arms. He's just my type. Billie once joked that my love language is physical touch, but I didn't need to take a test for something I already knew.

"I saw you walk in," he says loud enough to be heard over the music. Of course, he did. It's a pity I don't remember his name. I'm trying to rack my brain as to where I know him from. "You look as beautiful as always, Ivy."

Listen, I don't need sweet talk, but it definitely helps a girl's ego, that's for sure. I'm not model size, but it's never been relevant when I learned at a young age to embrace my curves, and that confidence will stop any man in his tracks. I have hip dips, a chubby midsection, and thick thighs accompany my luscious ass and large tits. Every single man I have been with has worshipped my body because *I* worship my body. I would never let a man talk ill of me. And I wouldn't do it to myself either.

"Any chance you want to leave soon and head to my place?" he asks, turning me in his arms. Then his mouth finds my ear, and he starts trailing kisses up and down my neck.

"To yours?" I question, deciding not to push him away because I like this type of worship. But also, the party has only just begun, though, and I'm tempted to string him along for the night until I'm ready to leave. It fuels me to know I can have him so quickly.

Before he can answer, someone bumps into us, and I barely miss having a drink spilled on me.

"What the fuck ma—" my toy boy starts, but then snaps his mouth closed and pales as he sees the size difference between himself and his opponent.

Hawke hasn't even noticed us as he makes out on the dance floor with his *sweetheart*. Her arms are around his neck, and her legs are wrapped around his hips as she grinds against him.

You have got to be kidding me.

The thing about Hawke is I never know when something is accidental or he's childishly trying to grab my attention.

I scoff at them loud enough that his gaze flicks over to me while he continues to kiss her. He's smirking as he pulls back and leans into her, biting at her earlobe, his gaze never wavering from mine, as if he's trying to taunt me.

I turn toward my guy, so I'm back-to-back with Hawke, and he doesn't have to deal with him.

"Not getting enough protein, obviously," I say snidely to Hawke as I set my guy's hands on my waist again.

"Just building an appetite," Hawke replies over his shoulder. I don't even bother replying because we could go back and forth with this shit all night. Though, it does give me smug satisfaction when his gaze drops to my ass before his sweetheart directs his attention back to her.

I push myself against the guy I'm dancing with. I really have an issue with remembering people's names. Despite being able to easily collect data on almost anyone, when it comes to men in person, they all seem to blur for me. Moving to the beat of the music, I drop my head to the side, giving my dance partner all the invitation he needs to start kissing my neck again.

"Let's get out of here," he says again, and I rub up against him, my hips moving faster. I can hear his breathing pick up and feel the slow rise of his cock. I love this power, knowing that he wants me and I'm in complete control of everything that will happen past this point.

It's a woman's gift, in my opinion, once we learn how to harness it.

Also known as pussy power.

He wants this.

Pity my mind is on the dickhead behind me, who, when I glance over my shoulder at him, is still watching me.

This guy is truly insufferable.

Luckily, the night is young.

I whisper into the guy's ear with a smile. "Come find me later. I'm not done with my girlfriends yet, but I'll go home with you."

"What, just like that, you're going to leave?" he asks, and I wave goodbye as I go back to where Hope and Posie are.

"Damn, girl, you're like a Venus flytrap," Posie says approvingly.

Hope is shaking her head. "Care to explain what's happening between you and Hawke? And don't tell me nothing. You two have so much sexual tension, it makes me want to be sick."

I laugh as a waitress comes over with a tray of drinks for us. We look up at Jewel, Eli, and Dutton, who are watching us. Jewel salutes with her drink, obviously, the one who sent the drinks. I definitely like her.

I grab what smells like vodka and Red Bull. Come to Mama.

"You girls don't fuck around," Posie says, throwing back her drink as Hope does the same. I try not to laugh as I finally respond to Hope.

"I like to toy with him, and he does the same in

return," I tell her with a shrug of my shoulders. It's not a total lie. I do love to toy with him.

"Looks like I'm not the only one playing games," I say as I look pointedly at her detective, who's pushing his way through the crowd.

Hope pauses when she sees Braxton. I can't help but smirk as I look back up at Eli and Dutton, who are staring at him. He's welcome here, to a degree, but everyone is still on edge about Hope's new boyfriend. He's shown his loyalty to her father, but respect has to be earned amongst these ranks. Macho shit, even though I'm certain they have already accepted him, they like busting newcomers balls.

I sense Hawke's approach and put my hand up in his direction before I even face him, knowing him well enough. He stops in his tracks, always overtly protective of the women in our group, like a big brother. He scowls at me, and I make a shooing motion with my hands.

Braxton joins us, and I can't help but feel overjoyed for Hope and the way she looks at him. She's found someone who accepts her exactly how she is. Yet there's a small part of me that feels like I'm being left behind. Basically, everyone is part of a couple now, and I still can't understand the appeal.

But that's above my pay grade. I grab another drink from the tray and hand it to Braxton. He frowns at it, but I encourage him to take it. "What's wrong, detective? A little sugar gives you heart palpitations?"

"I've been warned about what nights out with you can be like," he says with a charming smile as he accepts it.

Hope tries not to grin as he scoops her in for a kiss.

"It's not me you might have to worry about tonight," I say as I take another sip, my hips finding the rhythm again as I dance.

CHAPTER 6
Hawke

A vision in fucking pink, that's exactly what she is. She has curves for days that can hypnotize any man. The way she moves, the way she dances. Fuck, the way she dances. I couldn't keep my eyes off her on the dance floor, even with another woman in my arms. That's the hold Ivy has over men, and I'm but a mere mortal.

Hours of drinking and the countdowns begin. I wanted to give this party a theme of resetting, and have a countdown at midnight so everyone has a reason to take another shot and make out. And I love the way it makes the birthday boy uncomfortable. He's used to controlling everything, but he certainly doesn't seem to be complaining as Posie grinds against him. He whispers something in her ear, and she giggles. And in the next minute, they can't be found.

Billie and Ford came back for a little bit but have once again disappeared. I swear, my brother's new addiction would concern me if I didn't see the way Billie looks at him. I was in denial about the two of them when I first caught them in the act. I didn't want my brother to get hurt or for me to be forgotten on the wayside. I'm a selfish prick, I know that, and it seems ever since that day he got poisoned...

I throw back another drink. No matter how much I try to block out that day and the all-consuming grief around it, it repeatedly bubbles up. It doesn't matter how much I drink or how much sex I have. None of it is enough to push away the demons from that day.

I hear Ivy's laughter before I see her, which snaps me out of my depressing thoughts. I haven't opened up to anyone about that day I found Ford and Billie in the bunker, my brother fighting for his life. I haven't expressed that the dead, staring eyes of the woman I put a bullet in as she tried to escape the scene after attempting to kill him still haunt me.

We vowed never to hurt women.

And yet I had.

I follow Ivy's laughter from the bottom of the stairs back to the VIP area as it inevitably brings me back from those harrowing thoughts. They don't often appear when I'm out partying, but sometimes, like tonight, they do.

The woman I've been making out with all night went

to join her friends for a bit. I could've taken her back to my place hours ago, but I didn't, choosing to stay here instead.

My eye twitches as I spot the detective with my cousin, Hope, perched on his lap. I don't like him. He pisses me off... much in the same way I piss other people off, I suppose. But he makes her happy, supposedly, but the moment he hurts her, I'll happily break his legs.

Ivy goes to stand, but I block her path. She opens her mouth to curse, but when she notices it's me, she looks away. I push farther into her space so she can't focus on anyone but me. I can't help but tease her. Lately, she feels like the only one left who wants to have fun. And that's what I need right now.

When she looks up at me, those gorgeous blue eyes find mine, and I can't help but reach out and place a finger under her chin. I can tell the others are watching our interaction, but I don't care much for what anyone thinks. Ivy scowls at me, and the disapproving glare makes my cock twitch.

"Why so sour, lover?" She hates it when I call her that, and I love it. She is by far the best I've ever fucked, and the only one I would gladly keep going back to. Over and over again. Not that she's ever given me the chance. "You sure did give me a show." I wink at her. "When you were rubbing up on him, did you think of me?"

She places her hand on mine and smiles. That vicious little tug of her lips is more enticing than it should be to any sane man. Which I am certainly not. "Not much to think about is there?" she replies, staring directly at my cock.

I rub my thumb against her bottom lip contemplatively. She's at the perfect height to blow me, and her eyes dance with mischief as if she knows exactly what I'm thinking. "You didn't deny it, so I guess that was a yes."

"Eww, not in front of me," Hope squawks, and I laugh as I give Ivy space.

"Like you're one to talk, little red," I say as I sit across from Ivy and glare at Braxton. The fucker has the audacity to smirk at me as his hand slips under my cousin's top.

"I'm surprised they've left you unwatched," I growl at him, and Hope reprimands me immediately. I put my hands up in defense. How the fuck am I the bad guy for looking out for her?

"I could say the same for you," Braxton retorts. I feel my left eye twitch. I want to kill this fucker.

"Stop. Both of you," Hope says, exasperated. "Braxton, let's go get a drink." She stands up, pulling him with her. We all look at the numerous bottles in front of us, and I smile because it's obvious she's making him leave on my account.

That's when I notice Eli coming up the stairs. He's staring at Braxton the same way I am. Though he might be a dirty cop, it'll take me a lifetime to trust him, even if my cousin loves him.

"He's a smartass," I tell Eli as he taps me on the shoulder.

"Probably why you two get along," he replies. "My wife has decided she wants to make a mess of my back, and because I don't want to bleed all over my office, we're going home."

"Too much information," I say quickly. My boss and his wife have some blood kink. I ain't judging, but I'm not saying I want to walk in on it either.

I nod, and his gaze bounces from Ivy and then back to me before he says, "Play nice." I smirk as I turn to her. She's looking away, trying to ignore me as she takes a sip of her drink. When Eli's gone, the silence and tension between us build. I don't like silence. I also don't like being alone.

"Lover." Her gaze slides back my way, and I know she wants to say something, wants to let something slip from those beautiful lips, but she keeps them locked tight. She does this punishing game sometimes, and I love falling into her trap, every time coaxing her frustration out of her.

Moving to the seat next to her, I reach for her, and she comes willingly, sitting right on my lap.

"Going to blame this on the alcohol?" I ask with a smug expression. I've seen Ivy drunk plenty of times, and let's just say our bodies are a little more honest with one another once the alcohol hits. My favorite part is when our clothes come off, not that she's let me take her again. But that one time was enough to destroy me.

"Do you think you can just touch me whenever you want?" she asks in a seductive voice. Ivy knows too well what she does to me.

"Yes," I smirk and lean in. "Because you like it."

She doesn't deny it but simply *hmphs* at me as she slides her hand over her short blonde hair, making sure it's still slicked back. I love the way her hair is styled, how she looks, how she *smells*. My nostrils flare as I take her in, and I can tell she's trying not to smile.

"You think you're so irresistible to women, don't you?" I arch an eyebrow and look her up and down, making a point that she's exactly where I want her.

She smiles in that wicked way of hers, and it's like watching a switch being flipped. One moment, it's mean Ivy. The next it's seductive Ivy, and the latter is the most dangerous version of her because I know she'll lead me into something before dropping me short of letting me have what I really want. *Her.*

She grabs my hands and pulls them around her waist as she sizes me up as if she's about to kiss me. I'm staring at her, almost begging that she does. She starts rocking her ass against my cock, and her smile grows wider.

She knows I would never push her away or turn her down. I'm just a man, after all, and she's a woman, the most gorgeous woman I've ever laid eyes on. Having her on my lap feels right. Sexually, we're the perfect fit.

Ivy spots my "date" first, and her hips start moving faster. The woman's eyes go wide. Threesomes aren't for everyone, but by reputation alone, women know not to get territorial over me. I'm here for a good time, not a long time. And what fascinates me is everyone's sexual curiosity.

"Come, Hawke wants to tell you something," Ivy says to her, grinding her hips against my cock, which is standing at attention for her. Fuck, the weight of her feels good, my mind quickly thinking about her sweet pussy. I welcome my date with a smile as she steps closer, somewhat unsure of herself. I encourage Ivy's hips to move faster. Jesus Christ, the woman knows precisely how to unravel me.

Ivy beckons her to dip closer, and when she does, Ivy whispers into her ear, "He likes it when you flick your tongue on the tip." I groan. Not because of her words, but because of what her ass is doing to my fucking cock. "But don't expect him to last long," she bites out with a grin. I don't bother to reply, and she's quick to reach down and grab my cock. Hard. I groan again, losing any smart-ass comeback.

That's when Ivy finally looks at me and chirps, "Have fun with your date," as she stands.

I immediately grab her wrist. I don't know what it is about Ivy that drives me out of my mind. But it was her laughter that brought me out of the memories and thoughts I was trying to drown out moments ago. And I suddenly don't want to lose that.

"Stay," I command.

Her blue eyes narrow, and she almost seems disappointed. "No comment about not lasting long?"

"You know that's not true," I growl, more worried about my hardening cock that's no longer getting any attention.

"That's a no. Goodnight," she says with a smirk. She pulls out of my grip, her hips swaying as she walks away.

And I know that was payback for interrupting her date the other night.

Damn, that woman is amazing.

CHAPTER 7

Ivy

Hope is waiting for me at the bottom of the stairs. She looks exhausted, most likely from being out for so long and having to deal with so many people.

"Where did your detective go?" I ask.

"He's getting the car so we can go home. Want a lift?"

I search the dance floor. Most of the night, I kept tabs on the guy I was dancing with earlier until he started vomiting in the corner and was escorted out. There are other prospects here, but I'm not entirely immune to the way I was dry humping Hawke. It was hard to remove myself from his lap, and I know if I go home with anyone else tonight, I'll be more frustrated, and then I'll be having to use my vibrator.

Unfortunately, Hawke has that effect on me.

"I'm done for the night," I say. "Besides, tomorrow I have some work to do, and I promised to help Billie pack. Look at me being all responsible." That's all true, but my sexual frustration might also have a part to play. My pussy is pounding, but I refuse to give Hawke the satisfaction. And it makes me even more irritated at having to deny myself once again what was the most fantastic fucks I've ever had. But if I give in, the asshole will be so smug.

Hope briefly glances up toward where Hawke is watching us, then turns and leads us to the exit. "I'm not going to say anything," she states.

"Good. Because there's nothing to say." I smile at her sweetly. I don't bother looking back in Hawke's direction as we leave, though I can feel his gaze penetrating my back.

"Early night, Ivy?" the bouncer at the door asks, almost sounding disappointed. I chuckle as I tip him a hundred bucks.

"Just don't tell anyone. I've got a reputation, you know?" I joke, and he chuckles.

As promised, Hope's detective is parked at the curb, waiting for us. She slides into the front, and I hop into the back seat as I take in the ridiculous lineup of people waiting to get inside the club.

I sigh heavily.

"I need to get laid," I say, sulking.

Braxton coughs as if surprised by my honesty, and Hope laughs.

"That one vodka and Red Bull kicking your ass?" I ask. "You have your detective anytime you want sex. I have no one."

"Ivy Walker, you don't fail in getting sex when you want it. Most men would grovel to be in the same room as you, let alone have sex with you." I smile and lean forward to kiss her cheek.

"Thanks, Hope. You sure know how to boost a girl's confidence."

"You are the only woman I have ever met who needs no help in that department," she replies, and I wonder why I was sulking in the first place. I've often dealt with my sexual frustration easily, but lately, men seem to be irritating me more than usual. Or maybe I've just met too many bad eggs in a row, even if I'm only looking for fun.

I catch sight of Hope's hand in Braxton's, and I quickly look away.

Vomit.

All this relationship shit seems a little over the top. But as I look at their clasped hands again, I realize I've never seen everyone so damn happy. Even with their own personal obstacles, they're all glowing from their monstrous fucking. And I, the one known to fuck the most, seem to be going in the opposite direction.

A terrible thought comes to mind. What if I'm slowly turning celibate?

A moment of panic strikes me, and then I shake it off.

There's no way. I like to fuck just as much as, if not more than, most men. My libido is fine.

I pat myself down and sigh, relieved. I'm okay.

I just need to find the right man to fuck.

But tonight it will be my favorite vibrator and me.

CHAPTER 8

Ivy

One thing I like about my life as a freelance IT specialist is that I'm my own boss. While studying IT in college, I had to dilute my talents so I didn't stand out too much, mostly because I didn't want my father to realize how much I took after him.

My father is an absolute genius when it comes to tracking people; throughout my life, I've watched him work. There's an art form to it, really: following the leads, drilling down further and further. My parents never hid the fact that what he often did was not for the faint of heart, nor was it legal. But they always emphasized the risks. So, I pretended not to be interested in the dark web or having a side business that was unsavory.

As I got older, I naturally gravitated toward electronics, and it turns out I'm very good at it. So, when I picked IT as a specialty, my father was proud. He's never once tried to sway me into going down the same route as him, but I really enjoyed it and the mystery behind figuring out the unknown. I dabbled in other things, even picking up a camera and pencil for a while to see if I was any good at design like my mother. But I didn't have a knack for it in the same way that she does.

Most of the gigs I accept are above board, though I enjoy dabbling in tasks that not just anyone can complete. I've seen some shit and been a part of illegal activities from a distance. I always safeguard my identity and dealings in case anything goes astray. Anything is possible with a laptop or phone. But I always tread on the edge of caution and siphon my earnings from those jobs into an untraceable account. Who knows, I might use the money on a rainy day, or it might just sit there. I have everything I want, and my mainstream gigs pay for my lavish lifestyle and love for traveling. I come and go as I please, free as a bird.

Most of my friends are aware of my talents and know it's forbidden to let their parents or mine know of their extent. I'm just not entirely sure if that's the avenue I want to go down, and I know the moment my father finds out, he'll act like a big old Labrador, probably wanting to work together as a father-daughter bonding experience. I love my dad, but I leave his overbearing nature to be directed at my mother, who seems to love it. And she's not afraid to put him in his place when he gets to be too much.

"Are you sure all of these clothes are mine?" Billie yells from her room. I can't help but laugh as I untuck my legs from underneath my ass where I'm sitting at my desk, messing around on my computer after finishing up a work project. My current employer gave me a ten-hour window to complete the task, and I finished it within the first hour, but I won't make it live just yet. They've had three IT specialists fail at their expectations, so I'll wait a while before I upload it.

My room's covered in potted plants—some of them dying, some of them alive. There's a pile of clothes in the corner and wrappers on my computer desk in front of the three screens that give me an exterior view of the apartment complex. I never lift the blinds to look outside.

I head over to Billie's room and find her sitting on the floor, a pile of clothes scattered around her. I pick them up and compare them to my frame. "Well, not even my left tit will fit in half of these, so yeah, boo, they're yours."

"Gah, why do I have so many clothes? You did this." She points a coat hanger at me. I chuckle because I've definitely been known to be a bad influence when it comes to retail therapy, but as women, we're naturally an accessory that can be glammed up in any way we want.

Why wouldn't we want to style ourselves differently every day?

I sit on the floor with her. Multiple boxes surround her room, and the curtains are wide open, forcing my eyes to adjust to the lighting. We sit there in silence, taking in the chaos.

"I'm going to miss you," I say glumly.

"I'm not dying," she says, but it's a reminder that she had almost died once. I'd just returned from Ibiza when she was kidnapped, and she hasn't spoken to me much about it. I'd never felt so useless as a friend. I'd had no idea, and it was Hawke who contacted me to track down Ford when he realized something was amiss. It was a reminder that in this world we were born into, even if not fully associated with it, we're at risk.

"I'll still come around for movie nights," she says, laying her head on my shoulder.

"You better; we have a lifetime of popcorn in the cupboard," I joke as I rest my head against hers. We've been thick as thieves since we were kids. We went to college together and moved back to Manhattan together. It feels like Billie's getting her shit together, and here I am, almost twenty-five, and all I've really done is party. I haven't had to work especially hard for my lifestyle, and I haven't had to prove myself in any way like Billie and Hope. But that doesn't make me feel any less... lost. Shouldn't I have found some grand purpose by now?

I try to shake it off. I'm not one to reflect or beat

myself up about things I don't have or where I think I should be at this point in my life. I love my life, the end.

The front door opens, and I know it's Ford before I see him. Only he and Hope have access to our apartment, apart from our parents. He walks in, biting into a muffin, and I narrow my gaze. "That better not be the last blueberry muffin Billie baked."

"What my girlfriend bakes is only ever for me," he grumbles.

"Please. I was here before your dick was, and—" My words fall off as Hawke saunters in behind him. You've got to be kidding me. Hawke whistles as he scans the room.

"Damn. Nice place you girls have. Why haven't we had some parties here?" His gaze slides to me, and he smirks.

"Do they just let any stray walk in from the street now?" I ask Billie as she stands. She laughs as she walks over to Ford and kisses him.

"Hey, I'm here to help with all of this. I'm better than any moving company. Got a van and everything," Hawke announces as the other two leave, Billie explaining to Ford what has to go in the first load. I still don't understand why she didn't hire professionals, but she said Ford seemed excited to help.

Hawke offers a hand to help me up, but I uncross my legs and stand on my own. "You can't be serious. Seriously? A van?"

He seems proud of himself as he points to the window. I can imagine this big asshole driving a van. I can't help but peer outside and laugh. Yep, there's a fucking van. I feel him come up behind me, his arms wrapping around my waist as he pulls me against him.

"Where's your room, Ivy?" His breath is hot on my neck.

"Where's your sweetheart, Hawke?" I bite back. I can feel his semi-hard cock against the small of my back.

"You always dress like this at home? I should've come around sooner. I'm digging the pink booty shorts and crop top."

"No." I turn and shove at his chest. "I'm not usually wearing anything. Now, if you'll excuse me, I have some work to finish," I say as I head for the door.

"You think you've got the upper hand after fleeing the club early last night?" he asks from behind me, and I can't help but glance over my shoulder and smirk, looking pointedly at his semi-hard cock. I purposely bend over slightly, giving him a glimpse of the bottom of my ass.

"I don't need an upper hand, Hawke. You want what you can't have. Now, pick up your chin; you're drooling." I slip into the hallway, my smile growing and my hips swaying on the way back to my room.

I don't leave my room again, and I'm surprised when he doesn't barge in to bother me further. I'm entertained when I raise my blinds ever so slowly to watch him and

Ford carry boxes and furniture to the van. It makes them look so domesticated when I know they're anything but. These men are dangerous.

Hawke is dangerous. Yet anyone not paying close enough attention might think he's just a manwhore with the energy of a Labrador.

He's been a little off lately, and I don't know why, but I think it might have something to do with Ford and everything that went down with the poisoning. But I haven't asked because it's not how Hawke and I are. We don't have deep conversations. More precisely, we can't converse without sniping at one another or trying to rile one another up.

Like he can feel me watching him, Hawke looks up, his eyes landing directly on me, and he smiles. I slip back into the darkness of my room. I prefer to work in the dark with my multiple screens. But right now, it makes me feel like I'm hiding from him. It doesn't make me any less curious about the asshole and what he gets up to in his spare time when he's not being so... Hawke. I wonder if he has deeper layers. Or is this arrogant, cocky prick all that he is?

It grates on me that I'm curious because once something's grabbed my attention, I can't help but drill down until I get to the bottom of it. Whatever this thing between Hawke and me is, I've purposely avoided looking into it for years because I know nothing good will come of it.

Except, of course, orgasms. Which, in my opinion, is never a bad thing. But since our one and only time together, I've always held myself back, uncertain as to why and unwilling to explore it further.

I upload the task for my job and then decide to get dressed. Once they have it, I should receive payment, and I suddenly feel like I need to go on a shopping spree. There's nothing better than a woman with her own paycheck, purchasing all the brands she loves.

CHAPTER 9

Hawke

Even as Ford tried to act all calm and collected earlier, the moment he walked out of the house, I knew something was off. I always know. Now, my heart is pounding rapidly, adrenaline is coursing through my veins, and I have a live update of his car as Ivy tracks him for me. It's come to a dead stop.

I don't know why, but I'm feeling a sense of impending doom, and it has me sliding all over the dirt roads, if that's even what they can be considered. They're more like trails that lead me out into the middle of fucking nowhere. I end up at an ominous location that can only mean one thing— something underhanded is going on.

Ford tells me everything. We do everything together. But I'm totally in the dark about whatever situation he's walked into here.

I bring my car to a screeching halt when I spot his car.

There's another vehicle that I don't recognize parked nearby. I send a photo of the license plate to Ivy to have her trace it for me, but I don't even need her response when a woman runs frantically toward me.

I raise my gun in her direction. I've never killed a woman and never will. It's a rule, Ford, and I never break. We might be street rats, violent good-for-nothings that were sharpened into weapons, but we do have some standards.

She seems surprised to see me, but then her expression changes to one of calculation. "Well, well. I didn't think you'd get here so soon."

My brow furrows. I've seen her somewhere before, but I can't recall where. Was it a job Ford and I had? She doesn't look sane, and there's a crackle of energy around her that I don't particularly like.

"Where is he?" I demand. I know she has something to do with all of this.

"Dead," she says with wide eyes and a cruel smile.

Everything stops. All sound. My breathing. Comprehension.

My brother... my twin. My everything.

Dead.

No, that can't be right. My mind begins to spiral as graphic images assault my brain. We've killed so many people together... Ford is invincible. I'm meant to protect him. We protect each other... We...

The woman whips out a gun and points it at me. I want her to take me out. If there's no him, what's the point of me being here? But he wouldn't be taken out so easily... I won't believe it.

My finger pulls the trigger at the same time hers does. Two shots. Only one that hits its mark.

I can hear my heart pounding after the ringing of the shots fades. Blood seeps from a hole between her brows, and the force of the bullet hitting her has her reeling backward.

I know, right in this moment, I can never come back from this. I feel my demons invade me. It was only ever men we hurt. Cruel men, unhinged men, and sometimes innocent men. But never women or children... Never...

But now...

I want to take it back, but I can't.

My feet move before rational thought kicks back in.

The woman might be dead, but she's taken something from me. Something I can't get back and don't entirely understand. I'm running in the direction she came from, searching for my brother, ignoring the crippling reality that I've well and truly become a monster. And not one I can embrace. An ugly, disgusting thing that once vowed never to hurt something as precious as a woman.

I couldn't save my mother... even when I resented her the most. But I would never hurt her... Never...

I can hardly breathe by the time I stumble across the doors built into the middle of a grass plain. My harrowing thoughts focus again. My brother. Ford. Please don't be dead.

I throw open the door, my gun aimed at the gloom

beyond, only to find a fumbling Billie trying to drag my brother's dead weight up the stairs.

Everything stops once again.

I can't... He can't...

"Little Tornado," I rasp, a part of me jumping into action while the majority can't keep up with what's happening. I grab for my brother, who's bleeding from his leg and is a sickly, pale color.

I bury all of my demons, doing everything I can to bring my brother back. I'm willing to sell my soul to the devil in exchange for his life. If he's not here, what purpose do I have? He's the good one. The reliable one. The likable one.

I carry him across the field, Billie stumbling behind me...

And then I'm haunted by the woman's eyes—wide and empty. Lifeless.

Her eyes stare at me... haunting me... drowning me...

Killing me slowly.

I'm sucked into a void like quicksand, claws grabbing and dragging me down for what feels like eternity.

I bolt upright with a gasp. I'm panting harshly as I realize I'm in my brother's home, in his spare room designated for me. Sweat glistens on my chest, and the blankets have been thrown off the bed. I run my hands through my hair, trying to swallow despite my parched mouth.

I close my eyes again, pinching the bridge of my nose, trying to push away the imagery of the dead woman staring back at me. It's been months since the incident, but lately, these nightmares have worsened.

I roll out of bed and throw on a loose shirt. Checking the time on my phone, I see it's three in the morning. It's too early, but I decide to go to my local gym. It's the only place that makes me feel sane. I have my own gym set up at home, but for some reason, since the nightmares, I've been going to a twenty-four-hour one I found.

When I open the bedroom door, a soft meow has me tilting my head down. Felix, a black cat the size of my hand with bright green eyes, stares up at me.

I can't blame him for begging me for food before Ford and Billie wake up. I eat as much as I can, too, so I always spoil him with an extra serving they don't know about. I flick on the kitchen light and then give him a serving of food before I grab a protein bar out of the cupboard for myself.

Fuck.

That dream won't stop haunting me. And though I know my brother isn't happy about how often I sleep here now, especially on the first night Billie has officially moved in, I can't help it. I thought here, of all places, would bring me peace. But my demons have followed me to the one place I thought would be safe.

Being close to my brother was always the one thing that brought me peace.

But even I don't deserve that now, it seems.

I scratch Felix behind the ear. "Don't bring in too many mice for Billie. She might actually make you an indoor cat," I warn him quietly. He's too preoccupied by his food to acknowledge me. Fuck, it's bad if even the cat won't pay me any attention.

I leave the house, focused on the gym. I like being around people. Ford and I only had each other for a long time, and when we were on our own, trying to survive on the streets, we were overlooked. But now I've made myself so imposing in size that no one will ever overlook me again.

More importantly, I don't want to be by myself. I fucking hate it. Especially with these demons in my head.

CHAPTER 10

Ivy

It's been a week since Dutton's party and Billie's moving out, and I just returned from a four-day trip to Miami, where I worked on my tan and had a little fun. Coming home to an empty apartment, I decided to finish up two projects I took on during the week and then found myself bored.

It's midnight on a Friday night. I'd usually be out partying, but since I spent the last four nights doing exactly that, I don't feel the urge tonight, despite receiving multiple messages asking where I am from acquaintances who want me to join their party. I tuck my feet under my ass, still wanting to cure my boredom.

I go to the kitchen to get a bowl of cereal and milk, then sit back down at my computer. I push my hair to one side, thinking about a particular rabbit hole I've been trying not to fixate on as of late. My friends' privacy is important to me, and I'd never invade it unless I think it jeopardizes their safety in any way. Although I have the power to hack any of their things, I've made a point not to. However, there's someone I've always considered an exception to that rule. *Hawke.* Because he'd do the same thing to me if he had the ability to hack like I do. Hawke appears easygoing and goofy, but people underestimate his sharp mind.

I bite my bottom lip, my hands moving over the keyboard of their own accord. Maybe a little peek won't hurt. It's not the first time I've spied on Hawke, and I'm sure it won't be the last. At this time on a Friday night, he's probably not even home. He's most likely either on a job with Eli or partying.

Hawke once let it slip that he had cameras installed both inside and outside his home after Eli officially took over as the boss. I can only imagine their underworld dealings heightened with that change in leadership. He was bragging about installing the best of the best, which I took as a personal challenge to access. It wasn't a challenge whatsoever.

The first screen I pull up shows his garage. His Range Rover is parked inside, which doesn't necessarily mean he's home. I swear the reason he picked that car is because it's the only one that he fits comfortably in.

I eat a spoonful of cereal as I switch cameras. The kitchen is empty. Then I flick to his bedroom. Why he thought it was a smart idea to put a camera in his there is beyond me, but I'm not surprised at men in his line of work having paranoia.

I flick to the living room, and that's when I see him. He's naked and thrusting into a woman.

My, my, my, I couldn't have picked a better time to stalk the big oaf.

He has the woman bent over the couch, and she hugs a pillow clutched tight to her chest, holding on to it for dear life as he fucks her from behind. His hand slides into her hair before he fists it and pulls her back by it, angling her head toward the camera.

Hmm, pretty. She looks like a sporty type. Most likely a gym girlie. I don't recognize her, but then again, Hawke generally doesn't have the same person twice.

Hawke isn't aware that I have access to his cameras because, obviously, what I'm doing is highly illegal. Not that it's a deterrent for anyone in my family or intimate friend group.

I take another mouthful of cereal, leaning back and enjoying the show. The man is built like a god, one carved out of a mountain with the amount of muscle he carries, especially in his arms and chest. He has a nice ass too, and it's a shame I can't see it from this angle.

A small part of me wants to tell him how easy it is for me to break into his security, but another part likes that I can hold this secret over him.

Something begins to stir in my stomach. Anticipation. Desire. I'm imagining myself in the other woman's place. It's a dangerous type of torture, especially since I've almost gone a month without a man's touch, which is my definition of a midlife crisis.

I look down at the cereal bowl in my hands. Oh my God, I'm at home on a Friday night, eating cereal and watching Hawke fuck some random chick. Maybe I really have hit an all-time low.

That just won't do.

I put the half-full bowl down and then grab my phone. I scroll through my contacts until I find his name, hovering my thumb over the entry. Sure, I might be bored at home right now, but there's a reason why I wanted to spy on Hawke in the first place. Because, at the very least, he always promises fun. I hit call, curious if he'll answer.

I bite my bottom lip, continuing to watch the live footage as he smacks the woman's ass. That's when his phone screen lights up on the edge of the couch. He looks at it, his eyebrows furrowing, and he yanks harder on the woman's hair as he leans back slightly to grab it. He continues thrusting into her as he brings the phone to his ear.

"Lover," he purrs into the phone as the loud slapping of him thrusting into the woman echoes in the background. "You miss me?"

I can't help but smirk triumphantly as the audio filters through my ear. The woman he's fucking looks at him over her shoulder, and I just know she has a big smile on her face, thinking he's talking to her. Too bad for her; he doesn't speak to many women like that. He continues to slide his cock in and out of her, not slowing his pace, as he shakes his head at her, confirming it's not her he's speaking to.

"No," I reply as I lean back in my chair and kick my feet up on the edge of my desk. "A lot of noise over there. You okay?"

As I watch, his pace picks up, and I focus on his labored breathing. It does more for me than it should, but that low thrumming tingles down to my pussy.

"Getting my dick wet, lover, though I wish it were you who was wetting it." He grunts, and the woman begins to go red in the face from exertion.

"You're disgusting," I say, playing with my necklace because my fingers are tempted to play with certain body parts instead, and I refuse to give Hawke that satisfaction, even if he wouldn't know about it. It's torture denying myself, though.

"You love it," he growls back and slams into the woman. She screams, and he grunts as he jerks into her, coming. I can see the vein in his neck pulse as he holds her in place by her hip.

He licks his lips, satisfied, and the woman smiles in pleasure.

"Two pump wonder at it again?" I snark, focusing only on him as he smirks and pulls out of her.

"Would you believe me if I told you I lasted more

than three this time?" he asks, dropping the rubber to the floor and then wiping his cock with a shirt.

"Wow, even a caveman can improve," I reply, and his smile grows.

The woman turns to face him, and I hear her say, "That was my shirt."

He taps her on the ass. "I'll pay for the dry cleaning. You can clean yourself up in the hall bathroom. I'm on an important call," he tells her as he walks away, buck naked. She looks confused as she watches him, but anyone who knows Hawke's reputation knows not to get attached. But there are always those women who think they'll be different. She bundles her clothes from the floor and heads for his hallway.

I switch cameras just in time to catch him entering the kitchen.

"Now, why did you call me? It's not every day I get a call from the one and only Miss Ivy Walker. I must be in some serious trouble today." He pulls a jug of milk from the fridge. "Everything okay in Miami?"

"How'd you know I was in Miami?"

"You think I'd miss the opportunity to stalk those bikini photos in your IG story? I liked the baby-blue bikini the most, just in case you're wondering."

"Lucky that's the one I burned as soon as I got home."

He's smiling again as he puts the jug back in the fridge and then leans his elbows against the counter, stretching out in all his glory. The guy has no shame, but I can't ridicule him since I do the same thing.

"If you're back in town, is this a booty call?" he asks arrogantly but with a bit of hope.

I lean over my legs to grab my cereal bowl again and shrug nonchalantly. "Just wanted to give you some advice," I say before taking another mouthful of my cereal.

"Oh, this should be interesting."

I can't help but follow the movement of his body, the bunching of his muscles. Hawke is not easy to ignore with a body like that. The vivid memory of when my hands once ran over every ridge comes back to mind, making me almost salivate for it again. I ogle his tattoos; plenty more have been added since that night. His brother is the only one who tattoos him, and I can appreciate the art form on such a big-ass canvas. It's a shame his obnoxious, cocky personality overrides his physical perfection. Then again, it's the part I like about him the most, not that I'll ever admit it.

I've never seen Hawke in action, though I have heard stories that he can get crazy when pushed, I imagine it's very terrifying.

"I just thought you needed some tips," I force out, reminding myself I have to speak instead of drooling into my bowl.

"Tips? Now, what type of tips do I need?" he asks.

His gaze flicks toward the living room, most likely to check on the woman he was just fucking.

"With fucking," I reply.

He chuckles. "You know firsthand that I can fuck. You can say you just wanted to hear my voice, lover."

"The memory is a little hazy; we were both drunk. But I think I recall wondering when your dick actually entered me."

He laughs then, a monstrous boom, bringing a smile to my face. I like the way Hawke laughs. It always sounds so freeing, but lately, when we have outings, I notice he doesn't laugh as much.

"I remember every detail of your body," he purrs, and it goes straight to my already pounding pussy. "But enlighten me. What's your first pointer?"

I bite my lip, trying to decide how much of my hand I should tip. Should I let him know I've been watching him? I could keep it as my little secret, yet Hawke brings out my mischievous side.

"The way you just grabbed her hair and pulled on it was all types of wrong. You need to grab it from the roots. You see, as a fellow blondie, my hair is fragile, so it's imperative to take hold of it correctly. If you don't, you could break it.

His gaze immediately slides up to the camera, and he smiles. I bite the edge of my nail, grinning like a dumbass.

"Is it?"

Busted.

CHAPTER 11

Hawke

I vy is not only beautiful but one of the most intelligent women I've ever met, if not the most intelligent. I don't need to fuel her ego anymore.

"Lucky your hair is short, and I'm forced to hold you by your throat instead," I growl back. It fills me with satisfaction to know she's been watching me. Everyone says I have a loud mouth and can't keep a secret. For the most part, that's true, but it comes as a reward now if she's hacking into my home cameras to watch me. She can spy on me all she wants. I'll give her a show every time.

"Too bad, I think you'll look better with a collar. Do you think you'd crawl around for me like a good boy, Hawke?"

My cock twitches at the thought of this beautiful, bossy woman taking charge. "Do you want me to bark as well, lover? You can do whatever you want to me. You know that."

"So easy," she purrs.

"You can't tell me you called me while watching me fuck and then intentionally giving yourself away just for a friendly chat. Please tell me this isn't the first time you've watched me fuck other women."

I never brought women back to my house until I got the cameras installed. I got the idea from Jewel, who'd broken into Eli's home—this was before they were together—and installed her cameras. The idea of it, for this specific reason, intrigued me.

It's gratifying to know even Ivy falls into temptation. I've been playing by her rules, keeping my distance, but the moment she gives me the chance, I'll be on my knees, worshipping her.

"Do you think I have so much spare time?" she scoffs. "Goodnight, Hawke."

The line goes dead.

I smirk as I put my phone on the counter. Aside from fucking and partying, I'm also known for my unwavering determination to get what I want. And Ivy has been on that list for a long time. I fist my hardening cock and step closer to the camera, gliding my other hand through my black hair as I stare directly into it in all my naked glory. Just hearing her voice is enough to get my libido back in a short amount of time, and I stroke myself, knowing she's watching.

Right on cue, my phone starts ringing, and I can't hide my grin as "Lover" appears on the screen. I put that as her contact name in my phone to piss her off after that night we had together, but ever since, I've hoped it'll happen again. Even years later, I'm waiting like a good boy.

I take two steps back to answer the call, placing it on speaker while my hand stays wrapped around my cock.

"Stop that," she scolds, and it gives me a burst of satisfaction to know she's still watching. Like me, she can't resist the pull between us.

"Why, lover? Does it turn you on?" I ask rhetorically because I know it does.

The receptionist from the gym walks into the kitchen and stops in her tracks. She's dressed in a tight-fitted jacket, her dirty shirt in her hand.

"I'm still on the phone, but feel free to get on your knees," I suggest to the woman, and then fix my gaze back on the camera, all for *her*. My sweet, sweet Ivy, who's just as poisonous as her name suggests. Because after just one taste of her, I haven't been able to get her out of my system.

The blonde walks over, a devilish smirk on her face, and I remind myself about the hair thing, wanting to be more careful after the recent suggestion. She kneels in front of me and takes me into the back of her throat. And, as always, I think of another blonde I would rather be choking with my cock. These women... their faces, names, and bodies blur into one. There's only one woman I've ever savored or memorized their every touch.

"Cat got your tongue, lover?" I croon to Ivy. "Does it turn you on?" I repeat my earlier question. The woman on the floor nods her head, but it's not her I'm talking to. If anything, I'm now growing bored of the situation because it's not her mouth I want swallowing my dick.

"No," Ivy deadpans. There's a tendril of something more in her tone, and I can't tell if it's irritation or interest.

"How about this, then?" I thread my hands through the woman's hair and push her head down farther, encouraging her to take me as deeply as she can. She begins to gag on my cock, but I know her limits since she was sucking me off only an hour ago.

"Looks like she's looking for something more tangible to eat. Oh, excuse me, that's my door. My date must be here. Bye, Hawke," she says and then hangs up. I'm left on the edge, all my libido and the buildup of the anticipated sex talk coming to an end.

"Umm," the woman on her knees says. I look down at her, and my cock starts softening.

What the fuck?

It's like a double-edged blade. I always come, but there's an irritation taking over in its stead this time.

Did Ivy say she has a date?

I know it's not my right to be annoyed, but how dare

she hang up on me for another guy just as things were getting interesting between us.

Then again, I literally have a woman sucking my cock, and it's now deflating like a punctured balloon. I'm baffled. My dick and I have a mutual understanding. We make each other happy and always get off. I step away from her, and she looks up at me, confused.

I try not to laugh like a madman. This has never happened. Even drunk out of my mind, I always come. There's only one person to blame for this, and it's the only woman who's ever been daring enough to hang up on me.

Ivy

The balls on that fucking asshole. It's never bothered me before seeing him with other women. Hell, it didn't even bother me earlier tonight. In fact, I enjoyed it. But at the end, something twisted in my stomach, and I suddenly wasn't feeling inspired by any of it.

I lied about the date. I didn't want him to think he was the only one having fun. I finish my bowl of cereal and put it to the side. My room looks like a dumping ground. Billie always suggested we get a housekeeper, but I prefer having a chaotic mess around me. It's how I work best. If something feels too clean, it reminds me of a clinic or a display home. It doesn't feel lived in.

I received another project offer and looked over the details. I'm grateful for the distraction. I accepted the job and let them know I'll be ready to start on it next week, but it does nothing to take me out of my foul mood. Fucking Hawke. I walk into my en suite and turn the shower on cold, not bothering to strip my nightgown off. I want to feel the cold water washing over me, to calm myself down.

I've watched plenty of people have sex, whether it be swinging, sex shows, or threesomes, and none of it has really done anything for me. Sure, it builds up an appetite, but nothing compared to the yearning of my pussy as I watched Hawke shove his cock into that woman.

I hate that I think about him more than I should. He takes up too much room in my head. I've known him for many years, and he's always been attractive to me. But I never once thought we could, or would, be anything more. We both love sex way too much to stay monogamous, and after our only sexual encounter, I'd backed off, knowing if we became hooked on one another, it would most definitely mess with our friendship or ruin sex for us with anyone else.

I can hear my phone ringing from my room, but I ignore it and enjoy the bite of the cold water. I begin to shake, and goosebumps rise on my skin. *What the fuck am I even doing?*

"Looks like I can break into places as well," someone says.

I jump, grabbing the showerhead and pointing it in the intruder's direction.

Hawke takes a step back, looking down at his drenched shoes. "Really? A shower head is your weapon of choice if someone breaks in?"

"How the fuck did you get past my alarms? And I'll have you know I have a gun in the drawer beside my bed."

He shows me a key to my apartment. "I stole this from Ford. Figured he didn't need it anymore. And a gun? Really? That's so sad. I was hoping you'd have a collection of toys in there."

I roll my eyes. "I obviously have that as well."

His entire demeanor changes as he becomes very interested in that little tidbit. "I want to see that."

"Get out," I growl as the cold air suddenly registers on my skin. I put the shower head back in place, flip the water to warm and step out of the spray while it heats up. "Besides, I never broke into your house. And don't you have a little blonde to be entertaining?"

At that moment, I realize I must look like a crazy person, showering in a nightgown that is now saturated with water and clings to my wet body.

"Didn't you have a hot date tonight? And I've already checked under the bed," he says.

I choke in disbelief until I realize he's serious.

"You're just lucky I arrived when I did. I'm quite familiar with this showering business, and in my experience, you do it with your clothes off," he says as he pulls his shirt off.

"What are you doing?" I squeak as he steps into my space. The reason I wanted this en suite is because it doesn't have a door. I love the size and openness of the bathroom—it's how I like most things—open and big.

He comes closer as if he owns this fucking shower. My gaze dips to his cock as he shuffles out of his jeans. It's getting hard, and I lick my lips at the sight, fighting against all my natural instincts to do what my body loves the most, which is fuck.

But this is Hawke...

"You can touch it." He smirks and nods to his cock. "It won't bite... but I will." He winks and pushes forward until my back hits the tile. His gaze doesn't leave mine, and his almost-black eyes twinkle with mischief as he reaches for my body wash. "Fuck, you smell good."

"Buy your own body wash," I bite back as he squirts some into his hands and begins to rub it against his stomach. I can't help but watch as he glides over every ridge of his six-pack.

Fuck me, this man is something else. Nothing but sin and temptation, and that arrogant smirk takes me out at my knees.

I know I shouldn't play into our game. But, fuck, does my body want it.

He's killing me with a slow, torturous death.

I have to get out of here, or I'm going to do something I might not necessarily regret, but something that I'll undeniably get hooked on. And that's the reason why

Hawke and I haven't blurred the lines again. But it should be him leaving; he's in *my* shower, after all.

"Get out," I say through gritted teeth, my nails digging into the palms of my hands as I try to restrain myself and do my best not to give anything away. But his arrogant smile taunts me like he knows what's going on in my head.

"Can't. Have to wash myself." His hand trails down to his fully erect cock, and I swallow. Hard.

Nope. I literally have to force myself out of this room, or I won't come back from this. I cling to the only rational brain cell left and go to push past him. His laughter bounces around the shower as he blocks my way. And trying to move him would be like trying to move a mountain, so instead, I defiantly glare up at him, a move that has been known to make men whither within seconds. I shove at his chest, but he doesn't budge. My fingers then trail against the heat of his skin and the hardness of his muscles. *Fuck, fuck, fuck.*

Remove your hands, Ivy.

This is Hawke, remember?

No touchy...

I'm internally screaming at myself, but my mind and body aren't cooperating.

"I'd like to have that mouth all over me," he says. And when I look back up at his face, I see he's staring at my lips.

A flash of the woman who was sucking him off not

even an hour ago comes to mind, and I shove him hard enough this time to make him take a step back. "Fuck. Off."

"If you get me off," he retorts as I step out of his reach.

He continues washing himself as he watches me grab a towel and wrap it around myself. This asshole really isn't getting the memo.

Fine, I can teach him a lesson.

I head into the kitchen and open the pantry. I'm not much of a cook, but Billie has left plenty behind, and a devilish smile paints my lips as I reach for the first item I see. From what I've heard, Hawke might be tough and able to fight off multiple men at once, but let's see how he gets out of this.

I hide the item behind my back as I walk back into the bathroom with a sweet smile plastered on my face.

"Knew you couldn't stay away," he says, reaching for me. But before he can get his hands on me, I douse him in cooking oil. He seems shocked at first, but then his gaze hardens. He reaches out again, this time to grab the bottle still leaking oil. The moment he shifts, he loses his footing and falls to his ass. Hard.

An ugly snort escapes me as I bend over laughing. Tears stream down my face as I try to avoid stepping into the puddle of oil. I can't even see from how hard I'm laughing, and before I can wipe the tears away, a hard body slams into mine, and I slip. I anticipate the worst, trying to catch myself, expecting my head to crack on the tiles. But it's only my tailbone that hits hard. When I open my eyes, I notice his hands are cupping the back of my head, taking the impact. He's half on top of me now, my ass numb from the fall.

"You think that's funny?" he teases. I try to give him my angriest expression, but I snort and break into a fit of laughter again. I will never forget him looking like a baby giraffe on ice, hands, and legs in the air as his hard dick strained in the wind while he fell. I try to wipe away the tears, but they keep coming. "You can stop laughing now. What if my dick was hurt during one of those falls?" he grumbles.

"Maybe you'll have to rely on your head instead of your dick, then," I say, still laughing. When my laughter begins to recede, I realize how intently he's watching me. "What?" I barely manage to say because he looks serious. Is he really that mad? Okay, sure, it was an asshole thing to do, but it's Hawke. And besides, he broke into my home.

"I like it when you laugh. Maybe next time, not at the expense of my cock, though."

I bite my bottom lip, trying to hold in the next fit of laughter. Heat fills the room, and it has nothing to do with the hot shower still running behind him.

I feel his callused hand gliding up my wet nightgown. My heartbeat picks up speed, and I hyperfocus on his touch as it glides higher, his gaze unwavering. My thighs open of their own volition as I suck in a breath, antici-pating all the things I know this man can offer. I feel stupid now for resisting it for so long because I know how he can make me feel. I know how my body will come undone.

His hand curves around my thigh, and I steady my breathing as I feel the brush of his thumb against my clit. It's just a graze, but intentional enough to have me begging for more, which I refuse to do.

"Do you want me to slide that nightie up and fuck you?" he asks with a slow-spreading smirk that implies he thinks he's already won.

"No," I bite back at the same time my hips tilt, applying more pressure from his thumb on my clit. Treacherous body.

One of his eyebrows raises. "Are you sure? It feels like you want this."

"No," I say again, and he challenges me with his gaze, but his hand retreats from my clit, roaming down my leg the same way it had come up. This time, his touch sets a fire against my skin, and I want it back where it was before.

It's so hard to not give in to this man who already knows he's a god. He raises carefully to his knees, and my pussy is pounding, my heart racing at the thought of yanking him back to me. His hand, however, doesn't leave my body, and it feels like a tether between us.

"What if I'm just hungry?" he asks, his eyes devouring me.

"Then you better work on that appetite," I reply breathlessly.

He pushes up my nightgown. I'm not wearing any underwear underneath, and if he wasn't looking at me like he was going to devour me before, now I'm really in trouble. My legs fall open expectantly. I might not be able to admit it to Hawke, but I want him. Well, my body does.

"Just a little taste?" he almost begs.

And I find myself responding with, "Just a little taste."

His leash of control snaps. He leans down, pressing kisses against my lower stomach. "So fucking perfect," he whispers against my skin. His hand slides to my ass, a smear of oil left in its wake as his kisses trail lower.

Fuck me. I've needed this release for so long. I lean back on my elbows and tip my head back, focusing on the feel of him. He says something I can't understand, and then his tongue is inside of me.

"Fuck." Shit, I said that out loud. But I'm too committed now to care. He chuckles against my pussy, his hot breath ghosting against me as he begins to eat me out, his slippery hands gliding up and down my outer thighs, his fingers massaging the muscles.

My palms slide over his hands and arms. I love the feeling of how big he is. Hawke makes me feel small in comparison, and I fucking love the way he devours me as if he's a starved man.

I bunch up the bottom of my soaked nightgown, raising it higher. Guiding one of his hands to my breast, he squeezes it hard, the oil adding a sensual touch. His other hand continues rubbing up and down my thigh, as I roll my hips against his mouth.

Fuck me, he knows what he's doing with that tongue.

He continues torturing me, sucking, tongue fucking, and biting at me. Every tug, every lick teases my core, as if from only that one time together, he's mastered my body. But this is better than what I remember. Maybe it's because I haven't gotten off for so long. Or, maybe it's because... we've been building up for this for so long.

I want to blame my month of unintentional celibacy as the reason I'm allowing him to slide his mouth between my legs right now, wanting to ignore the fact of how deeply attracted I am to him.

I don't touch him, letting him worship me. He spreads my thighs farther apart, giving him better access, and I cry out, surprised by his ability to tongue fuck me deeper. I glance down at his black hair; all his attention is on servicing me. The sight is beautiful. I can see how hard his cock is, but he continues only focusing on me.

I fist the edges of my nightgown as he flicks his tongue faster, his strong hands pinning me in place.

It feels like I'm struck by lightning, the orgasm tearing out of me as I crash over the edge. I cling to his forearms, needing something to anchor me as I buck against him. He's stroking me from the inside with his tongue as if entitled to my every wave of pleasure. My head thumps back against the floor as I ride it out, wriggling against his mouth, trying to bring myself back into the here and now.

His tongue strokes become lazy as my breathing begins to steady.

My eyes burst open, and I stare at the ceiling, noticing the steam circling the room and how hot it is in here. The water hitting the marble floor of the shower comes back into focus as I come down from my high.

I feel the disconnect the moment his mouth leaves my pussy, and I raise up onto my elbows. He's on his knees, staring at the floor, most likely trying to figure out how he can stand without slipping again. The image of him falling on his ass flashes in my mind, and I burst out into laughter again.

"You laugh, but shouldn't you be thanking me?" he asks with furrowed eyebrows.

I realize I might've hurt his male pride. But that makes me laugh even harder. I scoot backward, out of his reach. He tries to grab me, but slips in the oil again. I snort, trying my hardest not to laugh. I use the counter to help me stand and shift the nightgown over my body to cover my nakedness. But even when I'm covered, it does nothing to deter that burning gaze.

"Thanks for your service. Show yourself out," I say, trying to contain the laugh at the idea of how he'll get up and out of the bathroom without slipping all over the place. "And I suggest you leave quickly, or I'll tell Daddy Walker you broke into my home."

Any desire falls from his expression as his eyes grow wide. "You wouldn't dare."

"Oh, I'd dare," I say matter-of-factly. I don't know why my father hates Hawke, but he always has, and he refuses to do any work if it's directly for Hawke. He's the only one he won't help, which is why Hawke comes to me. But it makes me laugh how quickly Hawke pales at the thought of my father. Hawke is literally double the size of my father, but he acts like a boy at the mere mention of him.

I have oil over my body, but I don't have it on my feet, which means I have the advantage that I can leave the room. After throwing on some dry clothes, I grab my coat and keys, knowing if I stay, it'll be more than him just tongue fucking me. So I decide to go to my parents' house, since they're traveling, to take advantage of their shower.

As I leave, I tap away at my phone, and by the time I reach the door, the power cuts out, and I smile triumphantly. Sure, I might be leaving my apartment, but there's fuck all he can do here without any power. Besides, I'm certain the threat of my father knowing he's in my apartment will have him hightailing out in no time.

CHAPTER 13

Ivy

That was the last message I received from Hawke. It's been two days, and I haven't bothered to reply. But it amuses me to think about how many times he landed on his ass, spread eagle.

My father presses a kiss on my mother's cheek as she shows me her recent design for a new office in Dubai. I've only partied in Dubai a few times, but if Mom's setting up there for a few months, I might have an excuse to join her. For moral support, of course.

My mother has continued building her interior design empire over the years and is excited to create a new office space. She's selective when it comes to the projects she personally takes on. While she loves her work, she and my father also enjoy the freedom to flit off on trips whenever they please. They're the ones who've curated my unquenchable thirst for travel. Though we spent most of my early childhood in Manhattan, we also often traveled to London, the two main office locations my mother worked out of as she continued expanding her business.

My mother's lips curve into a smile as she gazes up at my father, who's sporting a few more grays lately. I enjoy giving him shit for it, and I'm certain the only reason he hasn't dyed his hair out of vanity is because my mother said she likes the silver fox look.

"This is the new space I'm drafting," she says, handing me the tablet. I zoom in on the design. It's elegant and unique.

"It looks nice," I tell her, enjoying my chai tea. "The staircase is cool."

She smiles, and my father quickly says, "The stairs were my idea."

"Yes, good job, dear." She pats his head, and I roll my eyes at how he enjoys the obvious praise.

My parents have a beautiful marriage. They're one another's best friends, and I grew up in a household that prioritized freedom to have fun. It's mostly where I learned to become mischievous and a slight prankster. But on top of that, they always spoke to me like an adult, educating me on anything that piqued my interest and encouraging my excitement around certain subjects. I was like a sponge.

I'm not opposed to the idea of having a partner in crime, like they have with each other. There just hasn't been a man who can keep my attention long enough for me to even consider not being able to live without them. It'd be nice to have a man look at me the way my father looks at my mother—with undeniable devotion and respect.

Men worship me, but it's only surface-level. They worship my body, which, up until now, has been perfect for my needs. Until that changes, I'm going to continue to live life the way I want to live it. People judge me, sure. But the fact of the matter is, I don't really care. The only opinions I care about are those of the people who love me. One of my favorite quotes goes along the lines of: *everyone has an opinion, just like they have an asshole.* It's kind of become my mantra in life.

I finish the chai tea as I make a couple of tweaks and suggestions to the office design. I don't have an eye like my mother, but it's almost encouraged that my father and I make minor contributions. Every time she keeps a suggestion of ours, I think it's her way of having a little bit of us and her home in each project.

"Any recent conquests?" my mother asks, and she always purposely does it in front of my father. It's been an ongoing joke for years now to make him uncomfortable with those types of questions. He groans in complaint.

Out of nowhere, the memory of Hawke between my

legs flashes into my mind, and I'm quick to push it away. I haven't seen him since he broke into my apartment. And I've been doing my best to avoid him, simply for the fact that I can't get him out of my head, which is torturous and all-consuming. I sometimes contemplate making a friends-with-benefits arrangement with him, but I feel if I say anything, it will boost his ego even more. And anyone who meets him already knows how big his ego is, and he doesn't need anyone to stroke it for him.

I've also managed to keep myself from hacking into cameras again, not only because he knows I was doing it but because I think I need to separate myself from him.

"I think it's actually getting serious with a guy I recently met. He enjoys bird watching," I deadpan, and my mother and I look at my father, who pales.

"A what?" he grits out in his thick British accent.

I try to keep my expression neutral.

"You know. Like, he'll go and watch birds for hours and take photos of them; he also made me this super-cute friendship bracelet. So, I'm pretty sure it's escalating quickly. He doesn't want to have sex before marriage, so maybe we'll have a quick wedding, you know?"

"You're fucking with me again, aren't you." His frantic gaze bounces between me and my mother, both of us trying not to break out into laughter.

"Maybe we should start picking out dresses," she says, nodding agreeably.

"Over my dead body. You two think you're so funny, but you're not," he grumbles as he leaves the room.

My mother and I look at each other and begin to laugh. "It's just too easy," I say, wiping away a tear.

She taps the tablet's stylus on her chin. "Maybe next time we should go with a cowboy theme. Nothing will put a bee in his bonnet more than a countryman trying to take his little girl to the middle of nowhere on a farm."

I can't help but laugh as I spring off the chair when my father walks in with a basket of my clothes and places it on the counter.

My mother likes to iron clothes. I'm not really sure why. My father tells me to let her do it when they're in town because it makes her feel more involved in my life. They don't have to twist my arm to let her take of a chore I abhor anyway, so it's become an excuse for me to come back home whenever I please, not that I really need one.

"Oh, there's a small pile I have to iron quickly. One second," my mother says as she hurries out of the room.

"You look beautiful, by the way. Where are you off to?" Dad says to me.

"A party. One of the girls I went to college with invited me. Good way to spend a Friday night," I reply.

"Don't let your mother pressure you into thinking you need a man because you don't. If anything, I'd prefer you remain single for the rest of your days."

I sarcastically nod my head. "Absolutely. It's why I've sworn to remain a virgin."

He cringes at how casually I say it, and I can't help but laugh. I love riling him up like this. It's ironic because he tends to push everyone else's buttons—forever a smartass—and yet my mother and I beat him at his own game.

"Be safe tonight," he says, the same way he has since I was old enough to party.

I've never given them a reason not to trust me, even when I was younger. Sure, I've been impulsive when it came to some things, but nothing they haven't thought I couldn't handle myself. "Come over for dinner Sunday night before your mother and I fly out."

"I'll mark it on my calendar." I beam at him.

"Here," my mother says, coming back into the room and adding another two shirts to my basket of clothes. To be honest, I can't even remember when I wore those last. She scoops me into a big hug. "Be safe and have a good night."

"I'll see you Sunday night," I say, pressing a kiss on her cheek and then giving my father the same treatment.

As I'm in the elevator, riding down to the lobby from their penthouse, I look at my reflection in the mirrored back wall of the car. My short blonde hair is straightened and slicked back, showcasing my large silver hoop earrings. I live by the philosophy: the bigger the hoop, the bigger the ho. They've become a staple piece in my wardrobe from the first time I heard that.

I'm wearing a short black dress that emphasizes my curves, with matching red-bottomed heels. I absolutely love these heels; they're one of my favorite pairs. I look at the time on the Rolex my father gifted me on my sixteenth birthday. It's a must-wear every day. Everything else gets switched out, depending on my mood that day.

I'm late, but then again, I'm always late. I don't usually do it intentionally. I just have a habit of misreading the time. Thankfully, for my career, I work on my own schedule, or otherwise, I'm pretty sure I'd be fired.

My phone buzzes again, and I pull it out, noticing a missed call from Hawke. The guy's persistent, but that's not my problem. Tonight, I'm planning on getting laid. That will definitely wash away this weird fixation I have with Hawke as of late.

CHAPTER 14

Ivy

When I arrive at the party, it's already in full swing. Makayla was very popular in college. She was known for her party-girl ways, which is why we naturally gravitated toward each other and became friends.

On the nights Billie wanted to focus on her studies, Makayla and I went out on the town in London. I don't talk to her as much now, other than a few social media comments here and there. She moved to Manhattan—around the same time I came back—to be closer to her on-again, off-again boyfriend, Jared, who is originally from here. Despite our infrequent communication, there's one thing we can depend on each other for. If there's a party, it's go time.

There are only a few people here I recognize, but I don't need people I know in order to have a good time. I could be placed in a room full of strangers and still have the most epic night. It's one of my many talents. Like my father, my mother always told me I'm a total extrovert. I do, however, enjoy my own company and sometimes prefer that, but I draw my energy from large groups of people.

The restaurant is cute and has been designed to create a mini-club vibe, and it's often rented out for special events. I don't know whose birthday this party is for, and I don't care. There aren't many guest lists I can't get on.

I spot Makayla straight away, Jared basically attached to her hip. I don't know why those two stay together. They're always cheating on each other, hooking up with complete strangers to make each other jealous. Yet they always work their way back to one other, even knowing how toxic it is. I told her what I thought about it once, and I've never bothered to repeat it because it's not my life.

Jared notices me first and immediately pulls me in for a hug. "It's been a while. We've missed you. You've been quiet on the town lately," he says, and before I can reply, Makayla pushes Jared out of the way and screams so loudly that we both cringe from what might be close to a pierced eardrum. She throws her arms around me, the force of her embrace causing me to take a couple of steps back. I quickly realize how drunk she is already.

"I've missed you," she slurs in her British accent.

"She's already ten shots in," Jared explains. Then he motions to the guy next to him. "This is my friend Lester."

Makayla steps back and looks at me seriously without giving me time to greet their friend. "You have to catch up," she demands as she grabs a shot glass from the table they're sitting at and hands it to me.

"Don't have to tempt me with a good time," I reply, then throw it back. She claps loudly as she grabs a second shot glass, and I hold up a hand.

"Let me breathe first," I say. She might be ten in already, but I want to at least enjoy the taste of a drink. The night's young, and I want to savor it as I circle the room and see who grabs my attention.

"Ohhhh, any new boys on the radar for you?" she asks, leaning into me as if I'm harboring a great secret, and begins to scan the room. Jared doesn't seem impressed but takes a seat beside me with a group of people I haven't yet met.

"Ewww. We fuck *men*, Makayla," I tell her with raised brows. "And, no, I'm not seeing anyone exclusively."

One thing I've noticed about my college friends, especially my fellow party girls, is the moment they shack up with someone, they ask when everyone else will be in a relationship. And then it's like they try to relive their glory days through me while pitying me at the same time. I really don't give a shit about any of it, though. I'm grateful I don't have to deal with that from Billie and Hope.

"But you want to be?" she asks. That's when I notice her eyes are dilated. Okay, maybe she's done more than just drink. Don't get me wrong, I've tried party drugs before, but I've never been dependent on them to have fun. Makayla looks like she's pumped full of them right now.

I go to tell her no, but then her hands are on my face again. "Oh my God! I have the perfect idea," she squeals, and Jared rolls his eyes, obviously exhausted.

Makayla grabs my hand, then glances around the table, realizing it's full of empty glasses. Then, she looks behind her at a table with a half-full wine glass on it.

"I just need to borrow this for a sec," she says, swiping it from someone who looks at her confused but says nothing. It's the usual reaction when Makayla is up to her antics.

She places it in front of me and then scoots Jared's glass of whiskey closer.

"Now, you hold this, and you hold this," she instructs. Jared is now holding the whiskey glass, and my fingers dance at the base of the wine glass. "We're going to play a game. Jared, get closer to her."

He shoots me a puzzled look but does as she says, and I wonder where she's going with this. I'm all for games and pranks, but Makayla's are sometimes... not fun.

"I played this game with Jared once," she says proudly, and he rolls his eyes.

She reaches for my purse, and I pull it out of her grasp.

"What are you doing?" I ask.

"I need your phone. Trust me." I don't trust her, but I'm also curious. "Unlock it, please."

Jared takes a sip of his drink and casually asks me, "How long are you in town for this time?"

"I live here now," I tell him, and he pauses his glass at his lips. "I'm still traveling a lot, though."

"She's been complaining about you not coming out much lately," he says as Makayla stands behind us and clears her throat.

"Cozy up and keep the hands close," she directs as she takes a photo of only our drinks and hands, then posts it to my Instagram story, along with a tag of our location.

From an outsider looking at the photo, it appears like I'm on a date with a mystery man.

"Why did you do that?" I ask, and she bounces between us, shuffling to sit on Jared's lap and then winding her arms around his neck. She's chuffed with herself.

"Well, I like to call it dick roulette. The guys on your account who are obsessed with you will most likely arrive, and it'll be entertainment for us. And, bonus, you'll get laid. Win-win." She claps her hands excitedly. I look to Jared, who shrugs and wraps an arm around Makayla's waist. She reaches for another shot and sets it in front of me, and I decide to make more room for them by sitting on the other side of their friend, Lester.

"Glad I have company now," he jokes. He's attractive but not really someone I'd go out of my way to sleep with. Maybe after a few drinks, I might think differently.

"Better buckle up; it's about to get fun," I say as I cheer with the second shot. Jared is staring at us. He often does that—watches me when we're all out together—and I'm certain he's not a fan of me sleeping with any of his friends. If they're single, they're free game.

I start talking with Lester, and it quickly becomes apparent that he's not my type. My ovaries shrivel by the second as he talks grotesquely about Instagram models who would be out of his league even if he theoretically met them. Snooze.

I slip away and start mingling with the other guests. I notice a girl vomiting in the corner, which isn't surprising at these types of events. One of her friends is holding back her hair, and the poor waitress looks like she doesn't know what to do. Someone else walks past with a bucket of bottled water. I swipe one, my stomach stirring at the thought of being in the same situation as that poor girl.

Maybe there's something in the air because I start feeling nauseous myself. The alcohol is hitting me, which is weird because I've only had two shots and can usually drink far more before I start feeling sick. I pull out my phone to check the time. I haven't even been here for an hour. I feel my forehead. Am I sick? No, I don't think so.

I struggle to focus on the person speaking to me, their words blurring and their voice getting fuzzy. I can't quite comprehend what they're saying.

"Ivy." I don't know who says my name, but I wave them off and try to find somewhere to sit. I think I need another glass of water. Did I eat today? Maybe that's why I feel tipsy. I usually eat before I drink because otherwise, I feel sick. I don't exactly feel sick right now, but something isn't right.

CHAPTER 15

Hawke

I'm in a bad mood. Not only did the deal between Eli and one of his distributors go well, but he's also advised that Ford and I can finish early for the night. This calm shit is starting to make me restless. I thought I'd be able to carve at least one person up tonight, but everyone seems to be falling into line. It's fucking weird.

"Pearl?" I suggest to Ford as he drives. He side-eyes me. We've just dropped Eli off at his mansion, and I already know the answer. "You're boring now that you have a girlfriend," I say sulkily.

He sighs. "You know, I never enjoyed going to those clubs anyway. I always went to make sure you didn't get into trouble."

I smile. "Aren't you worried I'll get into trouble now?"

"Always. Maybe you should pick up another hobby besides drinking and fucking."

My jaw drops. "Blasphemy!" I exclaim as I open my phone and begin scrolling.

I'm looking to see what everyone else is up to, and that's when I come across a recent story from the one and only Ivy Walker. My eyebrow raises. I can see now why she couldn't answer my call. She's too busy getting cozied up with some dickhead. Ivy never posts images of guys. And, okay, it might just be his hand holding a drink, but I already want to fucking break it. More so because I know without seeing the body attached to the said hand that, I'm a lot more fun. That's all I'm looking for tonight— some fun. And I have a roadmap directly to that location.

The moment we arrive at Ford's, I'm out of his car and into mine. He looks at me like I've grown a third head. "You're not coming in tonight?" he asks.

The truth is, I know he and Billie want their own time together. Everyone jokes that I can't read a room, and although Ford and Billie don't treat me any differently, I know I need to create space for them that's independent of me.

"Not tonight, brother. One of us has to have some fun." I wink and put the car into drive. I blast my music as I tap my thumb against the steering wheel.

It seems my little lover thinks she can go on a date

without me. But it's like she wants me to find her with the tag of her location.

She posted the story over an hour ago, but I'm gambling on the chance that she's still here. If not, I'll track her down in my own way.

I park my car at the curb, and before I've even opened the door, a bouncer approaches with his hand outstretched. "You can't park there."

I step out, coming to my full height, and square him up. I make a point to lock my car as I step up and loom over him. The dickhead actually pales as I calmly ask him, "You sure about that?"

He gulps. Part of me hopes he says it twice. I wasn't able to entertain myself tonight, and if he's the only fucker coming between me and fixing my boredom, then it'll be his downfall.

"M-maybe just once is okay," he stammers, and I give him a bright smile as I pat his shoulder.

"Make sure no one scratches my car, or I'll make you personally accountable for it," I say as I head for the restaurant's entrance. I fucking love my car.

The moment I step inside, my ears are assaulted by loud chatter and even louder music. Drunk women are laughing and dancing in groups scattered throughout the space. Trays of alcohol are being distributed, and I sift through the bodies, looking for the curves I've memorized by heart.

My gaze catches on the hand of some guy at the bar,

and I change course to head in that fucker's direction. He has the same tattoo on his hand as the guy in Ivy's photo; however, he currently has that hand around another woman. Honestly, the ugly-ass tattoo looks like it was done by a two-year-old. Without hesitation, I walk straight up to him. The woman he's with turns and spots me first, her lips curve seductively as she scans me from head to toe, like she just found a new snack. When he turns around and catches sight of me, he pales. I don't blame him. I plan to cut that hand off him.

"You here with Ivy?" I ask him. His eyes go wide, and the woman he's with laughs.

"I know you. I've seen you out before," she slurs. "I'm Makayla." I really don't care. "And this is *my* boyfriend. We made a joke and posted a picture on Ivy's stories to see which guys would fall for the bait. Did you see it?"

I don't care what the reason behind it was; it's all the same to me.

"So you didn't touch her?" I say to him, ignoring her obvious smugness. She can lump me in with whatever men she wants to. Any man would be fucking lucky to lay eyes on Ivy.

"No," he says a little too quickly.

"Hmm." I size him up, unsure if I should still kick his ass. I break out into a bright smile. "I guess you can live tonight." He tries to laugh it off, but I don't share the humor with him.

"Where is she?" I ask her friend.

She waves to her left. "She's probably over there, sleeping on the table. Needed some fresh air or something."

Sleeping? Ivy is a night owl through and through, and I've never seen her drink more than she can handle. I walk in the direction she indicated. There's a small outside area where a few people have congregated. My stomach twists as I spot her. She's sitting at a table with her head propped in her hands. A guy is sitting beside her, his hand gliding up and down her leg, getting too fucking close to the hem of her dress for my liking. Something's not right. This isn't the bright, flirtatious Ivy I know. And she'd certainly never give a douchebag like this the time of day.

"Ivy." The man jumps as I call out her name, his hand immediately pulling away as if he knows he's in the wrong.

Not going to fucking happen, motherfucker. I grab the collar of his shirt, and he immediately raises his hands defensively. "I-I don't w-want any trouble."

"What did you do?" I growl, aware that the couple sitting closest to us are quick to head back inside. I can feel eyes on me, but I don't fucking care. Never have and never will. I've never had any restraint, and I certainly don't have a tether when it comes to *her* or anyone willing to fuck with her shining light.

"Nothing, she wants me, man," he tries to say confidently.

"She doesn't. Of that, I'm sure."

"Look, I was told she was easy. You know how it is—" I grab the back of his head and slam it into the table. I hear the satisfying crunch of his nose. Then I throw him around like a ragdoll. He falls to the floor in a heap, and I kick him hard between his legs, ensuring he won't be using that area anytime soon. He's choking on sobs and shock as blood pours out of his nose, but I'm far from done. I bend down and raise his arm, the one he was touching her with. I smile, the buzz of murderous intent coursing through my veins. An old friend, a lover, the part of me that has always gone unchecked and kept me alive.

His eyes go wide in horror as if knowing what I'm about to do. He tries to tug his hand back, but it's too late, and I'm double his size. I snap his wrist, and he screams. I stand to my full height, watching him whimper and pale as he stares at his limp wrist before I kick him in the head. Hard. He immediately goes still and quiet.

I couldn't care less if he's dead or not.

Ivy mumbles something. It's incoherent but enough to draw me back to her. I want to pummel this guy into nothing but a fleshy puddle, but my focus lies elsewhere. I crouch beside her, trying to see her face, but she's barely able to hold her head up.

Fuck. She's not okay.

I scoop her into my arms, holding her close to my chest, and her body goes limp as a noodle, and her eyes are a sliver open. People stare and make way for me as I stride back through the party. No one tries to stop me, but if they did, I'll kick their fucking heads in as well. I hear her friend calling out, but I ignore her. Shit fucking friend she is. If I were a woman, I'd kick her head in as well.

When I walk out of the restaurant, I head straight for my car. I shift her weight so I can open the door and place her in the passenger seat. I buckle her seat belt, then wipe the smudged makeup under her eyes. This isn't the Ivy I know. How much has she had to drink?

"Ivy, baby, how much did you have to drink?" I ask her, lightly tapping her cheek.

Her head rolls to the side, and she mumbles something incoherent, but then she holds up three, then four, then two fingers before her head rolls to the other side, and she passes out cold, lightly snoring.

"Fucking hell," I curse. My fear is confirmed. She's not drunk. She's been drugged.

CHAPTER 16

Ivy

My head and body ache like I've had way too many drinks. My mouth is dry, and my eyes feel like they're glued together. I eventually manage to crack my lids enough to see I'm in a dark room. Dread fills my stomach as I realize this isn't my room or my bed. *Where the fuck am I?* I start breathing heavily as panic grips my throat like a vise. The last thing I remember is that guy Lester was trying to talk to me while I drank some water because my head was spinning.

"Water is next to you." I jump at the sound of the voice, my heart rate picking up speed until my brain registers that the voice is familiar.

"Hawke?" I ask carefully. He shifts in the seat he's sitting in beside the bed. I can just make out his bulky silhouette in the dark.

"I'm here, baby," he says gently. Ordinarily, I'd reprimand him for using a nickname like that on me, but right now, I'm just relieved he's here. "This might hurt a little."

A side table light turns on, and my eyes immediately close, affronted at the brightness. He quickly dims it and then hands me a bottle of painkillers. I try my hardest to push myself up, but I just feel like shit. Everything aches. He holds out a glass of water. That's when I realize I'm in his bed. I try to put pieces together, but it's just blank. Why am I here? I don't remember seeing him at the party.

The party...

I swear I only had a couple of drinks. I'm so confused right now, and when I reach for the water, my hands are so shaky that I drop the glass and spill it all over the floor.

I want to cry. I don't know why, but I just do. I'm overwhelmed. The pain, the unknown...

"It's okay," he says quietly as he leans over to pick it up. He's looking at me like I'm some wounded animal, and I fucking hate it. *What happened to me?* "I'll get you some more." He walks into his bathroom to fill the glass with more water.

I run my hands through my hair. I look under the blankets, comforted a little, when I find I'm still wearing my dress.

"Why am I here?" I ask when he returns. I reach for the glass again, but my hands won't stop shaking, so he puts it to my lips. My eyebrows furrow in confusion, but I feel so out of sorts that I let him.

"Drink." I do as he says and take a sip. It immediately moistens my mouth, bringing relief, but it also brings on an unsettling wave of nausea in my stomach. I take another two mouthfuls and pull away.

"Did you accept drinks from anyone?" he questions, now sitting at the edge of the bed. The mattress dips to the side under his weight.

Dread fills me because there's usually only one reason people ask that question. And I know the truth of it even when it's unsaid. I was drugged.

"Yes," I say quietly.

Blank. It's all blank. All I remember is walking into the party. Having a few shots. And it becomes hazy after that. Then nothing.

"Drink," he says again as if distracting me from my spiraling thoughts. This might be the gentlest I've ever seen Hawke. But underneath his cool demeanor is a rage I'm too scared to draw attention to. I'm used to his brother being quiet and calm. But Hawke is full of expression. Not right now, though. He's as terrifying as he is gentle.

Sure, I've seen him pick fights, but those times feel different from now. This is a palpable tension, reminding me just how dangerous he truly is.

"You know better than to do that. Did you forget where you come from?" he scolds.

"Please don't reprimand me right now," I quickly bite back as I try to keep the tears away. He looks up then as if seeing me for the first time, and I see the remorse in his eyes.

"I'm sorry. I just—I feel so useless right now." He blows out a breath.

"This isn't your fault," I assure him as I put my hand on his shoulder. The motion of me stretching toward him must be too much for my stomach to handle because the water I drank comes up just as quickly as it went down. I vomit all over his arm and the side of the bed.

I sit back, mortified.

The big oaf doesn't even move, unfazed, as he brushes back my hair. I try to tell him to stop. That it's gross, but I vomit again. I'm gasping as I fight back and forth with whether my stomach is settled.

"I'm sorry," I whimper as I wipe my mouth.

"You have nothing to apologize for," he says as he pulls back the covers and swiftly scoops me into his arms. His sea breeze-scented cologne hits my nose, but it's overpowered by the smell of my vomit on his shirt. He carries me into the bathroom and places me gently beside the toilet, where I'm quick to vomit again, clinging to the bowl.

I hear water running, but before I can lift my head to look, I'm throwing up again with slight relief that at least it's in a toilet and not all over a six-foot-two mountain of a man.

He brushes back my hair, and just when I think I have nothing left to throw up, I'm heaving again. I wish I hadn't drunk that water, even though at the time, it was the best water I'd ever tasted.

When my vomiting eases, he slowly unzips my dress. I don't even bother pushing him away because I know, for once in his life, he isn't trying to fuck me. I feel like a rag doll as he reaches under my arms and lifts me as if I weigh nothing. Other men struggle to lift me, while Hawke does it so effortlessly. He holds me up with one hand and slides the dress off so I'm only in my underwear.

My head feels like it's bobbing from side to side, and the room seems unbearably hot.

He proceeds to take off my underwear and then carries me toward a claw-footed tub where the water is running. I catch a glimpse of myself in the mirror, and if I had the strength to open my eyes all the way, they would bug out of my head at the sight of me. There's dried vomit on my cheek, my hair is a disaster, and I'm pale yet flushed. I look like death warmed over, and honestly, I don't even recognize myself right now.

He lowers me into the bath, and the water, though only coming up to my waist feels like heaven, relaxing me almost instantly. "Don't drown yourself," he says, then turns to the sink. He grabs his toothbrush and puts toothpaste on it.

His actions seem automatic. As if he's done this a million times before.

He holds out the toothbrush, and I take it from him, my arms feeling like Jell-O. I brush my teeth and scrub my tongue, and when I'm done, I hand it back to him and watch as he throws it in the trash.

I'm freaked out about the blank spots in my mind, and if it weren't for Hawke, I might've actually spiraled and lost my shit. I'm a level-headed woman, but this is a woman's worst nightmare. What-if scenarios race through my brain, and I immediately shut them out. *No.* That didn't happen. If I'm with Hawke, that means I'm safe.

Hawke grabs a bottle of body wash and places it on the edge of the tub. "Give me your hands," he gently orders. I do as he says, fascinated by this side of him. It's like seeing him as a completely different person.

"How do you know what to do?" I ask. My voice comes out in a rasp, and I can tell the sound of it grates on him. For such a big guy, he looks so small right now. I'm not yet ready to ask him what state he found me in. I'm too scared of the answer.

"My mother was a drug addict. The memories I remember most are of putting her to bed and making sure she didn't choke on her own vomit in her sleep.

Cleaning her up became second nature," he says matter-of-factly.

My heart breaks as I imagine Hawke as a child. It's so strange to think of him as anything but this giant. I'd heard they'd lived on the streets before Anya adopted them, and although I've been tempted to dive into Ford's and his history, I've always refrained from doing so. If he wanted me to know, he'd tell me himself.

"What happened to her?" I ask. I can't even imagine living in a home like that. I almost feel guilty for having the parents and upbringing I did.

He looks at me then as if realizing I'm curious about him. He silently requests my other hand. I give it to him, and he cleans it just as gently as he did the first one. "You don't have to ever be shy to ask me questions, Ivy. I'm an open book," he says as he leans over to put the cloth in the water and run it over my skin. "She overdosed when we were twelve. We didn't have any other family to go to, and we have no idea who the fuck our dad is, so Ford and I lived on the streets.

"It was always just us. I always felt like I had to protect him, you know. He's smarter and can hold his own, but I was always bigger than him. I mean, I had to be all brawn if he was the brains." The last bit is said in a joking manner, but it hurts to hear. I've never once thought of Hawke as stupid. An impulsive, open book, yes. But never stupid.

"We lived on the streets until we broke into Anya and River's home when we were fifteen." He smirks at the memory. "Anya put a gun to both of our heads when they found us, and it was River who wanted to give us a second chance. I don't know why, but he saw something in us. I think he also pitied us, but as I came to know them better, I learned that pity isn't exactly something our mother feels."

I've met Anya Ivanov plenty of times, and that woman is terrifying.

He then looks up as if recalling another memory. "Ford and I also learned how to help each other out when Anya introduced us to micro poisoning to build our tolerance. She said it'd come in handy, but I thought she was paranoid. Turns out, it's exactly what saved Ford's life when—"

His circles on my arm come to a stop abruptly, and I can see the moment he recedes back into himself.

"What happened that day?" I ask quietly. Not even Billie gave me details, and I didn't want to push her too much about it. I know she was poisoned. Was this what it felt like for her when she woke? I inwardly curl into myself, the terror rising at the thought of what might've happened during the time I can't remember.

"I don't want to talk about it," he says, immediately closing up despite just telling me I can ask him anything. A tangible weight fills the room. My curious mind wants to push him further, but the exhaustion from last night and the warmth of the water are quickly sapping every-thing out of me.

"How did you know where to find me?" I ask. I want to ask what state I was in and what happened, but those questions just won't leave my lips. He looks at me then. Despite being naked, his gaze has not once wavered from mine.

He pulls out his phone and shows me the IG story Makayla posted. I completely forgot about that. I don't want to inquire about Hawke's motivations for showing up at the party because, frankly, I'm just grateful he did. When I needed someone the most, he was there. Even when I didn't ask him to be, he just was, like he is now.

"I didn't post that, for what it's worth," I tell him.

"Oh, I know. But I'm grateful your shitty friend did," he says, that lethal edge creeping into his voice.

"You can't kill her, Hawke," I say, rolling my head to the side.

"I don't kill women," he snaps, and it's so startling that we just stare at one another.

"I'm sorry. I—" He cuts himself off abruptly.

"I know you wouldn't. It's okay. I'm sorry for saying that." I'm certain he wants to burn the world alive right now, and it offers me a sense of safety to know that someone cares about what happens to me. I know people care. I just... It feels different with him.

I curl my knees into my stomach as he looks over me with concern. "Are you feeling sick again?" he asks.

I shake my head, exhaustion grabbing at me again. The pounding in my head begins to take over again. I close my eyes and say, "Hawke, please don't tell any of my friends or family about this. I just want to work it out on my own first."

I'm surprised when he takes my hand in his. I open my eyes again and look at him. "Nothing happened to you. I found you at the party an hour after the picture was posted."

Relief washes through me. Although he can't guarantee nothing happened to me, knowing he found me so quickly makes me feel a little better. "Thank you for coming for me," I whisper as I sleepily close my eyes again. "And I'm sorry about your bed. I should go home," I add absently, my mind slowly being pulled under a haze.

"You should sleep. Don't worry. I'll look after you," he promises.

I feel him lifting me out of the bath and wrapping me in a towel. I come in and out of coherence as he puts one of his shirts over my head and helps guide my arms through the sleeves.

I can keep my eyes open long enough to realize he's changed the sheets and blanket on his bed before he places me down gently and tucks me in. This Hawke is different. Maybe it's all just a dream. Or a nightmare.

"Go to sleep," he coos. But I don't need his encouragement as the darkness takes over.

CHAPTER 17

Hawke

"Not many people surprise me. I certainly wasn't expecting it from you," Braxton says, standing at my front door late the next evening.

This guy pisses me off, and I can't believe I felt the need to actually call him myself. I stayed with Ivy all fucking night and all morning. I don't think she realizes how much she slept. And I stayed in that fucking chair, imagining all the ways I should've killed that fucking dickhead who thought he could take advantage of her. But make no mistake... he will die.

"You just going to stare me down or put cash in my hand?" Braxton says.

"You're such a dick," I grumble, reminding myself of all the reasons why I called him and why I shouldn't kill my cousin's new boyfriend.

"And you're an asshole. So what do you need?" His smile brightens, and I wonder if the reason I don't like him is because we're similar. Most likely. He's cocky, opinionated, and antagonizing. Had we met under other circumstances, I might've liked him.

He puts his hands in his pockets as if he has all the time in the world. But I don't. "Early hours are usually the best for murder, wouldn't you say?" I'm not surprised that he figured it out so quickly since he tracks anything Ivanov-related. I was messy, kicking that guy's ass at the party, and reports most likely have already been made. Ones that only this fucker can make disappear. Something he's been doing for years without us realizing.

"Which hospital is the fucker at?" I ask.

"Cough up the money first." He smirks. I pull out my phone and transfer the money. "I could've texted the address to you, so why did you call me over?"

I grind my teeth. I didn't exactly want to call him. But I also refuse to let that fucker who tried to hurt Ivy still be breathing by the time she wakes up again. She asked me not to tell any of her friends or family. If I call Ford, who I trust the most, he'll tell Billie. I could call my parents, but the Walkers are good friends with my uncle Alek. We're all interwoven, and this new fucker seems like the only option who can clean my mess, even after I murder the fucker in the hospital.

But most importantly... "I need you to watch Ivy

while I'm out for an hour." I step to the side, inviting him into my home.

His eyebrows furrow. "Why are you asking me?"

"Because I know you'll keep your mouth shut. You want to be accepted into the family, right?" I grit.

"Hope's mom already loves me," he says matter-of-factly as he steps inside. This guy is such a dickhead. "You know, this is usually something my little shortcake would handle. This guy is just her type, you know—a man who hurts women." It's only become recent knowledge for a lot of us that my cousin is a serial killer who targets men who try to hurt women, but this asshole is mine.

"This is personal, and I'm not a patient man. I have cameras around the house, and I swear to God if you touch her or—"

He puts his hand up. "Let me assure you, the only woman I like to fuck is your sweet little cousin." *Asshole.* "I didn't think there was anything between you and Ivy Walker anyway."

"That's none of your business. And besides, we look out for one another here," I say as I push past him. I don't want to leave her, but I'll self-implode if I don't finish the job. I wasn't thinking clearly when I found her like that. I wish I'd killed him then.

I'm walking toward my car as he calls out from behind me, "Nothing happened to her, by the way." I turn to face him. "I watched the footage just to make sure." Relief rushes through me, but that knowledge doesn't change anything.

"Just because it didn't happen this time doesn't mean the same fucker won't try it again to someone else." I turn and continue to my car, that lethal edge cracking through to the surface. This part of me, that I summon like a god, has a mind of its own. I know I'm impulsive. I know I'm consumed by it. But every time I welcome it, I enjoy the thrill of power it offers me.

I'm checking my cameras on my phone constantly, even as I walk through the hospital, ignoring those I pass as I stride in purposefully, still with vomit on my shirt. I see Braxton standing across the room from her as she sleeps curled up in a ball, short blonde hair fanned over my pillows. I wanted someone with her in case she vomits again and doesn't find the bucket beside her.

I walk down the quiet corridor, my temper following me like a shadow as patients sleep. My family has a lot of connections, and despite disliking the detective, the fucker is handy. Buying out doctors and erasing records is done within seconds with the right people in your pocket.

I come to a stop at his room, thinking about Ivy last night and the state she was in. I wish she could see this. Feel the satisfaction and relief that will come from it. But

I know it's better to keep her away from it. She might not be able to spill blood, but I'll gladly do it for her.

The door silently opens, and I find the fucker passed out in his hospital bed. His arm is in a cast, and he looks bedridden. I guess it sucks to be him. I shut the door behind me, then pull the curtain so no one can see through the door. I loom over him, and the fucker has no better sense to stir awake. I reach inside my jacket and find my spiked gloves.

When Ford and I survived fighting on the streets, I learned that my greatest weapons were my fists, while he prefers crowbars. Even when we began working for Eli, we never changed our methods. I like feeling bones break and blood splattering my skin. The spikes on the knuckles of my gloves make everything far more explosive and effective. Instead of putting them on as I usually would, I put them on the opposite hands, so the spikes are on the palms so whatever I grab will feel the bite of them.

These gloves have taken many lives. But this one, I think, will be one of my favorites. I flick off his machines, and a moment later, his eyelids burst open. Horror mars his features as his gaze quickly flicks to the gloves and then back to my face as if he can't believe I'm standing here. I bet he wishes it were a nightmare. But I imagine he's used to being the monster haunting plenty of women's dreams. How many women has he done it to? How long has he thought he'd go unpunished?

"Hello, Lester." I smile like the devil himself, embracing the part of me that only wants to see a price paid in blood. "I bet you thought you'd seen the last of me." I lean down and pull the blankets off him. He cries out and tries to fight against me, but no one will hear him. And even if they do, no one will come. Turns out, having influential parents and a dirty detective in the family makes things really easy.

"I-I didn't d-do anything," he stammers. I don't care what he has to say. I saw what he was doing with my own fucking eyes. That was all the proof I needed. "I didn't know she was your woman," he says in the next breath, which very much says he knows what he was doing. "I didn't supply it." I would really like to take this nice and slow, stretch it out, slowly run my glove up and down his skin, but I have a woman to return to. "I'll give you names," he says in a pleading tone.

"You talk too much for a dead man," I say, reaching for the pillow behind his head and taking the pillowcase off with my free hand, then stuffing it into his mouth. He tries to pull it out, but I hold his arm down, the spikes of my glove digging into his skin and making him wince. His other arm is already in a cast, including his fingers, so he can't use that at all. Such a shame. So helpless. As most cowards are.

I pull his hospital gown up, and when I do, I see a sad excuse for a fucking dick. I bet women laugh at it; probably why he drugs them because it's the only way he can fuck them. The fucking asshole.

I'm a cold-blooded killer, make no mistake about that, but what this man does is disgusting. And all people like him should be put six feet into the fucking ground. He tries to pull his arm free, but I'm a lot stronger than he is. I wrap my other gloved hand around his cock. His screams are muffled by the pillowcase as he tries to kick and wriggle from the hold I have on him. I squeeze harder, and blood begins to ooze from his cock.

A man like him isn't deserving of a dick. It should only be used to please women or to be pleased by a willing partner. And it seems this man has his priorities all mixed up, so I've come to fix that for him. I squeeze a little harder, and blood starts leaking onto his bed. His eyes roll back in his head, and he quickly passes out, taking much of the fun out of this for me. Fucking pussy.

I grab his throat, the spikes on my gloves puncturing his flesh. I squeeze, satisfaction bubbling up inside me as I feel the life draining from him. I focus my hearing on his labored, unhinged breaths as his body tries to keep him alive. Too bad the Grim Reaper has decided it's his time to die.

It's like watching a worm wriggle until his breathing comes to a stop. I can't even find satisfaction in the kill as I blink once and then twice. How long have I been choking him? Blood has spread all down my gloves and is seeping through the blankets.

I release him and walk over to the sink to rinse my gloves. I sometimes lose myself in moments like these. I get so excited by the kill that it becomes patchy for me. When I step out of the room, two men are waiting in the hall with a small rolling bin. They're the cleanup crew.

They nod their heads and then enter the room. Pulling out my phone, I immediately check my home cameras, thankful to find her still sound asleep.

CHAPTER 18

Ivy

I'm not sure how long I've been here, but the second time I wake up, I feel a lot better than I did the first time. My stomach gurgles with hunger, and I'm thankful it seems to be settling down. My mind feels clearer, and I don't feel so sluggish and dead on the inside. I turn to my side and find him in bed next to me, his back against the headboard, his arms crossed over his chest, sleeping without a shirt on. He most likely had to shower after I vomited all over him. I take the opportunity to study him closely.

Tattoos cover his chest and arms. There are only a few spots without any ink, and I know, without a doubt, he'll find something to fill them. I'm jealous of the asshole's thick eyelashes, and his hair looks effortlessly styled despite just being washed. Hawke is beautiful, and it's strange to view him the same way I might've days ago, after how carefully he treated me. It's a sobering thought to think about how fucked-up his childhood was. I wonder who looked after him. I have the urge to curl my fingers through his hair, but refrain because I don't want to wake him.

I turn back around, reach for the glass of water he left for me, and take a sip. There's a small package of crackers there as well, and as if my stomach senses them, it growls loudly, and I curl into myself, willing it to stop.

"You've been asleep for almost two days. You need to eat something," he says from over my shoulder. Damn, I always thought he was a heavy sleeper.

"Sorry for waking you," I say as I turn back to face him.

"I was only resting my eyes." His eyes are still closed, and he looks so tired. This is a side to Hawke I've never seen before. I wonder if anyone but his brother has seen this part of him that almost seems... sad.

"What time is it?" I ask, looking for my phone and spotting it on his side table.

"Four in the morning on Sunday."

"Sunday?!" I yell, sitting upright. He opens one eye now, his almost-black gaze finding me.

No wonder I feel like I've slept like the dead. I've literally slept for almost two days. When was the last time I slept like that?

Memories come back of spewing all over his bed, and I instantly feel guilty. I always assumed someone like him would have a housekeeper and that he wouldn't do things like that, but I guess I've been wrong about a few things when it comes to Hawke.

"I can pay your housekeeper bill. For the sheets. Thank you for looking after me."

"I've already washed them."

"You do your own laundry?" I ask, amused. I know Hawke has money, a lot of it, so imagining him doing something so domestic is... I try not to smirk. "Why?" I'm spoiled because my mother does mine, and I'd much rather buy a new outfit than wash laundry. I'm not incapable of it. I just hate it. I immediately try to imagine Anya doing the ironing, and the image is easily replaced by River doing it.

He casually shrugs. "You'll laugh at me."

"No, I won't," I say, promising myself I won't laugh at him.

He seems hesitant but sighs and then explains, "I come from nothing, so while it's nice to have money and do all the fancy things we dreamed about when we lived on the streets, I always told myself if I could just get a washer, I'd do all of my laundry myself. So when I bought this place, it was the first thing Anya gave me, and I still use the same one."

"She gave you a washing machine?" I ask in disbelief. I never expect these types of responses from him. I thought all Hawke did was fuck, party, kill, and lift weights.

"Yep. Our first Christmas together, she asked what we wanted. Ford remained quiet, and I blurted out, I wanted a washing machine. Trust me, when you live in the same clothes for weeks on end, you want one." A cheesy smile spreads on his face. "I just didn't think she'd buy me another one when I moved out and bought this place when I was eighteen."

It's crazy to think how quickly they turned their lives around. Sure, the twins had had help from Anya, but they honed their skills enough to impress Eli and ended up working for him. I grew up around those guys and know they're as ruthless as they come. Maybe I'm desensitized to it all because I'm not scared of them. Never have been and never will. But that's a luxury I know only a few have.

I don't comment on his living situation because I can't relate, but that doesn't mean I don't have empathy for everything he's been through. I was raised by two loving parents who literally showed me the world. We are different in a lot of ways, but at the same time, we're somehow alike.

"Have you traveled much?" I ask. Hawke has a social media account, but he rarely posts anything. And the number of women who follow him anyway is mind-boggling. Most likely, they're just sliding into his DMs. But I've never heard about him traveling.

"Nope. I think I have a passport somewhere. I've just never had the urge to since I'm by Eli's side all the time," he says, closing his eyes once again. "But you love to visit other places, don't you?"

Grabbing the crackers, I put one in my mouth, chew it up, then swallow it before I say, "It's my favorite thing in the world."

"Maybe we'll go somewhere together one of these days, and you can show me around," he says through a yawn. I turn to face him, place the second cracker in my mouth, and see he's already fallen asleep. I soften toward him a little more. I've heard about how heavy a sleeper he is, but it looks like he hasn't slept in months.

I think back on our conversation last night. I wonder if this has anything to do with his outburst on not hurting women. There's something vulnerable about Hawke that I've never noticed before. Despite his size, I'm reminded that he was once a little boy. Actually, it's clear as day that that little boy is still in there somewhere because he still acts like a big guy. It's part of his personality that often drives everyone insane.

I quietly climb out of his bed, hoping not to wake him. I head downstairs to the kitchen, still wearing one of his shirts that comes to my knees. I like Hawke's home; it's flashy, sizeable, and far too large for him to live in alone, especially compared to his brother's modestly-sized home. I wonder if that's because he never had this as a kid. But I can't help thinking about how lonely it must be living in a five-bedroom home without anyone else.

Maybe that's why he's always partying. I don't think he likes to be alone.

When I pull open the fridge door, I'm not surprised by how stocked it is. I try not to laugh. It couldn't scream "bachelor" any louder even if he tried. It's full of various meat, eggs, and protein drinks. Protein. Protein. Protein.

I don't expect anything less from a man who loves to eat as much as he does, and it takes a hell of a lot of food to maintain a body that big, I imagine. I settle on making a sandwich since he has bread in the fridge, which, okay, is kind of weird. But it'll do. I grab some meat and settle for that since he literally has no greens for a salad.

I make two sandwiches, one for myself and one for him, because he never turns down food. I take a peek into his personal gym before going back upstairs. I've seen all of this through his cameras, but being here. Seeing it all in person is different. It smells like him. *Feels* like him.

One of his eyelids peels open the moment I step back into the room. I'm certain it has less to do with my presence and more to do with the instinctual knowing that food is within his vicinity.

"You don't have any salad," I say, handing him the plate.

He curls up his nose. "You don't make friends with salad."

I shake my head as I take a seat beside him. It feels strange not having the sexual energy between us. Just simply being. Sex is the last thing on my mind right now as terror grips my lower stomach at the thought of what might've happened that night at the party. I side-eye Hawke, once again feeling a rush of gratitude for my unlikely hero.

I pick at the sandwich, making a decision to take back my power. This incident has deeply affected me, and I'm sure I'll have to figure out a way to overcome it completely. But my curious mind needs answers. I need to know what I'm dealing with.

"Did you find out who drugged me?" I ask, trying to be nonchalant as I take a bite.

"Yep," he answers, already having demolished his sandwich. Okay, I should've made him two. "It's been handled." And that's all he gives me as he lies down, his massive arms flexing as he tucks his hands behind his head. I don't even want to ask what his definition of "handled" is. If he's anything like my father or the other men we're associated with, it means the guy is on a magical boat to hell, most likely sent there by an excruciating death. Suddenly, I've lost my appetite.

"Do you want half?" I offer.

"You should eat more than half."

"I can't. It hurts my stomach," I tell him, and he's quick to devour it.

I lie down beside him, staring at him. It feels surreal and intimate. I've never done this with a man... just laid in bed beside them and not fucked. But it's his ease with the situation that scares me most. He must've done something very bad. I just hope he doesn't get himself in trouble for my sake.

"What did you do to him?" I whisper.

His dark eyes study me carefully as he casually tucks a piece of my hair behind my ear, as if not realizing he's giving in to his impulses. But it feels comforting, even if it is foreign. "I informed him what he did was wrong."

"Yes, but what did you *do*?" He doesn't answer. "You know I can find out, right?"

"Oh, I'm well aware of your tracking and hacking abilities, lover. Just because you try to keep some of it a secret doesn't mean I don't know." He winks. "Now, go back to sleep."

"I should probably go home." Despite how much I've slept, I want to close my eyes again, willing this all to be over. I might've been saved, but how many other women hadn't been? And the unknown, that blank space in my memory, haunts me. Because anything could've happened. I've always lived so freely, and this weekend has shaken me to my core as if momentarily clipping my wings.

"Sleep now, woman." He reaches for me, and I let him pull me close, my hands resting on his chest as he wraps his arms around me. I don't even want to fight him. Instead, I embrace the comfort he offers. For once, I'm grateful Hawke is able to speak in a language I understand well. A language spoken with his body. Because right now... this... it gives me all the comfort I want.

I nuzzle into his warmth, surrounded by the smell of his cologne. My mind begins to circle with the what-ifs, and every time I'm swept away by them, I focus on him again, bringing me back to the now. To the security of being safe in his arms. I can tell when he starts drifting off because his arms turn into dead weight, loosening enough that his hand drops to my hip.

He might be an asshole, but I will forever be grateful to Hawke for this moment. I close my eyes and try to follow his lead, not yet entirely ready to face this day or the new reality, knowing already that it's changed me. I'm not sure if it's for the better or the worse.

* * *

When I wake up, he's gone. I wipe my eyes, a sudden sense of loneliness overtaking me at his empty spot. I grab my phone from the side table, trying to adjust my eyes to the bright screen. He has blackout curtains, so it's a surprise when I realize it's midday already.

I didn't hear him leave, but then again, I slept like the dead. I feel even better than before. I've never slept this much in my life. I sit up and find my outfit washed and folded at the end of the bed. I have no intention of wearing that dress again. The heels, however, I'll keep.

I pick them up from the floor, but still take the dress and underwear with every intention of burning them. I don't ever want to think of that night again. Still wearing his shirt, I put on my heels. It might not be the most stylish thing, but I'm confident in pulling off almost anything. And I just need to get home.

I look over my shoulder to the camera that I know is hidden there and give it a small wave before I leave the bedroom. Downstairs, on the kitchen counter, I find my purse. I take that as well as I check my phone. I have a missed call from Billie, a text from Hope, and two messages from my mother about dinner tonight.

As I go to call a cab, Hawke's name appears with a photo attachment. I burst into laughter at his selected image. It's a mirror selfie of him shirtless, with that killer playboy smile. Fucking poser.

I bet he took that this morning and saved it as his lock screen for whenever he calls.

"You added a photo to your name?" I say in way of a greeting.

"I did. So you don't have to check on me through the cameras when you want to see me. Now you can just look at me on your phone. I saved plenty more for you as well. You're welcome."

"You're weird."

"You have a car out front waiting. I'm on a job, but I will come by when I'm done to see how you're doing."

"You don't need to do that," I'm quick to say. Whatever twilight zone Hawke and I have been in, I know the moment I walk out his front door, we'll return to how we've always been. We have to. Right? "I'm okay,

Hawke." I wish I knew if that were true. "Besides, I have dinner with my parents tonight."

"Good, Alina loves me," he gushes. It's true, she does. She fusses over him, which we all know he loves.

"Bye, Hawke," I say, walking out to the car that's waiting for me. The driver is already holding the door open. I greet him and then slide into the back seat. I open my photo gallery and flick through the twenty-two new images taken at eight this morning. All of them of Hawke in different positions. In every single one of them, he's entirely naked.

I can't help but snort as a bubble of life flutters through me, shifting the heavy weight on my chest. This arrogant asshole really doesn't care that he just left nudes on my phone that I could use against him. He knows I could easily share them with the world. Then again, he'd probably love all the attention he'd get from them. Because he truly does look incredible. I tilt my head to the side. I'm not one to enjoy dick pics, but I'll make an exception for this killer. Not that I'd ever admit that to him. I place my phone in my lap, impressed he didn't save one of them as a lock screen.

I look out the window, releasing a steady breath. Right. Time to move on. I try not to let things get me down for too long, but even as I try to push out from the dark cloud now hanging over me, I know something isn't entirely resolved yet. And it fucking sucks.

Hawke

The moment she hangs up, my recently updated screensaver, a picture of her sleeping, appears on my phone. I know if she finds out, she'll yell at me, but I don't give a flying fuck. It was the most beautiful thing I've ever seen.

Before she left my place, she must've stolen back the keycard to her apartment that I'd stolen from Ford. So here I am, at her door, knocking like a gentleman. Or something along those lines. I considered climbing up the fire escape, but since she's on a popular street in Manhattan, I didn't want others noticing me and giving her a heads-up, which would ruin the whole surprise. So instead, I'm holding a bouquet of flowers and wearing a collared shirt, which I fucking hate.

I knock once. Then twice. I look at the time on my phone. Hopefully, she hasn't left already. I go to knock a third time, and the door swings open before my knuckles can connect. She's wearing shorts so short that I know I'll see the bottom of her ass cheeks when she spins and a shirt that just covers her tits, which I know are the perfect handful.

Her gaze narrows on the flowers. "What are those?"

"For your mother, when we go over for dinner."

She crosses her arms over her chest. "Hawke, you're not coming with me for dinner at my parents' house."

I shove past, and into her apartment, not deterred whatsoever. "If there's free food involved, Ivy, I'll be there. I don't give a shit whose parents they are. What time are we heading over there?"

I know her mother. Alina won't have an issue with me coming over. I love her mother. As a teenager, I used to watch her steal things from her husband. She'd giggle and wink at me when I'd notice what she did far before he would. While my mother isn't particularly close with Ivy's family, my uncle Alek and Will are, in a surprising way, considering their different temperaments, best friends. That grace was never passed over to me because her dad can't fucking stand me.

She throws her hands in the air, frustrated, and I know I've gotten my way. My gaze dips to her ass. Yep, as perfect as I thought she would look.

"Stop looking at me like that," she chastises as I follow her down the hallway to her room. It's dark in here; three computer screens giving off the only light.

"Like what?" I ask, raising a brow.

"Like you want to eat me," she says with her back to me as she removes her shirt. The fucking tease. She throws another top on.

"Well, I haven't had dessert," I say matter-of-factly, basically salivating at the sight of her curves.

"Gosh, you're annoying." She goes to remove her shorts, but then looks over her shoulder at me. "Do you mind?"

"You love it," I smirk as I turn my back, still awkwardly holding the bouquet of flowers. I once bought flowers for my mother on her birthday. She looked at me like I'd grown a second head, unsure of what she was supposed to do with them and forgetting the fact it was her birthday. As far as Anya Ivanov is concerned, she doesn't age. To be fair, she doesn't look like she's aged since she first adopted us.

"My dad's going to be pissed if I bring you," she says as I stare at the wall.

"As if you're not excited by that," I reply, imagining that she's smiling right now.

I wanted to make sure she was okay after Friday night. I know Ivy is a strong woman, but the fact that she hasn't yet told anyone else about what happened, at least not that I'm aware of, doesn't sit right with me. I want to be here if she does need to talk about it.

But I'm not so wholesome. I'm also a completely selfish asshole. Sleeping beside Ivy for only those few hours was the first time in months I hadn't been haunted by nightmares. It was a fucking miracle, and I wonder if somehow this little viper is my cure.

I'm desperate for peace, and I can't deny the fact that she's one of the people I have fun with the most. She'll eventually push me away once she gets fed up with me, but if I can have some fun until then, then why wouldn't I put on one of my best-collared shirts and bring flowers to her mother? Especially if I get free food out of it.

She walks past me, her hips swaying in a flowing skirt, and I admire her ass as she does. I like Ivy's fashion sense because she doesn't have only one style. Every time I see her, she's wearing something different. It very much matches her playful nature.

"You're driving, then," she says, grabbing her phone off the counter. I look around her home. It's emptier now that Billie has moved out. Two bowls and spoons are sitting on the coffee table alongside an empty bag of chips. I never noticed it before, but she's a bit of a chaotic mess.

She's waiting for me at the door. "You just going to gawk, or do you actually want to be fed?"

"Just checking things out," I say as I step through the door. She has to move to the side, as do most people when I'm often the width of the door.

I like her apartment; it's not too flashy or oversized, unlike my own home. I wanted to get the biggest house when I had enough money to buy a place outright. Anya then helped me fill it up with furniture because... well, besides my gym and bedroom, I didn't think that far.

"I'm telling you, this is going to be a disaster," Ivy singsongs as we head to the elevator. We turn to one another with matching mischievous expressions.

"Just make sure your dad doesn't shoot me."

"No promises, Mr. Ivanov. I don't know what you did to piss him off, but he really can't stand you. I can't wait. But that's the only reason I'm letting you come with me." She's quick to add, "Don't tell anyone I was nice to you, or it'll ruin my reputation."

I pretend to zip my lips and lock them. "Your secret is safe with me, Ivy Walker."

CHAPTER 20

Ivy

Hawke has balls. I'll give him that much. Although my father is easygoing with most people, he's always made it obvious how much he can't stand the louder of the younger set of Ivanov twins, even going so far as to warn me off of him. He doesn't seem to have an issue with Ford, though. Maybe it's his father's intuition. I think tonight will be hilarious, though, and I'm sure my mother will enjoy it just as much.

Besides, it's nice to know he came to check up on me. I'm far from a damsel in distress, but it's nice to know he cares.

He stands on my parents' porch, adjusting his collar, looking like a complete dick. Don't get me wrong, he cleans up nicely, especially in a suit. But it looks like he's about to announce his intention of marrying their daughter, which I'm pretty sure isn't something Hawke even wants.

He knocks on the door, and I don't bother to remind him that I have a key to my parents' home. I just wait for it all to unravel.

My father opens the door, his smile falling from his face the moment he sees Hawke. "What the fuck are you doing here?" he barks.

"Hi, Dad," I say, waving at him. But he doesn't look at me. He and Hawke are too busy glaring at one another.

"Mr. Walker." Hawke offers his hand, and my father stares at it as if willing it to burst into flames.

My mother peeks over my father's shoulder and then shoves him out of the way when she sees Hawke.

"Hawke, is that you?" she says, pleasantly surprised, and brings him in for a hug, her arms barely able to wrap fully around his bulk. My father's eye actually twitches at her warm welcome.

"Good evening, Mrs. Walker," Hawke says politely, and I'm trying my hardest not to laugh at his formality, which is so unlike him.

"To what do we owe this surprise?" she asks. When she releases him, she looks between the two of us.

"Ivy owes me a dinner, so I've come to collect," he says, patting his stomach.

"I think the housekeeper threw a few scraps in the

trash," Dad bites out as he grabs Mom possessively by her hip and pulls her into him.

"I'm sure they're delicious if your wife's the one who cooked it," Hawke retorts.

My mother bursts out laughing as she turns and taps my father on the shoulder. "Be nice. He's a guest who is welcome anytime."

"Since when?" Dad grits, and it takes my mother steering him from the doorway to make room for us to step inside. When the door is closed behind us, she steps to my side, and we watch the two men silently walk beside one another, the tension between them palpable.

"Did you put him up to this?" she whispers. "Much better than a cowboy."

I try not to laugh. "No, he came willingly."

We try not to laugh even more as my father glares at him when we enter the dining room, already set up with a spread. I don't know how to tell Hawke this, but my parents very rarely cook, much like myself.

"Oh, these are for you," Hawke says, as if just remembering he's still carrying the flowers, and hands them to my mother.

"You walk into my home with my daughter, but bring flowers for my wife?" Dad growls from the head of the table.

"Yes. And aren't they beautiful? It's been a while since I've received flowers, so thank you, Hawke," she says pointedly.

My father's jaw clenches as he quietly says to her, "Are you displeased? I'll buy you a thousand blooms every day and far more beautiful ones than what this punk got you."

I can see Hawke's trying not to laugh, and I jab him in the side. It's very possible my father might have a heart attack after this dinner. Hawke and I take a seat beside one another, and his eyes grow wide as he scans over the food. There's enough to easily feed eight people, but I'm certain there won't be any leftovers with this tank sitting beside me.

My father pours a glass of wine for my mother and then offers me some. My stomach rolls at the idea, and I politely decline. His eyebrows furrow because it's very rare that I refuse a drink.

"I'm a little hungover," I'm quick to explain. Because all of this is a nice distraction, but the reality is I don't want to touch alcohol any time soon.

He looks at Hawke then, who gives him a cheesy grin. "Don't worry, Will, I'm driving, so no, thank you."

"That's Mr. Walker to you," Dad growls.

"Roger that, Captain." Hawke salutes. My father's left eye twitches again, and my mother and I are barely holding in our laughter. Suddenly, I've found a new appreciation for Hawke and his inability to think before he speaks.

"So what have you been doing with yourself, Hawke?

It's been a while since I've seen you. I think Dutton and Posie's wedding was the last time," Mom says, serving herself. I follow suit, adding food to my own plate.

"Yes, you couldn't be found for half of it, and I believe I saw you with two different women that night," Dad sneers as he takes a sip of whiskey.

"It was actually three, sir," Hawke corrects. "And I've just been doing my duties working for Eli. Buying property. Trying to stay out of trouble."

"I didn't know you were buying properties," I say, surprised.

He looks at me and casually shrugs. "I've got to do something with the money, right?" I don't know if it shocks me that Hawke does any type of investing, but I'm realizing there's more to him than I've ever known. I guess I've never really looked beyond the surface with him before.

"And when did you get so chummy with my daughter?" Dad questions, draining the rest of his glass. He's one to usually savor the taste of expensive liquor.

Hawke rests an arm over the back of my chair. "We've always been good friends."

"*Friends*," Dad repeats.

"Yes, Dad, friends. You should try it sometime," I say, rolling my eyes and shoving Hawke's arm away because I know he's intentionally trying to piss him off.

"I have plenty of friends," Dad replies, and my

mother pats him on the back as if soothing him, and yet again, my mother and I try not to laugh.

We change the subject to their trip to Dubai and what Mom already has set up. My father watches her lovingly as she speaks about what she's most passionate about. Besides the few jabs between my father and Hawke, the evening is actually the best I've had with my parents for a long time. Don't get me wrong, I always have fun with them, but I was especially nervous about coming over tonight after the weekend I'd had.

My parents are perceptive and can tell when something's wrong. And with a father who can knuckle down my every step in a matter of hours, I don't want to give anything away. Not unless I want to tell them. *Nothing happened*, I keep reminding myself. But it doesn't make me feel any less spooked by the situation and the what-ifs that play out in my imagination.

But I'm barely thinking of that as I listen to my mother explain color matching and interior design ideas to Hawke. He listens to her intently as he shovels food into his mouth, and I'm surprised by how right having him here feels. I never would've thought Hawke would be a knight in shining armor, not that I ever believed in those types of notions. It seems he's full of surprises.

I catch my father watching us. I don't know how long I've been staring at Hawke, but I'm quick to shovel a forkful into my mouth. I've never brought a guy home, not to our family dinners. To events, yes, but not like this. I don't want my father reading into it because there is absolutely nothing happening between me and Hawke.

At least, I don't think there is.

CHAPTER 21

Hawke

"I'm not fucking you," Ivy states as I pull up to the curb in front of her apartment.

"No, you did me one better. You fed me," I say, patting my stomach. Dinner with her father was the hardest I've ever had to work for a meal. The asshole was killing me with questions and snide remarks.

"I know what it is you really want to eat," she says matter-of-factly, and I lean over to grab a lock of her hair. Oh, all the ways I wish I could have this woman.

"Is it so bad to want you?" I ask honestly. I'm hopeful she at least invites me in. If I can get another few hours of peaceful sleep, that'd be ideal, but I don't know if it was just a fluke.

"No, you're only human. And I'm hot."

"I'm hot too," I fire back. It's why we're such a perfect fucking match.

She's opening the door as she looks over her shoulder. "Goodnight, Hawke." But she pauses before she gets out of the car. "And thank you for this weekend. I'm okay. I promise."

I don't entirely believe her. Or maybe that's what I'm telling myself because I don't want to leave her side.

"You know, you and I could hang more like this," I suggest. "Everyone else in our group is coupled up, and as you've recently discovered, you have pretty shitty friends. I could be a good friend."

She smiles as she jumps out of the car, then leans down to say, "Hawke, you and I can't just be friends."

"Don't tell me you haven't been tempted by the perks, lover," I say arrogantly.

"Goodnight, Hawke. I hope whoever you're fucking tonight gets more than two minutes of your below-average hip thrusting."

"Below aver—"

She slams the door, cutting me off. I open my door and stand, declaring, "I know I have the biggest dick you've ever seen. Women love my hip thrusting. And it definitely lasts more than two minutes. You've experienced it!"

Everyone within hearing distance stops and stares at me. Well, it's better for the word to get around if she keeps saying shit like that. I have a reputation to uphold.

She looks over her shoulder, that mischievous smirk wreaking havoc on me as she waves goodbye.

That woman knows how to chew a man's ego within seconds. Lucky for me, I have plenty of it.

I shrug and get back into the car.

I'm singing to the music blasting through the speakers when it cuts out and is replaced by the ringing of my phone. Dutton's name appears on the screen. I answer, "Yo! Need advice on spicing up your marriage so soon after the honeymoon?"

"You're such a dick," Dutton replies. "I need you to come to Pearl. I've already called Eli and Ford. I've got a problem."

Dutton doesn't give us orders because we don't work for him, but the four of us are close, and we always look out for one another. "How come Eli isn't the one calling me?"

"Let's just say he was in a compromising position when I called."

I chuckle and hang up on him, taking the next exit. I tap my fingers against the steering wheel to the beat of the music, a sense of anticipation filling me at the hope I might be able to finish the night with some killing. Some might say killing people is a job for the already depressed. I would like to argue that. I'm a very happy person. Well, I was up until my brother was poisoned. Now, there are ghosts that drag me down, but even then, I try my hardest to run away from them.

I don't see the point in getting depressed about things for the simple reason that I grew up not knowing if Ford and I would make it to the next day. It all changed when we met Anya and River. We were given a second chance. And I don't take things personally unless they are.

Out of the two of us, Ford is the one who looks like he could be depressed, even though he lives with the same reverence for the life we've built that I do. The only time I ever really see him happy, though, is when he's with Billie or tattooing. And it hurts a bit to know I can't give him that same feeling.

I enjoy my adoptive parents' company, too, but it's different. My mother would judge half the shit I get up to, which is exactly why she's worried I'll be the one bringing grandbabies to her doorstep. Their relationship is dysfunctional at best, mostly because Anya is outright crazy. River is the only positive male role model we've had, and he's the one who taught us that women are to be worshipped.

Before they welcomed us into their home, no one ever really loved us. And while I can say Ford and I loved each other, it's not quite the same as being loved by parents.

My mother has unorthodox ways of expressing love, like teaching us how to micro dose on poison. Some would call it child abuse, but in the world we live in, it's a matter of survival. And she was right. She was the first to teach me what a powerful woman is, and in my line of work, I've realized how women can be just as deadly, if not more so, than men.

Eli's wife is the best sharpshooter I've ever seen. And Hope loves to kill people for her art, which is a little morbid, but whatever. And then there's Ivy. I haven't completely figured her out yet, but I'm becoming more curious by the day. My beautiful little hacker who likes to keep what she does hidden. I don't understand why she wants to keep it a secret. She's good and, in my opinion, probably better than her father. But I might be biased.

Everything is changing around us, and I can't help but feel like I'm being left behind. So when Dutton calls me to Pearl, I jump on the opportunity because right now, I feel like my work is all I have to give me purpose. I don't think I'm depressed, but I'm certainly not having as much fun lately. And I don't know if it's a dangerous thing to expect Ivy to help with that.

Ford's car is already parked outside. When I walk through the back door of Pearl, I see the action is in full swing. I peek past the curtains to see one of the dancers beautifully angling herself on the pole. I fucking love women; they're the best. They have a grace that men just don't have.

"Hey, big boy," Mike, one of the bartenders, says as he steps up behind me. "I hope you plan on paying." His tone is flirty as I turn to face him.

"Here on business tonight, unfortunately," I reply.

"Pity," he says, looking me up and down before

hooking a thumb over his shoulder. "They're in the office. Still sure you're straight?"

I shrug as I walk past him with a smile. "I'm not sure on much, but that I'm sure about. I'll let you know if it changes."

"Flattering," he coos as he continues on his way to the bar.

Eli, Dutton, and Ford are already in the office. I close the door behind me. Dutton is sitting behind his desk, sipping a glass of whiskey. Eli is standing beside him, doing the same, and Ford leans against the bookshelf, scrolling through his phone.

"We have a problem," Dutton says, not even greeting me first. He tosses some photos onto the desk.

I walk over and frown at the images. Anger immediately pumps through my bloodstream.

"Who did this to her?" I ask, looking Dutton dead in the eyes. No one gets past Dutton's security, especially here at Pearl or any of his other clubs. They focus solely on their women's safety, so how the fuck did one of his dancers wind up dead? I know her. I've partied with her. And although I can't remember her name, no one deserves this.

"That's what we're trying to find out. We have a few men who have been rounded up who weren't regulars with whom she danced with that night. This happened last night after her shift. Her boyfriend called me this morning saying she hadn't come home. She was drugged. Obvious struggle. Abused. Killed," he tells me.

My jaw tics. All I can see is Ivy's smiling face. This could've been her.

What if I hadn't been lucky enough to intervene in time?

"I've had a few reports that drugs are circulating that aren't our product," Eli says. "This is the first woman who has been drugged and attacked. It hits too close to home." He lights a cigar and takes a deep inhale. "Another woman went missing."

"It's not just the drugs or attacks. We might be looking at a sex ring coming into town," Dutton growls.

My hands curl into fists, and the tension in the room shifts. We might not be good men—we profit from power and making men bleed—but we don't stand for women being hurt.

That stir of guilt rolls in my stomach as a set of wide, shocked eyes flash in my mind. A woman, dead because of me. I try to push it away.

Is this related to Ivy or just a coincidence? I open my mouth and then close it. I can't tell them about Ivy when she asked me not to say anything.

"We need to deal with this before it becomes a problem," Eli says, stating the obvious. "So now we hunt. I want us to track back to whoever the fuck thought it was a smart idea to put this shit out on my streets. We'll make an example of them so everyone knows the consequences of angering the Monti's."

CHAPTER 22

Ivy

I haven't seen Hawke since we had dinner with my parents. He messages me daily, checking in to see how I am. I don't usually reply because the moment he thinks I'm not okay, he'll be on my doorstep. Besides, I've picked up more projects this week to try and keep my mind occupied.

I have absolutely no interest in going on any dates, and the itch to find someone to satisfy my needs shrivels when I think about the effort. I just hate that I don't feel like myself right now.

Makayla tries calling me several times, and I ignore her. I don't blame her for everything that happened, but I'm very mad. Who even was that guy, Lester? I've never seen him at one of her parties before. Is she even aware that he's doing this to women?

I finally decided to answer her a week later and

agreed to meet up with her. While I wasn't ready to speak to her last week, I think my mind is clear enough for it now. I needed some time to work through things before confronting her because Hawke is right; she's a shitty friend. Not that I consider her that anymore, but I have to know how many other friends she's let that happen to. Or was she just so fucked-up herself that she had no idea?

We meet for coffee in a cafe we've been to before. It's pretty, with pink and blue flowers hanging from the ceiling, but I can't appreciate its atmosphere as I approach where she's sitting.

She stands as soon as she sees me, but I make no attempt to give her a hug. I don't even pretend to smile as I take the seat across from her, and her smile falters. I don't blame her for what happened, but I'm pissed that she didn't check on me that night. She knows how much alcohol I can drink and not get sick. So for her not to be concerned that I was acting wasted after I only had a few shots was perplexing.

"Have you been avoiding me?" she asks, then takes a sip of her drink. Her nonchalant attitude pisses me off further.

"Yes."

Her brows scrunch together in confusion and she begins to play with her nails, as if thinking that would magically dissipate the tension between us.

"Can I get you something?" a waitress asks me.

"No, thank you. I won't be here for long," I tell her, keeping my gaze pinned on Makayla.

Makayla's focus snaps to me again. She's not used to me being angry at her. I'm always happy and up for a good time. But that's because I'm not usually hurt or in danger. I'm nice until I'm not. I was raised with sophisticated thugs, so not much scares or irritates me. But this does.

Having my power of choice taken away is a completely different situation, one I would never wish on anyone. And I'm so thankful that Hawke found me before anything serious happened, but I can't say the same for anyone else.

"I was hoping we could have mimosas, but okay," she says. She flags down the next waitress and orders a mimosa. "The latte was just to get something in my stomach." I don't even have it in me to dispute her logic. "You're always up for a drink. You're not pregnant, are you?"

"No, I am not," I grit out, my last nerve so close to snapping. Is this all she has to say to me? After everything that's happened? I knew she was self-absorbed, but this is next level.

"Good, that would suck. You're one of my only friends I can depend on for a good time. Everyone else is becoming so boring."

I don't look at pregnancy the way she does. I wouldn't think it sucked if I were pregnant. But I don't indulge her. I'm actually shocked when she starts talking about her boyfriend as if this is the most casual conversation in the world. As she's talking, her drink is brought out. She thanks the waitress and then gets embarrassed when a small amount of blood trickles from her nostril. She pulls out an already soiled tissue and wipes her nose.

I don't know what drug she's on, and, to be honest, I don't care.

"That hay fever gets bad with the pollution," she explains before telling me how she and Jared might move in together. She then dives into a story of her accidentally cheating on him the same night I was drugged.

"I told him it was an accident because I was drunk, and now he won't answer his phone. I need you to find him for me. I'm scared I've lost him forever." She sobs and wipes at her tears. "Well, say something."

Only my closest friends know the true extent of my hacking and tracking abilities. Makayla has only seen a fraction of what I can do. Stalking social media pages was commonplace back in college.

I'm so baffled by her ability to focus only on herself that I don't just get up and leave because I'm concerned she might need psychiatric help.

"I was drugged." Her gaze shoots up to mine, and her hand, that was stretching out for her half-empty glass, pauses for a moment. "At the party you invited me to."

She stares at her drink before taking a sip. "You left

with your *friend*." I don't like the way she seethes the word "friend."

"He didn't drug me. One of your friends did," I tell her, and she begins to sob.

Oh, for the love of God.

"I'm sorry. This is a lot for me, and I can't take on your stuff as well. Not only is my relationship with Jared rocky, but one of my friends has gone missing too, so it's a lot."

My mind blanks. Is that the only reaction I'm going to get from her? I didn't expect much, but is that all she's actually capable of? I feel bad for anyone who might've considered her a real friend, and I'm grateful I have Billie and Hope, who I know would both literally kill for me.

How fucking drugged out of her mind was Makayla that night?

"That sucks" is all I can manage to say. I do have sympathy for someone dealing with something sketchy, like the disappearance of a friend, but I refuse to take on her shit, especially when she doesn't deserve that type of friendship from me.

"Yeah, Lester is a good friend. Maybe that's why Jared's not talking to me."

A shudder runs through me. Lester is the guy who was trying shit with me when I couldn't even stand.

I hacked the security footage from that night. Someone tried to wipe the recordings, most likely covering Hawke's ass, but I was still able to retrieve them.

I watched the moment Hawke came in and beat the shit out of the guy who was making advances on me. I was mortified to see myself in that state. Never again. Never again will I be helpless or unguarded like that.

When I drilled down deeper, I discovered that Lester had been taken to the hospital. But the night after the event, he disappeared completely. I don't have to ask too many questions to figure out who was behind it. I don't have any remorse for him. How many others had he hurt?

"You know it was Lester who was trying shit on me when I was drugged out of my mind, right?" I say.

She throws her hands in the air. "It's not all about you. I might not remember what the fuck happened that night, but I know it was *your* friend who beat the shit out of Lester. He goes to the hospital, and then, *poof!* He's gone. Do you not care?!" she exclaims, slamming her hands on the table.

"No, I really don't." Her mouth drops open in disbelief at my reply. I don't give a flying fuck if it looks like I've sided with the devil himself.

"How can you say that?" Her bottom lip wobbles. "How can you side with a monster like that? He's obviously done something to Lester. Something so bad that he's run away terrified."

I try to hide the cruel smile as I stand because I'm not mean enough to tell her that Lester's most likely dead. But I really don't care. "Because I don't sympathize with a man who drugs women to take advantage of them. That might be your scene, but it's not mine. We're done. Clean up your act and get off the drugs."

I grab my handbag, sliding the strap over my shoulder. Her jaw's still open in disbelief as tears stream down her face. I pity her. Part of me wonders if she was secretly in love with Lester. Either way, I don't give a shit. Hawke isn't the monster. He just does what most are incapable of.

When I turn to leave, she yells out behind me, causing a scene. "Your *friends* can't go around doing that. I heard rumors, but I didn't actually think they were true. You're not above the law!"

I pause at that last statement. "How does the law protect women from people like your friend?"

"He's not like that. Stop painting him as the monster when your friend is the real monster!"

My nails curl into my palms. This monster she speaks of—Hawke—is the same man who washed me, clothed me, looked after me until the drugs were out of my system. He's far from evil in my eyes, and I need to make something very clear. I'm not special because I have him and other true friends and family who would kill for me. I can protect myself. Perhaps it was my mistake for never quite letting that lethal side through as I partied all these years.

"You don't speak about him again. Do you understand? You're not worthy of having his name on your lips." At this point, I don't even think she remembers his name, and it's irrelevant because he's not the only one she needs to be concerned about. I look her dead in the eyes as I lean down, getting in her face.

"The fact that you're mad at me instead of mad about what your *friend* does speaks volumes about you as a person. Keep my family and friends out of your mouth because the ability to make people disappear isn't only his, Makayla. I can always find you, and I will make your life a living hell if you *ever* try to approach me or my friends again."

Tears stream down her face, and I'm not entirely sure if she's comprehending this conversation right now. But I do. It gives me back some of my power, reminding me of who I am. What I'm capable of. I can't believe I even hung out with someone like this for so many years. Sometimes it's fun until it's not.

I stride out of the cafe and decide to go for a walk. I'm close to Hope's studio, and though she doesn't usually like visitors, I'm one of a few she'll allow in. Not that I intrude on her often. I just need a real friend right now. To remind myself of how blessed I am.

But first, I pull out my phone. I bring up Hawke's number and call him. He answers on the first ring.

"Hey, lover. I'm not against a midday booty call, but I'm working."

"My schedule's full."

"The only thing you'll be full of is my cock... as soon

as you start replying to my messages," he says, and I smirk at his attempt to try and banter with me.

"I've been preoccupied. Lester..." I trail off. I've been intending to speak with Hawke about what happened with Lester because I'm not someone who wants to be left out about the details. I'm not a damsel in distress, and I've seen some shit before. But I'd wanted to confront Makayla first. Now that I have, I'm ready to close this chapter in my life. Although it wasn't my actions directly that led to this, a small amount of blood is on my hands, even if it wasn't me who took Lester out. I don't think I'm capable of murder, but I understand it serves a purpose and is sometimes necessary. Especially in the world I was raised in.

"So, no sexy time?"

"No sexy time."

He sighs, and I hear him mumble something about busting his balls.

"I was surprised it took you this long, my little tracker," he says. There's a commotion in the background, on his end of the line. Then, what sounds like a chainsaw revving. I have the good sense not to ask what he's up to right now. "Ford cut it for a moment." I hear a scream and definitely know I shouldn't ask questions. "Worthless piece of shit." Hawke laughs.

I'm not saying Hawke is innocent—the man is definitely a little unhinged—but I'll never be able to see him differently after the night he looked after me.

"I've known about what you did to Lester for a few days," I manage to say.

"So why didn't you call me back?" he asks.

"Be careful, Hawke, you're starting to sound needy," I purr as I look up at the building Hope works in. She usually starts around midday, so hopefully, she's here. "I just wanted to say thank you." I didn't think I'd ever be thanking a person for killing another person, but deep down, I'm very thankful.

"You seem to be doing a lot of that lately."

"What?"

"Thanking me. And I haven't even been between your legs for weeks," the cocky asshole says. I bite the inside of my cheek. Dangerous. Very dangerous. "So, does that mean I can come over tonight?"

"Goodbye, Hawke." I hang up with a smile as I enter the elevator. He tries to call back, but I don't answer.

I knock on Hope's studio door. "Who is it?" she calls out from the other side, and there's a bitter edge to her usual sweet tone. I smile as I open the door because I know how much she doesn't like being disturbed.

"Sorry, I'm not a six-foot-something detective," I say in greeting, and her demeanor changes.

"I wasn't expecting you today. But I guess you're the next best thing."

She's sitting in her usual seat, dressed in overalls, with clay everywhere. She goes to the sink to wash her hands, and I take the opportunity to appreciate her space. A water fountain gurgles in the center of the room, classical music plays in the background, and tons of natural light pours through the skylights. I begin touching things I probably shouldn't be touching, but she says nothing.

When I turn around to face her, she pulls me in for a hug. I'm surprised, but I wrap my arms around her. She's the shortest out of us, and I've always looked at her more like a little sister and best friend combined in an awesome bundle. But Hope isn't a very affectionate person; none of us really are.

This is just what I needed to remind me what good friends I have. Billie is currently on a business trip, but when she gets back, I plan on having one of our girls' nights.

Hope and Hawke are very close, and Hawke has a problem with keeping secrets. Dread immediately runs through me. *Does she already know?*

"What has he said?" I ask carefully.

"He didn't say anything, but I heard he went on a little rampage, beating a guy almost to death at some party you were at. I assumed he went to stir up shit. Sorry, you have to deal with my crazy cousin."

I sigh in relief, although I feel bad that Hawke has taken the brunt of it without anyone knowing the real reason behind it. It's nice to know he's been able to keep my secret, though.

I consider telling her, but it sits at the edge of my lips, not quite ready to come out yet. I don't know why I don't want to talk about it; it's not like anything actually happened, but I feel stupid. I can't believe I put myself in that situation, and I don't want to worry her.

"He's not all that bad," I say as I check out her recent work. Hope's beyond talented, and I know the public image and pressure get to her.

"It's his redeeming quality," she jokes. "Did something happen with you two that night?"

Images of him looking after me come to mind, but I find myself saying, "He wishes."

She brings me a cup of herbal tea. Not my usual go-to, but okay, seems like the day for it with the sun spilling in and serene music playing. "I'm just waiting for the day that it all clicks into place for you two."

I laugh because Hope has always said things like that about us. I wonder if there's something I'm not seeing that she does. "What makes you say that?"

She shrugs as she takes a sip of her tea. "Don't get me wrong, I don't want to see you two flirting, but I think you'll put him in his place. And we all know Hawke needs that."

True.

"And what do I get out of it?" I ask.

She looks at me then, those beautiful blue eyes striking against her vibrant red hair. "Someone to keep you on your toes so you don't get bored."

"Maybe," I say thoughtfully. No one would be surprised. My father might have a heart attack, though.

But I'm not even sure if someone like Hawke is capable of a relationship. Besides, it's a little presumptuous.

"But if you start getting bored, you can come out for dinner with me and my detective." She waggles her brows.

"That sounds awful," I whisper in mock horror because third wheeling is not my idea of fun.

"You know you want to," she teases, and I can't help but sit on the floor cross-legged beside her despite there being another stool. I just want to appreciate what I have and who I have. And it's nice to see Hope living out a happily ever after... in her own little morbid way.

CHAPTER 23

Ivy

When I decided to have a Friday night to myself instead of going out, I thought it would be me sitting on my couch naked, eating a bunch of takeout during a movie marathon. The six-foot-two, tatted asshole standing at my door with a cheesy grin thinks otherwise.

"I thought I said no to you coming over tonight," I say.

"When did we have that conversation?" He pushes past me and into my apartment. I shake my head as I close the door behind him.

"I'm not going out tonight. You'll have to find someone else to party with."

Hawke shrugs as he looks around the living room and kitchen. He's always looking at the mess I leave around, but he hasn't commented on it yet. Everyone else does, and I don't care. "It's only a party if you're there, Ivy. So if you're not out there, then I'll come here. Come on, we can order in food and braid each other's hair. *Fuck.*"

I smirk, leaning against the counter and giving him a full cleavage shot. His gaze dips to my tits, and it gives me deep satisfaction at how responsive he is to me. I'm wearing matching shorts and a tank PJ set with lemons on them. The only reason I'm wearing anything is because the last time I ordered a pizza, the delivery guy almost tripped over himself when I answered the door naked. Then Billie got on my case, saying something about protecting the male species from unrealistic expectations.

"What if I don't feel like having sex with you?" I ask.

He looks at me as if I'm crazy. "Come on, Ivy, everyone wants to have sex with me. Besides, it's *us*."

He says it is as if *us* is all I need to know. The cheek of this asshole. I flop onto my couch and pull out my phone, then scroll through the delivery options for tonight, purposely ignoring him.

His weight makes the couch dip, so I lean slightly into him as he sits beside me. "So what are we ordering?"

I glare at him. "Pad Thai with chopsticks." I don't know why, but the thought of a guy this big using something as delicate as chopsticks makes me want to laugh.

"Awesome. And what are we watching?" he asks,

lifting my legs and hanging them over his thick thighs as he gets cozy.

"You're seriously staying in with me tonight?"

"Yeah. Why are you making it weird?" He gives me a look like I'm the one who's flipping the script between us. We don't do this. Ever. We tease each other and play pranks on one another. Sure, maybe in a group setting, we've watched the same movie, but this isn't our usual.

I think back on what Hope was saying earlier. *Are we a good match?*

Gah, my brain hurts. I've been doing too much of that lately—thinking. I pass him the phone and let him order what he wants. "I was watching a sci-fi movie."

"You like that stuff?" he asks, surprised.

"Thought all I did was watch pornos?" I ask sarcastically.

"Preferably. I'd rather we make them, though. Do you think we'd make bank if we created an OF account?" he asks as he pulls my feet toward him.

"Like you need more money. And stop that." I squeal and yank my feet away from him as he goes to massage them. His eyebrows shoot up, and I know I'm in so much trouble.

"Lover, are you ticklish?" he asks, his sausage fingers twinkling in the air mischievously.

"I swear to God, Hawke, if you— Stop!" I scream in a fit of laughter as he lunges for my ribs. I push at his face and try to wrestle against his weight. "Stop! I can't... I can't breathe." I accidentally hit him in the mouth, and he leaned back, adjusting his jaw.

"Nice hook," he says, his almost-black eyes twinkling with pride.

"I'll aim for your nose next time if you ever try that again," I pant, trying to catch my breath, the pump of adrenaline coursing through my veins.

"Women will still want me even with a crooked nose." His arrogant gaze never leaves mine.

"Are you wanting to test that theory?" I ask absent-mindedly because my body is only focusing on his hand that's still pinned to my waist. Heat rushes over me as I become acutely aware of him. His smell. His overbearing and all-consuming presence. Simply Hawke.

"There's another theory I'd like to test out," he says as our heads naturally gravitate toward one another.

"What's that?" I find myself whispering so close to his lips that I can almost taste him. This devil that's never worn a disguise. Hawke has always been Hawke. Torturous in the way he tempts me. And sometimes I'm weak. Especially when I have needs that I know he can meet.

I brush my lips against his carefully, and it's all the permission he needs before his callused hand is holding my face, and he plunges his tongue into my mouth. My own tongue dances against his, a small moan escaping from my mouth. The moment he touches me breathes me in and feeds me, I feel my body relax and quickly be taken over by a greedy need. I grab him by the shirt, pulling him on top of me.

He hovers his weight over me, his hand gliding up and down my waist before it trails to my tits. Oh, fuck me. Hawke is everywhere, kissing, biting, teasing. Hawke knows how to worship a woman, and my body is so receptive to his reverence.

I can feel his cock straining against my pussy through the fabric of his pants and my own shorts. He grabs my ass lifting me to press harder against his cock, and I moan, arching into him, knowing precisely how much trouble I'm about to be in.

The thing about a man this powerful is that once you get a taste of him, you can't forget it. Don't want to. And no one will ever compare.

I've run away from it for so many years, frightened about how he'll ruin me.

But right now, I very much want to be ruined.

CHAPTER 24

Hawke

S he's everything I've always wanted. I've been praying to a God I don't even believe in for the chance to taste her again. And now she's coming undone in front of me, and I've barely touched her.

"Fuck, you're beautiful," I purr, kissing along her neck that tastes faintly of salt and vanilla. I squeeze at her bountiful tits. I've always fucking loved them. I've loved every part of her even before she gave me the honor of pleasing her.

My cock is pressing against my zipper as I roll my hips into her, pleasantly surprised when she matches my rhythm.

I look down at her, those blue eyes twinkling with desire and mischief. It's what I've always loved most about her. Those fuck-me eyes. That sexual gaze that oozes with confidence and damnation. She's perfect in so many fucking ways.

I trail my hand up her inner thigh, intoxicated by the way her breath hitches, but she doesn't look away. No, this woman has never shied away from my touch or intensity. I continue gliding my palm along her skin until I can push aside the tiny booty shorts that wreak havoc on my mind, only to discover she's not wearing any panties. *Fucking perfect.*

I slide a finger into her, satisfied at the way her body arches and her lips part, but she still doesn't look away. I insert a second finger, pumping into her in a lazy rhythm, studying her every sharp breath and the way her hips roll greedily into my hand.

"Coat my hand like a good girl," I demand as her pussy begins to saturate my hand. Her body's naturally getting ready for me, and I can't wait to slam my cock inside her, branding her from the inside out.

I've waited fucking years for this.

To feel her around my cock again. To worship what has been the most beautiful body I've ever seen.

"Oh, fuck me, Hawke," she whispers, and her expression twists between absolute pleasure and confusion. I love how she looks when I please her. I lean back as I gently rub her clit with my thumb. I'm not willing to let her come yet; that will be reserved for my cock as she squeezes everything out of me.

She seems to get frustrated as my pace slows, and I

smirk as I undo my belt. Her gaze snaps to my hand, transfixed, but I hear no complaints.

"Not going to fight me on this today?" I arch an eyebrow as I rub circles on her clit. Her eyes flash with heat and defiance. She wants to deny this tension between us, but I knew my girl would break eventually. Something like this has to be seen through to the end.

"Are you ready for Hawke Junior?"

Her head hits the back of the couch, and she laughs. "You can't still seriously be calling him that."

I remove my hand, and she raises her head, pissed off by the immediate loss. I stand up, and she grabs my wrist. "You're not done here, are you?"

I smirk as I reach into my back pocket and pull out a condom. I rip at it with my teeth and say around the wrapper. "Sounding needy there, lover."

She relaxes back as I step out of my jeans and boxers. My cock springs free, and she stares at it with appreciation. I remove my shirt, and she bites her bottom lip, her gaze roaming over me from head to toe. I roll the condom over my cock as I yank at her foot, but she fights me.

"No. You sit down," she says. My jaw clenches. I much prefer fucking the woman. She raises a perfect brow, crossing her arms over her chest. "Do you want *Hawke Junior* to become a man or not?"

I throw my head back and laugh, then do exactly as I'm told. I sit to enjoy the show as she stands in front of me and removes her top. I salivate at those perfect tits. Then her hands glide down her sides as she pushes down those ridiculous booty shorts that gave me a semi the moment I saw them.

She's naked, her curves on full display, ready for my hands to grab and squeeze. There's so much of her that's perfectly built for me. She's the furthest thing from breakable and the closest thing to insatiable.

Ivy places her hands on either side of my shoulders, straddling my hips. She's spread wide to fit my size as she looks down at Hawke Junior between us, and I can't help but smirk. I know I have a big cock. I fucking love it; it's literally the best. What I love more is watching her slowly lower her hips and line her cunt up to its tip.

She pushes herself down, her pussy squeezing around my cock, so painfully tight that a guttural growl escapes me. She breathes through it until she's taken all of me, and then her gaze snaps back to mine.

Oh fuck. I clamp down on her hips for a second, shocked by the fact that I almost immediately want to come. That's never happened before.

"I'm in charge here," she purrs, almost angrily, and I'm too embarrassed to admit I'm about to shoot my load. *Come on, Hawke Junior, get your shit together.*

"This time, lover," I say smoothly, brushing one of my hands against her cheek and then grabbing the back of her neck. Her body moves to my touch. She's alive and breathing right beneath my fingertips, and the impending doom of blowing a load with one stroke passes.

It just goes to show how perfect this woman is for me. How much I've held out for her. My fingers at her waist dig in as she lifts herself and then lowers again, finding her own pleasure on my cock, riding me like a fucking bull.

I love the way Ivy oozes power and takes what she wants from me. If this is what she'll allow me to have, I'll take it for now because I know I'm going to take so much more from her, like it's my hellbent mission to destroy her.

Ivy's hands roam over my chest, her perfectly manicured nails clawing my skin as her momentum picks up. My hips naturally match her rhythm, meeting her every thrust, slamming into her from below. The slapping sound of our bodies meeting is the perfect accompaniment to our feverish fucking.

"Oh, fuck me," she curses as her eyes roll into the back of her head and she leans back. I'm so used to flipping women into different positions, but this is so perfect that I don't want to change a thing as we fuck each other into oblivion.

Her ass bounces on my thighs as I pull her in by the throat, kissing her, devouring her, selfishly wanting to swallow her every moan and acknowledgment that *I'm* doing this to her. That this is how *I'm* making her feel.

"You're going to make me come," she says breathlessly, looking dazed and almost confused. It was almost the same the first time we fucked. I think neither of us knew what was happening. That we were surprised we were so perfectly matched.

"Soak my fucking cock," I demand as I bite her bottom lip and tug. Fuck, I need her cum all over me, rewarding me.

"Fuck, Hawke," she growls, and her nails dig into my abs as she braces herself as she bounces. "Ungh." She starts panting out incoherent words. "I— I—"

I cling to the edge, begging my balls not to explode until she does, but the moment her pussy tightens around me, I'm a goner. I grunt as I slam her down on my cock, those villainous hips torturous as she tries to continue rocking back and forth, milking me of every last drop.

We can't stop staring at one another, the descent from the high bringing us back to reality as we pant into one another's mouth, still unable to stop wrestling with this deep, carnal need.

I grab the back of her neck, her short blonde hair skirting the edges of my knuckles, as I say, "Next time, I'm in charge."

She raises a suggestive eyebrow. "You think there's going to be a next time?"

"You better clear your fucking schedule because I plan on smashing this pussy every chance I get."

She smirks as she leans into my ear. I'm waiting for

her to speak when the doorbell rings. My head hits the back of the couch, and I groan in complaint, and she gets off my cock.

Fucking buzzkill. I never thought I'd be so mad at food being delivered.

"What the fuck do you think you're doing?" I jump up from the couch and pull her back, keeping her from answering the door naked. "You're not answering the door like that."

She pops a hand on her hip, gobsmacked. "It wouldn't be the first time. And it's fine."

"Well, it's the last time. Put those little booty shorts back on," I grumble as I rip the condom off and throw it in the trash beside the door.

I open the door, stretching back my shoulders to showcase my size. The guy's mouth opens, and he can't even meet my eyes as he hands me the food. I make sure I'm wide enough to block the doorway so he can't see Ivy.

"H-here's a f-free dessert, as well," the guy stammers, and I give him a brilliant smile.

"Well, why didn't you say so sooner?" I don't care much for desserts, but Ivy likes them. I'd eat it out of her pussy, though.

I turn and kick the door closed behind me. When my gaze finds Ivy, she's shaking her head in disbelief. Be fucked if that good-for-nothing delivery kid was seeing a prized gem for free.

CHAPTER 25

Ivy

I sometimes take on jobs that teeter on a moral edge. I don't look down on them because it's precisely the type of clientele my father has. Most of the time, they give me a thrill or challenge I don't get through my mainstream jobs, which can be boring in comparison.

I have a fake name and separate contact details for the jobs that are on the darker end of the spectrum. I don't always know how newcomers get my information, but it can only be found through referrals, meaning someone I've worked with before. There is always the caveat of my prices, so those who approach me know to talk a language I understand—money.

I have more money than I know what to do with, which is exactly why my prices are so high. If I'm taking time out of my extraordinarily fun life, then they will pay the price for it. Fair exchange.

Tonight, I've been paid twenty-five thousand to hack into a security feed and record everything that transpires in the room. I then have to send the recording before I receive the second half of my payment. Easy. I've done a few similar to this; sometimes it's meetings with cryptic information that their competition is trying to gain a jump on. Other times, it's for blackmail. Sometimes, it's outright murder. That goes into a gray area for me. I've seen some shit, but I remind myself as I go into every job that I'm a vault. It's fair to say there are many people's secrets I'll be taking to the grave with me.

I'm chewing on a protein bar that Hawke so kindly stocked up on for me. He's only been over twice since the night we had sex for the second time, and I certainly don't have any complaints. He hits the spot every time and looks like a kicked puppy when I tell him to leave when I want to go to sleep.

It's the only way I can separate the sex from being something more because I don't know what that something more even looks like. And right now, I just want to focus on my needs being met, like I always have. I'll never admit it to him, but the protein bars are actually a nice snack, and considering all the fucking we've been doing lately, I need to keep my stamina up.

Vampire Diaries plays in the background as I flick my gaze from the TV to my laptop, waiting for someone to enter the room. I polish off the protein bar and reach for the bowl of popcorn.

The place I'm watching is a club in Springfield, Massachusetts, that is closed for the evening. It didn't take me long to hack into the security system.

I look alive when two women approach the club and open the unlocked doors.

The camera is angled down at the club doors, so I can't yet see their faces very clearly. They walk farther into the empty club, and I admire one of their tight dresses; it's something I'd probably wear. One of the women glances in the direction they came in from, and my stomach drops.

What the fuck is Makayla doing there?

I jolt upright to turn off the TV, my popcorn spilling all over my lap. I look for my phone, wondering if I should immediately call her to tell her to leave. But I don't know what this situation is yet. I didn't ask questions about the job, but I have a bad feeling about it now.

I bite my bottom lip as someone in a hoodie walks into the frame. From their build and height, I'm assuming it's a male. This guy must know precisely where he has to be since they've been led into the prime position to be caught by the camera. Do they all know they're being recorded? In my personal experience, not usually. The guy's hood is pulled low, and he's careful not to face any of the cameras directly, which definitely implies he knows what's happening.

The two women, however, seem to relax at the sight of him, meaning they most likely know him. And Makayla approaches him flirtatiously, but he holds out a hand to stop her. I then question if this is some twisted sexual fantasy being recorded. It wouldn't be the first one I've seen.

Makayla reaches out and plays with the shoulder strap of the other woman's dress, and the woman seems unsure as she looks back toward the door. But the man says something to her and steps forward as if to reassure her. Makayla doesn't seem happy by the exchange.

My hands are covering my mouth, and I gasp before what's about to happen hits me. With lightning speed, he slices the woman's throat. The woman grabs her neck with one hand, the other reaching out to Makayla, whose expression I can't see from this angle.

Snatching my phone from the arm of the couch, I press call. She needs to get the fuck out of there. Whatever is happening is bad. I change to a different camera, but I still can't capture the face of the man in the hoodie.

The woman with the slit throat drops to her knees, and that's when I see Makayla's expression as her friend bleeds all over the floor, gasping for her last breath. She's smiling as if she didn't just watch her friend get murdered. Wait. Did she lure her into this?

Makayla pulls her phone from between her tits and frowns at it. She flicks her hair over her shoulder as she answers.

"Don't answer," I hear the male say as Makayla says at the same time, "Oh, so you want to speak to me today."

"You need to leave," I tell her. I don't know what the fuck is happening right now, but I do know she's in danger and clearly out of her mind on fucking drugs to have any part of this. I might not agree with her recent actions, but I know this isn't the type of woman she is. Well, at least that's what I thought.

"What are you talking about?" she says, looking around. That's when the man in the hoodie reaches for the phone, disconnects the call, and throws it to the ground. She doesn't seem fazed. If anything, she's acting like he's asserting dominance, so they have time to themselves.

I watch in horror, realizing *she* was the lure, and I can't look away as the feeling sinks deeper that this is all types of wrong. *What the fuck am I watching?*

She begins to remove her dress for the man who's still standing in front of her, holding the knife. Wearing only heels, she spins to show him her ass and bends over as if trying to seduce him. When she straightens, he approaches her from behind, squeezing her tit with a gloved hand. She smiles, satisfied. And still because of the angle, I can't see his face.

Why is she doing this? And why the fuck am I even watching? I'm so confused by the situation and the fact that she's completely naked as one of her friends lies on the floor in a pool of blood.

I choke on air as the man brings the knife to Makayla's throat and slices.

Makayla pauses, shocked, and it takes a moment for her hands to lift to cover her throat as she tries to step away, but the person behind her keeps her close. He whispers something in her ear, and when she turns, I can finally see a glimpse of their face, only to realize they're wearing a knitted mask, as well. This person is careful not to be identified.

He releases her, and she falls forward on her hands and knees, one hand landing at the edge of red, pooling around her friend. She slips, and as she does, her other hand leaves her throat, and more blood pours to the floor.

And then she collapses.

I gasp, looking for air I hadn't known I wasn't taking. She falls into the pool of blood, dead. Waves of panic roll over me, but I'm quick to let my analytical mind take over, thinking with rationality. All I know is I'm meant to send this video to get my money. Was this targeted? Do they know my connection with Makayla, or was it entirely random? It has to be random because I know my identity is completely concealed. Right now, all I know for a fact is Makayla and another woman have just been killed, and her last phone call was from me.

Fuck. What do I do?

I'm on my phone to Hawke before I even know why he's the person I turn to. But if anyone is equipped to deal with the aftermath of a murder, it just so happens I know the perfect killer.

"Lov—"

Before he can finish, I blurt, "Where are you?"

"Whoa there, lover. What's wrong?"

I feel stupid as I gather my thoughts, realizing I need to give him context.

Breathe.

Focus.

"I took on a job, hacking into surveillance cameras to record whatever transpired. I'm supposed to send the recording now, but... They killed Makayla and another woman. I don't know how or why she's involved, but I— I don't know what to do now."

"Damn, sucks to be her," he says. "You hungry? I'm at Five Guys. I can bring you a burger."

His nonchalant, almost emotionless response shocks me.

"Are you fucking crazy?" I screech in disbelief.

The man on the screen leans down to check Makayla's pulse, then proceeds to pick up her dress and use it to wipe the knife before heading back in the same direction he entered from. I track him through the cameras, trying to trail him to catch anything I can use to my advantage. But I just can't think right now.

"Yes, it's part of my charm. But are you a lot calmer now?"

"No, I'm pissed off at you," I say, pointing out the obvious.

"Good. You work best when you're thinking of me anyway," he arrogantly replies. "I'll be around shortly. We'll figure this out."

I notice then that I do feel better. Well, I can think much more clearly, at least. And maybe, just maybe, Hawke said what he did to bring me back from the verge of hysteria. There's something comforting in his promise of figuring this out together. I've never depended on anyone for this type of stuff. Hell, I don't even go to my father for this stuff. I mean, I've never had to before.

"Do you want cheese on your burger?" Hawke asks.

"Hawke," I growl out. He might be used to people dying around him, and I thought to a degree, I was desensitized too but it's never been someone I've been so close to. For the first time, I'm experiencing what it's really like in this dark world.

"Bacon, too?"

"Gosh, you're annoying," I grumble as I hang up, fighting a smile because it's unreasonable at a time like this. But I also appreciate his ability to keep me grounded when I'm having a reality check of what it really means to be a part of this world.

Hawke

I ring Ford and tell him and Billie to get their own burgers because I have a date. Then I hang up before he can ask who because I don't fucking date. I know it's not a date, but hearing the concern in Ivy's voice makes my skin feel like it's being peeled from my muscles. I want to stop her immediate pain and confusion.

I contemplated telling Ford, and it took everything in me not to mention her predicament because I know he'd want to help. But the truth of the matter is I don't know what it involves, and I'm pretty sure Ivy doesn't usually share information about her jobs with anyone. I'm surprised she called and told me, but it shows her desperation.

I go to knock on her apartment door, but she pulls it

open before I can make contact and looks at the bag of food.

"I can't believe you actually got burgers and fries," she scoffs.

"And milkshakes," I say, offering her favorite flavor. Vanilla. She shakes her head but swipes the milkshake from my hand before turning and going back over to her laptop, where it sits on the coffee table.

The TV has been muted but is flashing with that *Vampire Diaries* bullshit she told me she likes. Something about vampires banging, which I guess I'm not entirely against. Popcorn is scattered on the floor.

I follow her to the couch and cozy in behind her as she rewinds the footage for me. I chow down on the burger as I casually throw an arm over the back of the couch. She spares me a look but doesn't reprimand me, too focused on the screen.

"My friend is dead," she says the moment the hooded figure slits her throat. I glance at her, expecting tears, terror, or something, but she looks more confused than anything.

"Do you know the other woman in this footage?" I ask, trying to silently encourage her to eat her burger, but she ignores it. She stands with the laptop and walks into her room, and I trail behind her.

"No. But I can figure out who she is." She plugs the laptop into her three screens. The room is pitch black, other than the glow from the screens. She tucks her feet under her ass as she starts typing away on the keyboard. "I don't know if this was something I was meant to see personally. I'd say it seems pretty targeted, but my identity for these types of jobs is concealed."

Different tabs and searches appear for the mystery woman's face. I'm absolutely amazed as I watch Ivy work, her fingers rapidly moving as different codes and screens flick quickly by. I don't know how, but she seems to know exactly what the fuck is happening. "I need to send this footage within thirty minutes of it being recorded. Which means I have eight minutes left. There!" she says triumphantly as the name and image of the woman come up on the screen. Her name is Elizabeth Carinne.

She continues typing, and within seconds, a whole profile comes up. "Her father's a politician. Maybe this was targeted." I sit back in awe. I knew she was hot shit, but this has my cock hard. She's not only beautiful, but she is hands down the most intelligent woman I've ever met. "Yep. The email address I'm sending this to belongs to her father. Which means they got involved in some shady business. But I don't know why Makayla was there. It doesn't make any sense. She's a party girl. Not some criminal."

She looks at me then as if I might have all the answers. "I don't think we can judge on appearances when it comes to criminals. I look like one. You don't, but what you're doing right now is not deemed acceptable by society... or the law. AKA, you're a criminal."

"Thaaaanks," she says slowly and looks back to her screen, but I notice the small smirk on her face.

"Are you still going to send it?" I ask.

She lets out a shaky breath. "I need to know who was behind this. Not just because Makayla was my friend, but this feels bad. There's something wrong here, and I can't explain it. Why did I have to watch?" She sighs. "Either someone just paid me a generous amount to watch on purpose and have me involved, or there's another reason why I saw this."

The likelihood of that is substantial. She begins typing away again, and I whistle as I adjust my rock-hard cock. "I knew you were hot shit, lover, but watching you work really does it for me." She looks over her shoulder with a promiscuous smile. "I mean it. You're really good at this. I knew you were talented, but... it's mesmerizing."

A flash of something crosses her blue gaze before she looks away. I'm not entirely sure what that was about, but then something grabs my attention.

"Wait. Go back," I say, pointing to the screen. She seems confused, but does as I say. "Pause." She does, and the image on the screen freezes. "Isn't that the same ugly-ass tattoo your friend's boyfriend has on his hand?"

She narrows her gaze, peering more closely at the image, and then her eyes widen. "Jared lured them in?" she says, baffled. "But why?"

The question of why doesn't concern me too much. It's more so the fact that he was at the same place at the same time Ivy was drugged. It could be a coincidence, but I highly doubt that.

"Only one way to find out. And that's where I get involved," I say, cracking my knuckles with glee.

Ivy bites her bottom lip as she looks at the time. Five minutes left to send it. "If I don't send this, they'll think I'm somehow involved. The only way to see this through is to find out what they were trying to accomplish with it."

"Blackmailing dirty politicians isn't unheard of," I say as I lean against her desk.

"No, but they're careful to cover their tracks." She points to the screen, and in real-time, we watch as the club goes up in flames. She stares at the blaze, and I know she's thinking of her friend. Even if she is a fierce warrior, she's not heartless. It must impact her in some way.

I offer her the burger again. "I'm not hungry. You can eat it."

I nudge it toward her again. "Send your video and eat. We'll get to the bottom of this together."

She's slow to take it as she looks up at me, those blue eyes twinkling with the screen that flickers with flames. "Thank you."

"Just don't expect me to be the brains of the operation. That's all you," I say lightly, flicking her forehead. She curses as she rubs the spot, and then her gaze lands on my very hard cock. I smirk. "And I'm here to work your other muscles too."

"You actually don't have an off switch, do you?" She rolls her eyes as she unwraps the burger and takes a bite.

"All is fair in love and war." I wink at her as I slip out of the room to make some calls of my own.

Ivy

The next evening, news has already broken out about Elizabeth's and Makayla's deaths in a suspicious fire that is being investigated. Only her father will know the extent of it all, and I feel dirty for sending him that video, but had I not, suspicions might've arisen about me, and that's precisely what we don't want right now.

Hawke's thumbs drum against the steering wheel cheerfully, but the dark circles under his eyes suggest he's not sleeping much. When I spoke to Billie only a few days ago, she said Ford hasn't been coming home much at all, which tells me that something big is happening in their world as well. I want to ask Hawke about it, but I know he won't betray Eli's trust. I almost feel selfish for dragging him into this. Even after he came over last night and I told him I'd handle it on my own, he promised he'd see it through with me to the end.

We're about to meet with Hope and her detective, Braxton, at an Italian restaurant. "Play nice with the detective," I warn.

Braxton and Hawke never get along, but if I'm asking Braxton for a favor, I need Hawke to be on his best behavior.

Hawke looks at me, baffled, before parking the car, and the two of us climb out.

"I'm always nice. Besides, he's a dick. Also, why do you still call him 'detective'?"

I smirk. "Because I don't give guys a nickname unless I know they're going to be sticking around. Plus, I love pissing everyone off by reminding them that he's a detective." It's highly amusing.

He stops dead in his tracks. "What's my nickname?"

I look over my shoulder and shrug. "I don't know. You've just always been Hawke."

"Not even Hawke the Great?"

"Definitely not Hawke the Great. Oh, wait. There is something else I call you..." I tap my chin thoughtfully, and he leans in with anticipation. "Asshole. Or arrogant prick. I learned that one from my mother."

His expression drops as Hope greets us at the entrance. I give her a hug, and Hawke does the same, holding her so tightly her feet no longer touch the ground.

"Too much," she says as she taps him on the shoulder. "Braxton is inside getting us a table. I just wanted to see how you were first."

I give Hawke a pointed look. He really can't keep anything a secret.

"What? We were coming here to discuss your friend's death anyway, so it made sense that I gave them that information first."

I roll my eyes as I walk alongside Hope, with Hawke following us like a bodyguard. It never ceases to amaze me the reactions we get when out in public with this man. Men look at him in horror, and most women salivate as if he's some deadly god. He looks so out of place in these settings, and his size is imposing, not to mention his monstrous laugh.

When Braxton spots us, he stands. He takes one step toward me, and Hawke's voice slices over my shoulder. "Don't you dare hug her."

Hope is smirking as she moves to Braxton's side, and I curse under my breath at Hawke. "I said play nice."

"Yeah, Hawke, play nice," Braxton says with a cocky smile. Oh fuck, this was a bad idea. I forgot how much these two hate each other.

"Is that a threat?" Hawke's quick to ask.

"Enough. You both have to be real dicks to ruin pasta for anyone. Sit," I say, pointing at a chair for Hawke to sit in.

He grumbles his complaint, but does exactly as he's

told. Hope giggles as she sits beside Braxton. The two men stare at one another, Braxton seemingly smug as he takes a swig of his beer.

"I'm sorry to hear about your friend. The one on the news," Braxton begins. I give Hawke a pointed look. I'm unsure how much he's told him. Hawke's gaze suddenly finds the ceiling very interesting.

"Thank you. I actually might need your help with something related to that. An opportunity for you to play hero," I suggest as the waitress comes over and offers us drinks. I ask for water, and can see Hope's surprise at that, but her jaw drops when Hawke asks for the same.

"I'm always interested in maintaining a good reputation," Braxton says with a conniving smile. The truth is, he's dirty as they come. But between him and Hope, I have no doubt they're as bad as each other. Christ, I didn't even realize she was a serial killer for years. Yet it feels strange to admit my own secrets. I suppose he's as good as any in the friendship circle.

"I was hired for a job. I received payment, and I was advised to record and send the recording to a particular email address. I don't usually ask any questions past that, for the record."

Braxton looks to Hope and then back to me. "A job like you've done for Hope?" he asks.

Hawke's eyebrows furrow in confusion, but I ignore him. He doesn't know what hand I have to play in Hope's business, and that's just one example of why I'm a vault. I put my hand on his thigh under the table, and it seems enough to distract him as huge plates of pasta are set in the middle of the table. Hawke's eyes light up as he sees the mountain of food. I try not to laugh as I wait for others in earshot to walk away.

"Kind of, but not the same," I tell him. "I still have a copy of the recording, even though I was told to destroy it. I have the evidence of what happened that night. I saw the whole thing."

His eyebrows raise. "Jesus. That's some damning information. Can I see?" he asks.

I look to Hawke for reassurance, but I trust Hope's instincts about Braxton, and if he so much as tried to fuck me over in some way, she'd kill him herself, of that much I'm certain.

I pull out my phone and show him the video. Hope leans over his shoulder as he silently watches it. Hawke serves me up a plate, as if him feeding me is an everyday thing.

"She knew him," Braxton says.

"Yep."

"It's possible you've been targeted in this. I don't know much about your line of... work. But do you think it's too much of a coincidence that you were the one to watch it?" Braxton asks.

"Have your men been able to track me breaking into your 'top secret' things at the station?" I ask rhetorically.

A vein pulses in his forehead, and I feel smug with that answer.

"Sure you haven't pissed anyone off lately? Broken someone's heart recently?" Hope asks, taking a small bite of some pasta.

An energy shifts between Hawke and me, and we glance at one another before I quickly look away. Why the fuck did he have to make eye contact with me right in that moment?

When I turn back to Hope, she's smirking, and I'm quick to say, "I'm always breaking hearts, but this is different. I know I haven't been compromised because there would've been at least one alert on my safety measures in place. But we think we know who it is."

This gets Braxton's attention, and he leans back in his chair.

"We think it might be her ex-boyfriend. We want to bring him back to town and get some answers from him."

Braxton looks confused. "So why do you need me?"

"We want to throw them off the scent," Hawke says around a mouthful of pasta. "I'm not happy about not killing him either."

I roll my eyes. "We want it to go public that he's been caught. We want answers. If it's who I think it is, he's not smart enough to be behind this. He's just a tool. Literally. I think there's more to this than we know."

"So why are you making it your problem? Didn't you

get the paycheck?" Hope asks. She knows that's always how I've been. I don't ask questions, and I don't go digging further. This time it's different. My throat feels like it's constricting. Because I now know what it feels like to be helpless and out of sorts. I might not have agreed with Makayla, but she was my friend at one point, and she deserved more than this.

"She was my friend," I answer. "I know it doesn't sit right with you either when men take advantage of women. It might just be a hunch, but I feel like there's more to this."

"I can understand the sentiment," Braxton says as he looks at Hope and I know he's talking about her and the months he tracked her every step, finally uncovering her secrets. "So my role in this is to take him after you get answers from him, and put him on public display, and then take the glory of finding the culprit so the big fish don't realize you're on his tail. Correct?"

"Correct."

"We should just kill the fucker," Hawke grumbles around a mouthful, and I kick him under the table. "Ow."

"You said I was running this show," I growl at him, and he rolls his eyes. Actually has the balls to roll his eyes at me.

"I can do that. And you'll bait him back here? How do you plan on doing that?" Braxton asks.

Hope smirks as if already knowing my answer. "Well,

he's just a guy. It should be easy to get him back after a few messages."

"I see," Braxton says.

And that's the end of that conversation as we enjoy our meal. Hawke has already demolished three heaping plates before I'm halfway through the first. We talk about Hope's upcoming show, and it's nice to see the way Braxton stares at her in admiration. He's utterly transfixed, and I know without a doubt he will never betray me because he will never betray her.

"So, what's happening between you two? You've been hanging out a lot. You're certainly starting to look a lot like a squabbling couple," she says, piercing a meatball with her fork. Hawke and I both look up at the same time.

"Us?" I look at him in disbelief, and the arrogant asshole has the nerve to smirk as he rests his arms along the back of my chair.

"Yeah, we'd make a pretty hot couple," Hawke says matter-of-factly.

"What the fuck?" I snap.

"Well, come on. It's obvious that I'm holding up the team here." He's so smug I punch him in the arm.

"You're such an ass," I say, throwing his arm off the back of my chair and then piercing a piece of my pasta. It's only then that I glance back up and see Hope and Braxton are watching us. Hope has a big-ass grin on her face. "What? We're just working on this stuff together. He fucking wishes we were together."

"See how she treats me?" Hawke says dramatically.

I roll my eyes. "Last time I checked, I treat you pretty well," I bite back.

"Only when that pretty little mouth of yours is being obedient."

"Please. My defiant mouth is the thing you like about me most." I glare at him and can't help but smile at his arrogant smirk and the way his gaze devours me. Fifty bucks says if I grabbed his cock right now, it'd be hard.

Braxton clears his throat. "Hawke, do you mind if I speak with you outside for a moment?"

Hawke's playful expression drops, and Braxton doesn't even wait for his answer before he's standing and pressing a kiss to Hope's forehead, promising he'll be back shortly. We watch as they leave, taking a palpable tension with them.

"I hope they don't kill each other," I say, wondering what that's all about.

Hope nonchalantly shrugs. "I think they'll end up friends."

"Really?" I ask, surprised she'd think that.

"Let's be real. They're both smartasses who like to push everyone's buttons." I think about that, concluding that's most likely why my father can't stand him.

"You sure everything's okay, though? You seem different lately. I just want to make sure you're all right.

And if my cousin is becoming overbearing, let me know, and I can shackle him in a basement for a week."

I laugh at that. Hope surprises me with some of the things she says. But it's reassuring to see this side of her slowly come to the surface. That she's comfortable enough with us to reveal all of herself instead of just parts. I feel almost guilty for keeping some of my own secrets, but I know I'll eventually talk about them. Right now doesn't feel like the right time as I hyper-fixate on getting to the bottom of Makayla's murder and whatever is happening behind it.

"I'm okay," I reassure her as I place my hand on hers over the table. I don't have the heart to tell her that I don't even think a chain and ball could keep Hawke down for a week. "Now, let's figure out what I should text Jared to bring him back to New York like a good little boy."

She chuckles. "From you, 'Hi' should be enough."

I smirk, validated by her confidence in me. Then again, catching a man's attention has never been difficult for me. It's the one who keeps showing up at my house uninvited that I'm unsure how to deal with.

Hawke

I follow Braxton outside, positioning myself so I can still watch Ivy. I see her throw her head back, laughing at something Hope says.

"This doesn't count as the favor you owe me. I'm saving that for something special," Braxton says, which immediately pisses me off.

"This was her idea. Don't worry. I'll still owe you a favor when the time comes."

Braxton nods. "Good. Is she okay? I know Hope's been worried about her lately. It's hard for me to keep secrets from my woman, so holding on to the knowledge of what happened that night gets more difficult by the day."

My jaw tics, and I look back at Ivy. I was hoping she would've spoken to somebody by now about what happened to her. It's not anyone else's business, but I know Hope, Billie, and Ivy are close, and I think there's been a small part of her she's been holding back since that day. Sure, she might think I'm hovering around to look after her, but it's entirely selfish because I don't want to spend any of my waking time with anyone else but her.

"She'll get through it," I say without a doubt. Ivy is one of the most resilient women I know, and she'll open up in her own time.

"Good." Braxton clears his throat. "Good luck with the not killing him part."

"You're an ass," I say as he smirks and shoves his hands in his pockets. He then walks back into the restaurant.

I take out my phone and call Eli. He answers on the third ring.

"Update?" he demands.

"Everything's in motion. We're going to bait him back to Manhattan so we can try and find a lead through him."

Eli clicks his tongue, and I can tell he's impatient with how slowly the pieces are moving. I'm not the brains behind most operations, and even now, this might be an unrelated lead, but we're grasping at straws. We've only been able to track down petty drug dealers. They're not the root of the problem of the recent distribution of date-rape drugs.

The moment Ivy told me about what was happening, I called Eli. Either way, I'd get to help her in the process, or it could potentially lead to our guy. I haven't told Ivy any of this because I don't want her thinking the only reason I'm helping her is because what happened to her might be connected to my work with Eli. I also don't want her to know I told them about the incident that happened that night. If she hasn't spoken about it to her friends, I don't want to betray her by telling the guys. But keeping secrets is torture for me. It makes me feel icky.

"Braxton is going to take him after we question him." Which means he's going to torture him, which I can't fucking wait for.

"Why?" Eli asks in a clipped tone. "Just cut the head off. No loose ends."

"Ivy thinks he's not the main problem, that it goes deeper, so she doesn't want his employers suspecting our involvement. She's good at what she does. I trust her."

Eli's quiet for a moment. "Why didn't you go to Will to have him dig deeper into this? He could track him down right now."

We're desperate using this as a lead, but in our line of work, we've learned to follow every thread, curious as to what den of vipers it'll lead us to.

I sigh, wishing that people wouldn't make me admit it out loud. "You know her father hates me and refuses to do any kind of work on my behalf." It's fucking true. Anyone can ask Will Walker for help, and he'll provide it for a high price. From day one, he's made it clear he will help anyone but me. "Besides, she's good at what she does, Eli. I think she's onto something."

Eli sighs, and I imagine him bringing a glass of whiskey to his lips. "Or it could be a waste of our time if it's unrelated. Just make sure you're focused on our objective and not thinking with your dick."

"You know I always think with my dick," I say with a smirk, then turn to look through the restaurant windows. I pause when I see Ivy standing directly behind me, furiously glaring at me. "I've got to go." I hang up on my boss. "How long have you been there?"

"Does it matter?" she bites out, and I can see the hurt in her expression. Fuck, this is bad.

"It's not what it sounds like?" I say, but it comes out as more of a question. Because I don't know what she overheard, all I know for sure is that she's pissed.

She scoffs. "So now you're just telling everyone my shit?"

My heart sinks because I haven't told them specifically, but the only one I alluded to was Braxton, so he could look after her. Guilt consumes me nonetheless, but I know if I hesitate with Ivy, she'll eat me alive.

"These are two completely different incidences. I can't give you the information about what we're working on, but they might not even have anything to do with each other."

"So are you helping me because you want to or because you're being told to?" she growls furiously. Shit, this is really bad. I've dealt with my mother's raging fits, and they often involve weapons, but I've never dealt with something that cuts so deeply as Ivy's scornful expression. It twists in my stomach, and I want to do anything to make it better. To tell her everything she needs to hear and to understand that I would never hurt her.

"You know I'd help you no matter what. I'm a simple guy. You know I want to help you."

"Especially because you always think with your dick?"

I don't know how to respond to that. Before I can reply, she throws her hands up in the air.

"You know what? It's been fun. And your dick is a lot of fun too, but maybe we should have some space for a bit."

"Space? What the fuck does that mean?" I ask, stepping toward her. She laughs as she steps back.

"Exactly what it sounds like, Hawke. No more you and me. No touchy. I can take it from here; I don't need your help anymore." She begins to walk off, but I follow her.

"You don't get to just call it because you're in a pissy mood."

She swings around. "Pissy mood?!"

Fuck. I said the wrong thing. Damnit, I'm not good at this shit.

"This is all just sex, isn't it? And we've had fun, and you can tick it off your list. Job well done, Hawke."

She turns away again, but I catch her wrist, unsure of what the fuck is happening right now. How is it spiraling so much, and I seem to be saying all the wrong things? I mean, I've always done that, but I want to be able to say the right things when it comes to Ivy.

"You're not just a tick on the list," I say, my eyebrows furrowing because I'm still not entirely sure if I'm saying the right thing.

"It just feels like we've been hanging out a little too much. Maybe you're lonely because you can't hang out with your brother anymore, but I'm not a consolation prize you can just fuck and use to entertain yourself."

I'm baffled that she would think that. And when she pulls her hand out of my grip, I let her because I have no idea what she's saying. "I thought we were having fun." I thought she was enjoying all of the time we spent together. Sure, we're at each other's throats all the time, but I thought that was our vibe. I didn't realize she thought I was *using* her.

"It's been fun. But now I'm going to find fun with someone else."

"What the fuck does that mean?" I growl.

"Precisely that, Hawke. We're not a thing. We can still fuck anyone else, and maybe we need to remind ourselves of that." She once again takes off down the sidewalk, and I storm after her. Despite her shorter legs, she picks up a ridiculous amount of speed when she's pissed. Onlookers watch us as we argue.

"Well, yeah. Obviously, it's easy for us to fuck other people," I bite back. I'm not even sure what I'm saying right now.

"Good." She throws her hands up, and somehow, some way, her speed picks up even more. Jesus Christ, this woman is on a mission.

"Yeah, well, good. I can probably pick up before you," I blurt, and a violent bubble of laughter comes to the surface. My cock twitches, and I internally argue with Hawke Junior that he should not find it hot when she's mad because I'm pretty sure this, right now, is serious.

"Want to make a fucking bet?" she challenges, those fierce blue eyes slicing over to me. Goose bumps erupt over my skin. She's furious, but I don't know how to stop the momentum.

"Yep. Game on."

She shakes her head, and I'm still at a loss as to whether I've done the right thing or the wrong thing. I scratch the back of my head as I follow her because this woman undeniably confuses the shit out of me. This isn't the straightforward Ivy I know. Or maybe she is being straightforward, and I've really fucked up.

I'm used to fucking up. But not like this. And I don't know how to stop it.

She's fucking furious with me. She told me to stop following her five times, but after the fifth time, she gave up.

Ivy is many things, but a coward she's not. If she's challenged me, we're going to see this shit through, or at the very least sit down and fucking talk about it. I'm familiar with the bar we walk into; I've been here twice before. It's mostly filled with tourists at the moment, but I don't care about who's here. I only have eyes for the furious little blonde who has far too much attention on her as she walks in. That is, of course, until they see me standing behind her, promising death.

She walks straight up to the bar and orders a water. When I come up beside her, she turns her back to me. I try not to laugh as I lean against the bar. I'm kind of pissed, but also I find this amusing. I can never quite understand Ivy, and maybe that's why I've always been curious about her. Just when I think I have her figured out, she throws a wild card at me like this.

A guy wastes no time approaching her as the bartender gives her the glass of water. I order a whiskey, trying my hardest to take the edge off because now I'm really starting to get pissed.

"Cute outfit," the guy says to her, and she tucks her hair behind her ear.

I loom behind her, glaring at the guy, and he pales when he notices me. She huffs out an irritated sigh, still not looking at me.

"Please ignore him. That's my brother," she says, and I can just imagine the sweet, flirtatious smile she gives him.

"He doesn't look like your brother," he says, still nervous. Good. I hope he pisses himself.

"I'm not her brother," I clarify. If the fucker has any brains or survival instincts, he'll run the other way.

"Oookay. Ah, I think my friend is calling me over," he says and then scampers off. I can't help but grin as the bartender hands me my drink. I triumphantly have a sip as I lean back against the bar. She still won't look at me.

"Stop glaring at men over my shoulder," she growls as she takes a sip of her water.

"I was actually looking at your ass." That does make her turn to face me. Damn, she is so fucking furious that my dick jumps again at the sight. This little vixen has no idea how much hold she has over me. "Lover, what are we even doing here? Let's go home and talk about this."

She points her nose up defiantly. Stubborn little wench. Yet, I still find it amusing. "We made a bet." There's never a dull moment with this woman.

"Yeah, yeah. Whoever can pick up first," I say, shrugging my shoulders and surveying the bar properly this time. There are plenty of beautiful women. But none of them will compare to *her*. "It's just that I have such an unfair advantage. Maybe we should up the stakes and make it two people."

"What, you think I haven't had threesomes?" she asks, folding her arms over her chest.

"I won't believe it until I've seen it for myself," I challenge.

"Um, excuse me. My girlfriend and I overheard some of your conversation," a somewhat attractive guy says, pointing out his girlfriend, who waves at us from the closest tall table to the bar. "We have a hotel room with two beds if you two feel like swinging."

Ivy and I glare at one another. The defiant little shit looks like she's willing for my head to explode, and a flush of red rises across her chest.

"That's what this is, isn't it? Role play?" the man pushes as his girlfriend approaches us.

She holds her hand out to me. "I'm Lucy."

I don't like the way the guy looks Ivy up and down, but she's smiling at him in that flirtatious way that gets her everything she wants.

My jaw tics as I turn back to whatever the fuck her name is. "Hi, sweetheart."

"Where did you say that hotel of yours was?" Ivy bites out.

A few months ago, I would've said this situation isn't surprising. Tonight, I can confirm that it's not only deflated a particular fantasy for me, but I also don't like how Ivy touches this guy. But I can't look away either. The woman in front of me gets down on her knees, undoing my belt. My cock isn't even interested until Ivy removes her shirt, and her perfect tits bounce free. The other guy is irrelevant to her, as her attention is on me. My cock twitches as the woman begins to stroke my cock, but it's not her I'm focusing on. It's a mischievous little liar trying to make a point.

And she will be punished for this.

CHAPTER 29

Ivy

I can't stop watching Hawke as he holds the women's hair and glares at me as they both sit on the bed.

I barely notice the man's mouth on my pussy as he tries to eat me out. He's shit at it, but I bite my bottom lip, pretending to enjoy it as I lie on my back and watch the woman work Hawke's cock with her mouth. I can't help but smirk with smug satisfaction watching as she tries and fails to take him fully.

I glide my hands up my body and to my tits, and his nostrils flair like a fucking bull. I love how he watches me even when he's with another woman. The guy's so bad at licking me that I start fantasizing about Hawke's tongue instead. Hawke watches me as I pinch my own nipples and moan. I wriggle slightly, and his hips buck, driving his dick into the woman's throat, making her choke.

His body moves as if it's mine he was fucking.

I'm so furious with him. When I stepped out of the restaurant to check up on him, I wasn't expecting to overhear basically my entire plan laid out on a silver platter. He said he hadn't told them about what happened to me that night, but I was gripped by a sense of anxiety at the thought of them casually talking about it. I'm not ashamed of it, but it's my business. But what really got to me was when he mentioned his dick.

I don't know when I started getting my wires crossed about us. Maybe it's because of the comments made about how we look like a couple. Or maybe I started getting too comfortable with him being around, even though I pretend I don't want him there.

It all felt like a fairy tale, so it was a rude awakening when that bubble was burst.

So, I go back to doing what I do best.

Fucking.

"I hope you last longer this time," I say to him with a shaky breath, exaggerating the rise and fall of my chest as if I'm actually into this guy between my legs.

He arches an eyebrow and slams his cock into the woman's throat again. "I pray you actually get off."

The man between my legs gives him a side glance but immediately thinks better of it when Hawke glares at him as if he's about to slice his throat. The man swallows hard and focuses on my pussy again. I push him farther down, trying to direct him to hit the right spot or at least come close to it. I need something more, but this isn't something you can teach a guy overnight.

"I'm getting there," I lie breathlessly.

"Really?" The guy going down on me perks up, surprised.

"Sure," I say, forcing his head back down. What the fuck is actually happening? I came here to make a point to Hawke, so why can't I keep my eyes off of him?

"She likes it when you nudge your finger into her asshole," Hawke comments. "Do you know how to find that... The hole?"

"What the fuck, man?" the guy says, throwing his hands in the air. I growl, irritated, tossing my head against the mattress. This is fucking pointless.

"I'm going soft," Hawke admits quietly as he looks down, disappointed.

The woman pulls away from his cock. "Rude. Fuck this. Whatever you two have happening between you is weird," she says and steps away from him.

I feel rather smug that he can't get off with her, but the reality is the guy between my legs is fucking awful, and I'm staring at the cock I really want.

"How long are you going to be a brat?" Hawke asks as he leans back casually on a shoulder. "Should I give him more pointers?"

"You know what, fuck this. I don't need this either," the guy says. "Look, you're hot and all, but this isn't my thing. You two need to leave."

"We're not fucking leaving," Hawke barks, splaying across the bed like some fucking God. Yet his expression radiates imminent death.

The guy is flabbergasted as he tries to force a semblance of manliness, which is the worst thing one could do with Hawke. "This is *our* room."

"Do you fucking own it? No, my boss does. Now, you have ten seconds to leave before I stomp on that pinprick dick of yours. You're just fucking lucky that I blessed you with an opportunity to look at my woman's cunt tonight."

"Hawke!" I snap. He's a fucking menace. The man pales, grabbing for his clothes, his girlfriend quick behind him as they run out into the hallway.

I sigh as I stare up at the ceiling, shaking my head. *What am I doing?* The only way I was getting off in any way was when I was watching Hawke. This is all just a mess.

"Does Eli really own this hotel?" I ask, frustrated by my needs not being met. If anything, I feel dirty with the promise of such a shitty lay.

"Yes." The bed dips beside me from his weight. I'm so mad, but I don't think it all has to do with Hawke. I just... It suddenly doesn't feel nice thinking that I'm another number to him, which is ridiculous because that's how I've always treated men myself.

"Lover, stop pouting. He was four inches too small

to please you anyway," he says as he reaches his hand out to my cheek.

I slap his hand away. "I had no issues getting off before you came onto the scene."

He smirks, and I realize I fed his ego far too much. And even that wasn't the truth. Men were often disappointing in the bedroom. I just forgot how bad it was because I'd been fucking Hawke.

"I'm sorry." His apology surprises me. "I didn't want you to know about the other stuff. I didn't want to worry you."

"Worry me?" I ask as I come up on my elbows. "I can handle myself, Hawke."

His dark eyes stare into my soul uncomfortably as he asks, "But is it so bad to be looked after?"

I'm still furious, but as my gaze roams down his impeccable muscles and tattoos, I can't help but trail a finger over one. It draws goose bumps to the surface, and I feel the heat and electricity between my thighs. Everything about this man sparks me to life.

Hawke is a simple man by nature. What you see is what you get. And I know a part of me twisted the narrative. I know that, and yet I can't entirely interpret the hurt. Maybe there's more to me and Hawke that I'm not willing to admit. Or maybe I'm starting to depend on him too much.

"Lover," he growls. "You better do something about Hawke Junior if you keep touching me like that."

I roll my eyes, trying to hold back the chuckle as I try to cling to my anger. I am still angry. But it's Hawke...

"I still can't believe you call your dick that."

He chuckles as he leans over and kisses me. It's slow and sensual, a very different pace to what I've felt with him before. His hand comes up with a towel as he wipes at my pussy. "I'm not tasting some other man on you."

"You better take that condom off because I'm not tasting some other woman's lips on you either," I tell him, realizing that just like that, my pussy is speaking for itself, and logic is losing control of the situation.

He arrogantly smirks as he throws the condom on the carpet.

"I bet he felt foul," he comments, and my heartbeat jumps at the possessive intent.

"I was so close to coming," I lie.

His eyebrows perk up in challenge. "Is that so?" He lines his cock up with my pussy, and I press my nails to his thick thighs, anticipating his size.

"Probably on the verge of the best orgasm of my li —" My breath is taken from me as he forces himself into me, impaling me. My lungs fill with air as I try to adjust to his size, but he doesn't show mercy as he slams into me again and again and again.

"Fuck, you feel so perfect on my bare cock." He groans under his breath. "Fuck," he grits out, and I'm too blinded by a mix of pain and pleasure. All I can do is brace myself with one hand against the headboard and the other on his thigh, as if trying my hardest to push him away because the guy is thick, pushing apart my hips to gain more access for his brutal pounding.

I stare up at him, bewildered, as tears stream down my face from the sheer force of his thrusts. I don't usually have unprotected sex, and I don't know if that's what makes this all the more impactful as the climb to the peak quickly builds, shaking my legs in anticipation. Or simply if it's because it's Hawke.

He's slamming into me like it's saving him from damnation, and I know, without a doubt, I'm mad at Hawke. I'm furious that he's making me feel all these things at the same time he's giving me everything I want.

"Oh fuck," I curse as I grip his hips, clinging on for dear life. "I'm about to come."

"Fuck," he pants, his face turning red as he jerks into me, and I feel his load hitting the spot. It breaks me, forcing me over the edge as I dig my nails into his thighs, keeping him in place as I feel him shooting inside me.

Fucking perfect.

I ride the wave, unable to look away from him as his lustrous gaze promises that for now, he's giving me all this, but he'd give it to me forever, too.

And that terrifies me.

Hawke terrifies me because I can't see him as only a big oaf now. He's far more than that.

He slowly slides out of me, rubbing his cock back and forth against my folds and then forcing himself back in as if making sure our cum doesn't go to waste. It turns me on more than it has the right to, which is exactly why the moment he leans over to get the towel to clean us up, I'm on my feet and grabbing my clothes.

"Wait? What's happening?" he asks as he wipes his cock. "I don't have sex with women without condoms, I swear. I was in the moment and—"

"I don't give a shit about that, Hawke," I say as I put my jeans and shirt back on. And I don't care. I don't have unprotected sex either, but it's the startling realization of how right it felt with Hawke that has me running out the door. That and I'm still wildly pissed about him not telling me he'd spoken to Eli about my secret operation. As a tracker, that information isn't to be given out. I pride myself on being a vault, so it should have only come from my lips.

"Then why are you running away again?" He looks like a kicked puppy.

I grab my purse from the floor and face him. "I'm not. We had sex. Good job. High five. I'm going home now."

I head for the door, and when he gets up to follow me, I stop him, knowing too well he'll walk out into that hallway butt-ass naked. "And you're not coming with me. I can handle it from here. Thanks for the sex."

I slam the door behind me and then close my eyes when I'm on the other side, taking a deep breath as I lean against the door, momentarily trying to steady my thoughts and racing heart.

Great. I think this is the first time I've ever run away from something instead of hitting it head-on, but I don't want to deal with the confusion of this situation right now. I only want to focus on unraveling whatever shit Makayla got herself into.

I just need a distraction from what might be an obvious thing.

I *like* Hawke.

I've never really liked a man before, and I'm not entirely sure what to do with myself. Because I've fallen for the one man who is known for liking every woman.

CHAPTER 30

Hawke

Eyes stare back at me. A trickle of blood ran down the bridge of her nose. I'm dirty. There's no pleasure in this. The calling of bloodlust and excitement that usually appears when I take a life is nowhere to be found. Instead, I feel hollow.

I'm a monster.

"You didn't need to kill her." Ivy's voice approaches me from behind. I've forgotten why I'm here. Wasn't I trying to find my brother?

"If I didn't, then... then..."

"Then what?" she asks, placing a hand on her hip. "You can't take this back."

I know. I know I can't.

But if I hadn't...

It would have damned Ford and Billie as well. Even if

the woman had shot me first, I couldn't have brought them to the hospital in time.

There's so much blood on my hands.

When I look up, Ivy is walking away. I reach for her, but she's already turning into smoke, slipping through my fingers.

I gasp, jolting upright in the bed. Shadows form around me in the darkness as I pat myself down, remembering where I am—Ford's spare room. The blankets are on the floor where I must've kicked them off in my restless sleep. I look at the clock. Damn, not even three hours of sleep. That's the most I've had all week.

I rub my tired eyes, my mind drifting to Ivy's disgusted expression. I know that didn't happen. I know she wasn't there that day, but it doesn't bring me any peace when Ivy hasn't spoken to me for almost a week.

The last time I saw her was that evening when we hijacked the hotel room. She ran out so quickly, and I couldn't make any sense of it. She looked terrified, and that scared me. I never want her to look at me like that again, and so that's what's been replaying in my nightmares.

I put on some loose pants and walk into Ford's kitchen. It's only three in the morning, but I want to keep myself busy, so I start to cook some bacon and eggs. Felix meows as he joins me, and I pick him up as I explain the basics of cooking bacon to him since the little shit always tries to swipe some off my plate.

I'm deep in my thoughts, and before I know it, I've cooked enough to feed four people.

I can't stop thinking about Ivy. When she doesn't want to be found or spoken to, she's sure able to make it hard to track her down. I've been so fucking busy with hunting down these drug suppliers that the days slipped by. And whenever I'm at her door, tempted to kick it down, she doesn't answer. Sometimes, I'm not even sure if she's there.

"Want to explain why you're cooking up enough eggs for a military camp?" Ford asks as he leans against the doorframe. I immediately dump the cat, not wanting him to detract from my manliness. But also because I know Ford and Felix hardly tolerate one another, and I know it pisses him off that his cat likes me more.

"Just couldn't sleep," I admit. "I hope I didn't wake Billie up as well."

A devilish smirk crosses his features. "She'll be dead to the world for a while."

I plate up a small dish for him, smiling sadly to myself. "I like this version of you. I like seeing how happy you are."

He sits across from me, studying me with eyes that match my own. Ford has always been the calculating one, the smart one, and I'd literally die for him. But lately, I feel like I'm nothing but a nuisance as I stay at their home almost every night.

"Everything okay?" he asks, ignoring the plate I offer him. I start digging into my own mountain of food. Food usually makes me feel better.

I lean back on the counter. I want to brush it off and tell him everything is fine. I don't want to be more of a downer for him, but there's been an elephant in the room from the moment he woke up in that hospital bed.

I'm not religious by any means, but I prayed that they would take me instead of him. Now that he's here, and their side of the bargain was kept, I don't know what to do with myself.

"I thought you were going to die that day," I say quietly. Finding him like that, pale and unresponsive... He always seemed invincible to me, the smarter of us. That type of dumb shit is expected of me, not him.

"So did I," he admits, and we can't look at one another eye to eye. A tension ripples through us. A possibility that one day it might happen, even when all this time we've felt like nothing can touch us. It's a fall from the pedestal I usually like to put myself on, and it almost makes me feel selfish, focusing on killing that woman instead of his experience at her hands. He almost died, for God's sake, and I'm being tormented by a ghost.

"I never thanked you for everything you did that day. For me and Billie," Ford says. I meet his gaze then. I've always looked up to him. We've always had one another's backs, and that will never change. But we've both changed since he was poisoned.

My fork pauses as I go to shovel up another egg. I look at the pleading eyes of Felix and throw him a piece of bacon, always a sucker for the little furball. "I— I—" I clear my throat, struggling for the confession. "I killed the woman who poisoned you. She pulled a gun on me, and I knew it was either her or me. And if it was me... I wouldn't be able to get to you. We always promised we wouldn't hurt women or children, and I... I feel like a selfish asshole since you were the one who almost died. And—"

"Hawke," Ford says, snapping my attention to him. "I will always be grateful to you, and I'm sorry it came at such an expense. You saved me and Billie, and I want to know what I can do to save you from this." He gets up and comes to me, then hugs me.

I'm so stunned that I don't say anything for a while. We don't hug. And yet, this embrace says something in a language that doesn't need words. He's here. Alive.

Even if I have to fight a thousand ghosts, isn't that worth it?

"I'll be okay," I say, noting that I'm tearing up. I clear my throat, then add, "I'm just glad you're happy."

"You know Billie doesn't mind that you stay here. Just no walking around naked in my house."

"Yeah. I appreciate that." I grab my plate and fork, overwhelmed with emotion. "I'm just going to go back to my room for a bit," I tell him and beeline for the door. I'm surprised when I see Billie leaning against the wall with her arms crossed over her chest.

"Hey, little tornado," I say in a big, bright voice, trying to be my usual larger-than-life presence.

She pulls me in for a hug, surprising me, as I awkwardly balance the plate in my hand. "You're always welcome here," she whispers into my ear. "We wouldn't be here without you."

More of that weird shit starts clogging my throat, and I clear it, pushing her back and giving her one of my dazzling smiles. I step back as I announce, "Well, if you ever want a threesome, just let me know."

"Don't push it," Ford growls, and I smile as I slip back into the dark bedroom. The moment the door is closed, I take a steadying breath, looking at my mountain of food.

It might not be the solution to keep ghosts at bay, but at least it makes me happy in some way.

CHAPTER 31

Ivy

I haven't seen Hawke for a week. He's tried, but I've kept myself busy drilling further into Makayla's death. Jared agreed to meet with me. The problem is, he's in Ibiza until next week. I tried to encourage him to come back sooner, but even my sultry sweetness didn't work. Apparently, he's there on "business" and also trying to deal with his "grief."

I tracked his movements in the days before the incident to make sure my hunch was correct and it was he who killed them. I've looked into any regular meetings he's had and his phone calls, but it's all still a puzzle where the pieces aren't quite lining up yet. What I'm certain of is he wasn't working on his own.

"I thought I might find you here," Billie says from over my shoulder. I look back at her, blinking a few times, my eyes adjusting from staring at the bright screen in the dark room. She switches on the light, and I squint.

"That's offensive," I grumble as she looks me up and down.

"So is your unbrushed hair. You living as a mole rat now? I know how you can get hyper-fixated on things." She takes a seat on my bed.

I run my hand over my hair, trying to remember when I last brushed it. She raises a brow at the takeout containers on the edge of my desk. "Glad I kept the key to the apartment so I could check up on you."

"Just working on things," I say as I close down the screens.

"I suppose if it's keeping you out of mischief, I can't complain." She flops back on the mattress. I join her, lying down and staring at the ceiling. It's kind of nice.

"I don't even know what day it is," I confess.

"It's Thursday," she replies and turns to face me. I mirror her movement. "You all right?" She tucks a piece of her long, honey-blonde hair behind her ear.

"Always," I answer with a smile that doesn't convince her of shit. I sigh. She and Hope have been so patient with me.

"Want to explain why Hawke has been at our house every night for a week, then?" she asks, and I roll my eyes.

"What has he said?" I growl.

"Nothing. I just know you two have been spending

some time together. Want to explain why? You know it doesn't bother any of us, right?"

"What doesn't?"

"You know... You and Hawke." She waggles her brows.

I laugh, enjoying the lightness of it, but sober at the reason we became close in the first place. I lick my lips and take a breath.

"I went out with a girlfriend one night, and, well, my drink was spiked," I confess. Billie shoots upright, and I pull her back down quickly. "Nothing happened to me. Hawke came and got me, and well... dealt with it."

Her eyebrows knit together. "Is this the guy in the hospital? He got lectured by his parents so badly for being impulsive and making it harder to clean up his mess." A wave of guilt runs through me. "But I wondered if it had something to do with you."

"What makes you say that?" I ask.

She gets herself comfortable again, the compassion rolling through her as she holds my hand. It reminds me of when we were children, building princess castles with blankets and pillows before Eli would come and destroy them, and Dutton would lecture him about ruining his sister's perfect creation.

"Hawke's always been particularly protective of you. And he didn't tell anyone what it was about. I mean, come on, it's Hawke. He's bad at keeping secrets, and the only one who has the power to swear him to secrecy is probably you."

"He did for Hope about her detective," I point out. And she shuts that down with nothing but a stare. Okay, point taken. He's bad with secrets.

"That explains why you haven't been drinking and partying much lately. Why didn't you tell me this sooner?"

"I wasn't ready. I felt kind of selfish unloading this all on you after your recent events and... I don't know. I know nothing happened that night, but it was scary when the what-ifs played out in my mind, you know? I can't stop thinking about how many times I've let myself be stupid drunk. I just never thought anything like that could happen to me."

Billie offers a small smile. "I'm glad Hawke was able to protect you, and I'm sorry I wasn't there."

I smile back at her because although we're best friends, we can't constantly be glued to one another. Only the fuckers involved, who think it's okay to do this, are at fault.

"What made you decide to come over today?" I ask. "Shouldn't you be at work?"

She rolls back over, staring up at the ceiling thoughtfully. "I took the day off to come see you." That's huge for Billie because the girl will still be working even when she's on her deathbed. "I overheard Hawke and Ford having a heart-to-heart this morning. It was actually really sad, but it was a conversation they both needed to have. It made me miss you. You're practically my sister, and I knew you were dealing with something, so I wanted to give you space until you were ready to talk to me about it. But I realized sometimes we don't always have tomorrow, you know? As morbid as that sounds. I just needed to know right now that you're okay."

Emotion bubbles to the forefront as I hold her hand again, and we lie there comfortably. It's like all of the lines of data and images I've been scanning and taking note of have quickly gone into the vault, giving me this space to breathe. Sometimes, when I hyper-focus on a task, I lose myself for days, and it's nice to know that there are people who accept that part of me, not just the fun, party version of me, and that they're also on standby to pull me out.

"Thank you for checking up on me," I say. "How are you after..."

"The getting poisoned, kidnapped, and watching my boyfriend almost die because of a crazy bitch?"

"Well, that's one way to put it," I say with a nervous laugh that brings a smile to her face.

"I wasn't okay. I even went to therapy for a month for it. The biggest obstacle for me is coming to terms with the fact that this is what Ford does for a living. He'll always be in danger, but I just have to trust that he'll come back to me. But it was the scariest thing I've ever experienced in my life. Would not recommend." She tries to laugh it off, but I can see the hurt and vulnerability there.

I couldn't imagine anything worse than watching the person I love be hurt right in front of me. Hawke's smiling face comes to mind, and I try to shove it away. It's not fair how the moment I step out of my bubble on the computer, he's who I think of.

"Thank you for telling me," I say, rubbing my thumb against her knuckles. "Let's not take so long next time to come to each other about things, okay?"

"That sounds like a good promise."

My phone starts buzzing, and it lights up at the end of my bed. I grab it and see I have two missed calls from my mother, two from Billie, and twenty-six from Hawke.

Billie whistles as she looks over my shoulder. "The boy has it bad. I can't believe you're still in denial."

I glare at her, and she puts up her hands. "I promise I won't badger you about it, *for now,* if you just answer his call. I think today he really needs a friend."

My eyebrows dip. "Is everything okay?"

She shrugs as she grabs her things. "If you want to know if he's okay, ask him yourself. I'm going to go and check up on Hope. Make sure you wash your hair. You stink."

"Rude!" I squawk, throwing a pillow at her, and she laughs as she leaves the room.

Fuck.

I'm torn about calling Hawke back. I haven't

answered any of his calls for a week, and these missed calls are only from the last two days.

I exhale as I head to the bathroom to brush my teeth, and when he answers, he's so frantic I can hardly understand what's happening. And my gut sinks for not having been there for him sooner.

CHAPTER 32

Ivy

"**I** *need your help. Please, Ivy.*"

Those were the last words I heard from Hawke before he hung up. I'm still kind of pissed at him and my lack of understanding of what's happening between us. But I've never heard him sound so desperate, either. Something serious must have happened. So here I am, at his mansion. I walk up to the entrance and open the door that's already unlocked.

"Hawke?!" I yell out, unable to keep the bite from my tone. "You better have a good fucking reason for this!"

I go straight to the kitchen, surprised he's not in here, and put down my purse. I try the next best thing—his home gym. "Hawke?!" I call again.

"In a minute!" he frantically shouts back from upstairs, and a wave of relief passes through me at hearing him finally reply. This house is too fucking big to be so silent. I walk back into the kitchen to get a bottle of water, but a box on the counter grabs my attention. I pick it up, flipping it back and forth in my hand before opening it. Inside, I find little blue pills.

Is that…?

No, surely not.

I pull out my phone to search what Viagra looks like, and a picture of exactly what I'm holding right now appears.

Why the fuck does Hawke have Viagra?

His larger-than-life energy hits the room before he does. When he appears, I'm holding up the packet. "You need help these days?" I ask.

He's still half soaked, obviously having just come from the shower, and a towel is wrapped around his waist, his cock straining behind it. I swallow, an immediate heat swarming in my lower stomach at how much I miss his cock; and it's only been a few weeks.

"It won't go down," he says, freaked out. Realization dawns, and I can't help but throw my head back and laugh. "Don't laugh, Ivy! This is serious! What if I lose my dick?"

"Are you trying to tell me you're taking Viagra now?" I try to say it without laughing.

"No. But one of the guys was selling them at the gym and, you know… after you were saying stuff that night…"

He looks at the floor. "I don't know. I thought I should try them."

I bite my bottom lip. "Oh shit. I didn't think you took that seriously. You know I was only giving you shit, right? You have plenty of stamina."

"Yeah, I know that!" he says agreeably. I try not to laugh. There's something wholesome about a guy this big taking what I said so personally. And here I thought nothing could shake his ego. "I just wanted... I don't know, it's dumb."

I fold my arms over my chest, now feeling partly responsible but also a little pissed. "Hawke, did you call me over for a blow job?"

"You're the only one I know who can get me off in seconds," he explains. When Billie said he needed a friend today, I don't know if she was implying this or something else, but Hawke seems very much okay to me right now.

I put the box on the counter. "Well, sorry about your dick, but goodbye."

"No, please. Ivy," he begs, racing over to me and pinning me against the counter. "I'll give you anything you want."

My devilish grin breaks free. "Really? Anything?"

"Anything," he breathes desperately. "Please make me come. I don't want to lose Hawke Junior."

I try not to laugh at the stupid nickname. "Even if I make you wear a collar and leash at our next party and walk you around in front of all our friends?"

He groans in complaint, and I push past him to walk away. "Wait! No, okay." He grabs my wrist and pulls me against his chest. "*Please.* You're the only one."

My heart falters, and it shouldn't betray me in such a way, especially considering the circumstances.

"How many did you take?" I ask, looking down at the *big problem.*

He shrugs a little and looks away. "Three."

"Three?!"

A nervous laugh escapes him now. "I thought because I was bigger, the normal dose wouldn't be effective. And so I wanted to try it, but I've been beating it out for thirty minutes already."

I snort, trying to contain my laugh, and his devilish grin matches mine. "You think this is so funny, don't you? You should be punished for that."

"Okay, well, it was nice to see you. I'm going now," I tease again. "I'm sure you can find someone else to help with that situation."

"Yeah, you." He nods, pressing his hard cock against me. My pussy starts pounding, and I struggle with any restraint as I look between us.

"What do I get out of this?" I purr as I trace my fingers against the edge of his towel. His breath hitches as he watches me tease him.

"What do you mean, what do you get? You get me. Making you scream my name," he replies arrogantly.

"Nah, I think I'm good." I go to push past him, but

he presses his weight firmly against me, all his games done with. Oh, he must be hurting.

"Little tracker." His tone is a warning. "You aren't allowed to leave until my cock has gone down."

I dance my fingers feather-light against his chest and then bring them up to cup his cheek. His eyes search mine desperately, forever with that mischievous twinkle. The games we taunt one another with. The back and forth. The wins. It's always rushing to the surface when I'm with Hawke. "Only if you agree to wear the collar and leash at the next party. Otherwise, your hand is gonna get a good workout."

He looks to the ceiling and curses under his breath. "Fine. Promise."

I raise my pinkie, victorious, as he hooks it with his. Then he grabs me under the ass and lifts me onto the counter. My heart is pounding from the way he looks at me, promising to devour with the urgency of saving his cock, which just so happens to be this man's life force.

"You so better make me scream," I say as I flick off his towel and look at the formidable opponent. His cock is very hard, and I wonder if it's actually painful, considering he just popped Viagra like it was candy.

"I'll do worse than that," he promises as his hands move to the hem of my dress, and he slowly drags his fingertips over my skin, lifting the material past my hips and exposing my black panties. I reach for his cock and clamp my fist around it. "Fuck," he curses as it twitches in my hands. "Fuck, you always feel so good. Taste good too," he says with a smirk as he drops to his knees, letting my hand fall to my side as he leans in and then bites my left hip. As he pulls back, he takes my panties with him and then proceeds to drag them down my legs. I thought we were here for him, but I'm all for how Hawke always worships me, even when he's in a very compromising situation. Not once has this man had sex with me and only thought of satisfying himself.

He proceeds to pepper my stomach with kisses and then drags his tongue lower. One thing Hawke is amazing at is pleasing a woman. And he knows it. He always takes his time with a woman's body and treasures every inch of it, not just with his hands but with his mouth as well. I think it's one of the reasons I've always struggled with other men, and I compare them to him. Not that I would ever tell him that; he doesn't need any help in the ego department from me, that's for sure.

His tongue moves lower to my slit, and he slides it between my folds. A moan escapes me as I bunch the dress in my fists. I'm already soaking wet for him. So while I enjoy his mouth being between my legs, my body is aching for the friction I know he can give me once his cock slides inside. He grips both of my hips as his tongue keeps sliding over my clit. My head drops back, and I pull the dress up and off until I'm naked.

"Stop," I tell him, and he does without hesitation. "Lie down." Again, he does what I tell him to do. He doesn't ever question me. He stretches out on the cool tile floor as I step over him until I'm standing above his hips, his cock below me. He places both hands behind his head as if he's relaxing, waiting for me to do something. I wonder how long I could make him lie there without trying to touch me. It'd be torturous for him, but I wouldn't be doing myself any favors either. Since having Hawke in my life like this, I've become needy, as if there's an urgency to be together as many times as possible before we won't be able to do this anymore. It makes me almost desperate. I drop down to my knees and hover just above his cock.

"Lover," he croons. "I'm happy to do all the work." He winks. And I know what he's saying is true. Instead, I lower myself until I feel him at my entrance. He keeps his hands to himself, giving me space to lower myself onto him. When he's seated fully inside me, I take a deep breath before I lean forward, place my hands on his tattooed chest, and start rocking my hips back and forth.

"Fuck, woman." He growls but doesn't touch me. He lets me do whatever I want to do. I ride him, and he lets me. Even when I can feel myself building and building, he makes no move to touch me. But as I look down at his face, I see he's biting his lip, and I can tell that he's restraining himself from touching me, letting me have complete control. I've never once noticed him let another woman take charge. Deep down, it makes me want to believe I'm special, but I focus on what we have now.

"Touch me," I command, and reach for his hand to place it on my tit. I know he fucking loves my tits and my ass; I always catch him staring at them. He doesn't waste any time as his hands cover both my tits, and they fill his palms. He takes them between his fingers and starts rolling my nipples as he shifts himself to sit up against the wall. I don't stop my movements as he takes one of my nipples into his mouth. He bites it and proceeds to bite all around my breast, and I know I'm going to have teeth marks all over me, which only turns me on more.

He's so in tune with my body because the moment my orgasm begins to crest, his lips slam onto mine as if coaxing it out of me, demanding that I give him everything. He consumes me, not letting me ride out this wave without every part of him being right there with me. He always reminds me who's making me feel this way.

The first orgasm that hits me breaks me apart as he devours me whole, grabbing my hips and rocking us back and forth to keep the momentum. I feel another build straight after the first, despite how sensitive I am. But he doesn't give me time to breathe or think. He just takes and gives, and I suddenly can't even remember why I'm mad at him. He just keeps my hips rocking, and his mouth devouring mine. Branding me from the inside out.

CHAPTER 33

Hawke

She collapses onto my chest, spent and completely done, but I'm far from finished. I pick her up, my very hard cock staying lodged inside of her, and take her to the living room. I set her on her feet, turn her around so her ass is facing me, then bend her over the chair. I slap her hard on both her ass cheeks before I thrust back in, pounding into her, trying my hardest to blow a load on her. Fuck, my dick feels red and raw.

"How about you take the condom off?" she pants, and I freeze, my hands locked on her hips. She looks at me over her shoulder. "We've been at this for an hour. Let me have a water break or something."

I pull out of her, staring down at my dick, confused. *What the fuck, man? You literally have the most beautiful woman in the world bent over in front of you, and you're not going to take advantage of it?*

"Hawke," Ivy says, clicking her fingers in front of me. "It's not falling off."

"It's not getting off either," I grumble as I whip the condom off. "You're not going to run away again if we don't wear protection?"

Her eyebrows furrow, and I wonder if I missed something again. Did it have nothing to do with the condom in the first place?

She takes a seat on the couch, and I'm confused at first, then she pats the seat beside her and says, "Let's talk for a second."

"You want me to talk about my feelings while my dick is splitting in two?" I ask incredulously and stare back at Hawke Junior.

"Yeah, it might help the little fella," she says, biting the inside of her cheek.

"Don't ever call him little when he's in the room," I retort, grabbing her by the hips and setting her on my lap. Her breath hitches as she casually grabs my cock and slowly strokes it between us. Fuck, it feels so good. I need to come.

In her, preferably. Always in her.

"I didn't run because we weren't using condoms," she states. "I just thought we needed space."

"Space?" I ask, and her hand clamps firmly around my cock to keep me in place.

Fuck, this is confusing, and I don't know if she's using my dick as a weapon against me right now.

"I'm also sorry about snapping on you when I overheard your conversation."

"Yeah, you were in a pissy mood."

She squeezes painfully hard, and I curse. "Okay, okay. I won't say pissy mood." I hold my hands up in surrender, and she smiles.

"Fuck, you're beautiful," I say as I grab the back of her neck and pull her in to kiss her. Every single day without seeing her has been torture. I've even stood outside her apartment, staring up at her window, watching the flashes of her screens just to know she's there and safe. With the amount of food orders being delivered, I knew she was in there. I don't even know if she realizes she hadn't ordered all her favorite foods. I had.

Hope had told me Ivy was prone to getting hyper-fixated on projects, but I was learning that my incredibly beautiful, intelligent woman will barely survive a week without someone looking after her. In all ways. My cock jumps painfully, and I growl into her mouth.

"Is your cunt ready for round five?" I ask, praying to whatever gods that I blow my load, but I'm torn between that and enjoying pounding into her sweet pussy all day.

I don't understand why she wanted space, but I'll speak to her in the language that I understand best, and that's marking her from the inside out.

She laughs as she throws her head back and shakes. "You're going to destroy me."

I fist her hair, holding her head back, and look down on her exposed throat. "But you fucking love it. Admit it."

Her shining blue eyes glare back at me, and she quietly whispers, "I love it."

That snaps my last thread of patience as I lift her hips and impale her on my cock, Hawke Junior gleefully soaking in her juices, and I'm almost certain that no other pussy will make him happy ever again.

CHAPTER 34

Ivy

My pussy is sore, so fucking sore that when he pulls out of me, I have to try and think of how I can make it stop.

He's fucked it, licked it, and smashed it with his cock and mouth. I'm not sure how much more I can actually take. I manage to step away, and when I glance down at his groin, I see his cock is still hard. I start shaking my head, and he just smirks as if he's enjoying every moment of breaking me. But even a girl like me has her limits. I thought I had stamina, but a whole day of fucking nonstop has destroyed me from the inside out, and I can barely use my legs.

"I have to leave," I say, finally throwing in the towel. "You need to go to the hospital for that."

"No, don't leave me. *Please*," he whines as he tries to reach for my hand. I slip out of his grasp, then go to the kitchen to find my dress and throw it on. All the while, he practically stalks me. Viagra or not, Hawke's stamina is unlike any man I've ever been with. I need to get out of this house while my pussy is still able to function.

I know the moment he grabs me again, my body will betray me, not listening to any logic. So I keep the distance between us so that he can't fill me with his cock again. It's not my fault he took too many Viagra, and now it's fucked up his penis.

I scoop up my purse and head for the door. I'm not showing him any more mercy; that cock is a sinking ship right now.

"Ivy, please!" he calls out, but I choose to ignore him, pushing through the pain this asshole has battered my body with. I'm sure hours from now I'll be grateful, but right now, my body fucking aches and my hips feel like they've been snapped off, trying to endure his size the whole time.

"Good luck. You know, with that." I point to his cock and quickly shut the door behind me. I hear him laugh, which also kind of sounds like he's about to cry, as I head to the car. He pulls the front door open, throws his hands up in the air, and screams my name, completely naked.

"Come back! We aren't done! You can't be serious, Ivy!"

I laugh as I drive away because there's no chance in hell that I'm turning around.

I haven't even pulled through the gate at the end of his driveway before he's calling me. He continues to call, and I ignore him, with very little sympathy as I pray for my pussy.

As soon as I'm home, I run a bath, not even waiting for the tub to fill up because my first priority is letting my sore pussy soak. She worked overtime today.

I sigh as I relax back in the water, a small smile curving my lips as I think about all the positions he had me in. Hawke loves to put me in weird positions, and I love it as well.

Today was strange. I was mad at him—still am, I think—but he was able to take me out of my head for a while and prevented me from obsessing about not being able to move forward until I see Jared.

My phone continues to ring, buzzing on the bathroom counter, so I lower myself deeper into the water until it covers my head and muffles the sound. I lie there, finally letting my mind decompress.

So much has changed, particularly because of one big oaf who keeps getting himself and his dick into trouble. Bubbles escape my mouth and rise to the water's surface as I laugh. Only Hawke would do something as stupid as taking three Viagra. It's fucking ridiculous. And hilarious.

When the water starts to turn cold and my skin starts to prune, I get out of the bath and check my phone. It's still buzzing. I don't even have to look at the screen to know it's him.

I can't help but be curious about his predicament, and so, after I dry off and dress, I grab my laptop and tuck my feet under my ass as I sit on my couch and hack into his cameras.

He comes up on the second camera, still in the living room. He's sitting on the couch, spread eagle, his hand wrapped around his cock as he pumps it, his other hand holding his phone to his ear. Persistent fucker. I almost feel cruel now. I flip my phone over and see his name appear again. This time, I do answer.

"Finally." He huffs, and I can hear his hand moving.

"How is your problem going?" I ask, biting the inside of my cheek. This guy, I swear…

"Better if you were here," he growls.

"I don't think you're allowed near my vagina until it recovers." I watch him on the camera and his hand pauses.

"So you're saying there'll be a next time?" he questions, and when I don't answer, he says, "Lover?"

"Maybe."

"Good. How about tomorrow?"

"Ummm, no."

"Today then?" he says. "Please, come back."

"I think you can take care of that yourself. Besides, you might not be home tomorrow if you're getting the blood drained from your cock in the hospital."

His hand freezes on his cock. "That's not really what happens, is it?"

"Sure is. Better get that hand working faster."

"Fuck," he curses as his speed increases.

"Put your back into it," I say cheekily, and his gaze darts straight to the camera. A slow smirk draws across his face as he continues stroking himself.

"You're enjoying this a little too much," he scolds. "Tell me, what did you like…"

"When I left," I joke.

"Liar."

"I liked it when you bit me," I confess.

When I was in the bathtub, I looked at my body, which happened to be covered in bite marks. And I liked it. I liked it even more when he was the one doing the biting. How and why I like it confuses me. And I know he wouldn't judge me because he loved doing it as much as I loved receiving it.

"Good, what else…"

"All of it."

"Are you wet?" he asks.

"No. I'm sore."

"I could make you feel better. My tongue could make you feel better."

"I'm going to sleep now," I say sweetly.

"It's daytime," he reminds me.

"Yes, and you kept me up all night, fucking me."

"And I can repeat that today if you like." I can't help the laugh that leaves me at his words as I hang up on him.

CHAPTER 35

Ivy

The next day, Billie pops over with a container of home-baked cookies. When I open it, I flip her off because she's written *Sorry about your vag* across them with icing.

"He was freaking out about it. It only just went down," she says, laughing at Hawke's expense. I'm shaking my head because I've been working on one of my freelance jobs since I hung up on Hawke yesterday. I uncurl myself from the couch enough to eat one of the cookies because my vagina deserves it.

I had texted Billie about how much Hawke really needed a friend and that he'd had a hard-on because he was playing with Viagra. We've been messaging back and forth all day, even while she was at work. To be honest, I'd been waiting for an update to say he went to the hospital to have it taken care of. So when she explains that he called Ford yesterday afternoon after I left, freaking out that his dick had been erect for twelve hours, I'm a little surprised. Glad I gave my best efforts for eight of those hours.

I didn't check back on the cameras when I woke up this morning. I just got straight to work, and then I fell back asleep. The situation wasn't urgent enough for me, considering he inflicted it on himself. The dumbass.

"So did he go to the hospital?" I ask.

"No. Apparently, a stern talking from Eli with a gun to his head for exposing himself to Jewel as he frantically asked everyone what to do was enough to deflate him."

My breath hitches, and then I keel over laughing. I roll on the couch, kicking my feet back and forth in hysterics. I wipe away tears. "He actually started showing everyone? That's hilarious! I wish I would have been there to see Eli's face. Oh my gosh! That's the best!"

She laughs as she takes one of the cookies and looks at me pointedly. "But what I'm more interested in is something you've been avoiding. You said your vagina is sore in the messages, and he may have let it slip that you tried to help him. Care to explain?" I bite my lip as she waggles her brows. "You helped him?"

I exhale and take the final bite of my cookie as I stand up to make us some coffee. "I was there yesterday after you said he was having a rough day."

"For what it's worth, I had no idea what he was

doing, and that was not what I was intending at all," she clarifies.

"Well, Hawke does Hawke things." I shrug as I put an espresso pod in the coffee machine. "But then I left him high and dry because my pussy was sore."

She can't stop laughing as she slaps her leg and joins me in the kitchen, leaning against the counter. "He was complaining about you and how it's your fault."

"It was not. I said he shouldn't have taken that many."

"Yeah, well, he clearly didn't listen." She shakes her head. "Apparently, he bought them from a guy at his gym, and I'm pretty sure he makes them himself, so Hawke was probably the first test dummy, and he should just be thankful his cock is still attached."

"Oh my God! So they weren't even legit ones?" I ask. He's dabbling with homemade Viagra?

"I mean, I guess the dude works at a pharmacy if that counts for anything."

"This is getting worse," I tell her, trying not to smile. Fucking Hawke. He's a big idiot.

"He literally thought he was going to die if his penis never worked again. He went to Eli's house in a panic and called an emergency meeting, then when everyone arrived, he showed his junk and asked them why it wouldn't go down." She keeps laughing.

"I bet Eli wanted to kill him." I can only imagine.

"Damn right," she agrees. "Soooo, care to fill me in on what's happening between you two now?"

"Nothing. I tried to help the situation, but when I got sore, I left." I pass her the first coffee, and she glares at me.

"That's not what I meant, and you know it. Stop avoiding the question, Ivy. Do you actually like him? There's always been something between you two."

I sigh. "Look, we fucked a few years back, okay?"

She slams her hand on the counter. "I fucking knew it!"

I try to hide my mischievous smile. "So, yeah, of course, I like Hawke, as unhinged as he is. He's a good time. But Hawke and I don't do anything past that."

She seems not to like that answer. "Hmm. You both like to fuck around, everyone knows it. Do you think it could be something more? Or will you both still fuck around?"

"I'm not trying to marry him," I sass, and she gives it back just as quickly.

"You want marriage and kids, Ivy, everyone knows it. You've drunkenly told Hope and me on multiple occasions. Stop pretending to be a big baddie. You just like sex too much, and everyone else bores you in the bedroom; it's why you keep fucking strange men."

Ouch.

"Way to call a woman out."

She raises her hands in the air. It's why I like Billie;

she doesn't pull punches. But damn. There's no reality check like a best friend's brutal truth.

"I'm just telling you, I think if you continue sleeping with Hawke, you need to set things straight and know what you're doing. Hawke's a simple guy; you need to spell it out for him."

"Didn't you sneak around for ages with Ford?" I throw back at her, deflecting from the answers she so obviously wants but that I'm not entirely sure I'm ready for yet. They were fucking each other for over a year before they got serious.

"I did, but he also knows what I want now," she says. "And I'm the happiest I've ever been."

"Okay, that's good for you. And when I know what I want, I'll be sure to tell the person I'm fucking that." I smile at her.

"No need to get mad, Ivy. I'm only looking out for you."

"That's the thing, Billie, I'm good with myself. When I'm ready to take that step, I will. But I also don't need to be lectured on it the same way people judge me for fucking whoever I please." I turn and bring my coffee to my lips, realizing what I just said. She's staring at me, and I'm quick to apologize. "I'm sorry."

"I'm sorry too. I know I should've told you about the Ford thing, and I'm not trying to pressure you into anything. I just want you to be happy. I think Hawke's an idiot, but he's a goodhearted idiot. You know, for a killer and all."

I laugh and take a sip of my coffee. "I've never really liked anyone. And Hawke's a gamble since he'll sleep with anything that moves."

She kicks her legs back and forth as she says, "But from what I've heard, he hasn't slept with anyone or partied for months." She swivels around on the bar stool. "Something must be keeping him entertained."

I shake my head as my phone buzzes with a message, and my eyebrows furrow as I see a text from Jared. Oh shit. He's back in town today.

"I need to get changed," I say quickly.

"For what?!" Billie calls out from behind me.

"For a date. Follow so I can explain!" I shout as I start pulling clothes from my closet. I've been waiting for this day, and my heart races with adrenaline. Finally, I'll be getting all the answers I need from this fucker. I'm buzzing with excitement that, finally, this asshole will be greeted with the punishment he deserves.

I'm just ecstatic that I'm going to be the sledge-hammer to his face when he doesn't even see it coming.

Sometimes the pretty enticements are the most lethal form of bait.

CHAPTER 36

Hawke

Eli is pissed at me. I didn't purposely show his wife my cock. She was just standing there when I was trying to calmly explain how it wouldn't go down. And I felt like I wasn't explaining it well enough, so I had to show them the issue. I figured once they saw it, they would fully understand. Instead, I got a punch to the jaw and a gun to my temple, attached with Eli's warning that if I ever do that again, next time, he'll chop my dick off.

Eventually, they called the private doc, and he sorted me out with some strong drugs to take so it would go down fully and I could finally fucking sleep. But I'm certain it's Eli scaring the life out of me that had Hawke Junior eventually shriveling.

The meds the doc gave me knocked me out cold, and

it's the only decent night's sleep I've had unless I'm in Ivy's bed, and she rarely lets me sleep over.

My wrist is still sore from all the jerking off I had to do. I felt like a teenage boy all over again, discovering his own penis. Nothing I did fucking made it go down. And Ford was fucking useless. All he did was laugh. He laughed so much that I told him to fuck himself and came back to my house to sleep instead of staying at his. Naturally, I grumbled my complaint the whole time until I fell asleep.

"Hawke." I turn over in my bed and make sure the covers are pulled up before my mother pushes my bedroom door open. My father stands behind her, trying to hide his smirk. "You're still in bed?"

"I didn't get any sleep last night," I mumble, still pissed off. She walks over to the blinds and pulls them open, letting the sunshine in as she looks over her shoulder at me.

"That's what happens when you stupidly take Viagra."

I squint at her and then glance at my father. "Who told you?" I ask, groaning and rolling over to the other side of my bed. Fuck those guys; I went to them for help. The only one who actually tried to help me was Ivy.

Hawke Junior twitches at the thought of all the positions I had her in.

Nope. Not happening. I am not getting a hard-on while my mother is standing in the same room.

"You should know everything finds its way back to me." She smiles and sits at the end of the bed. "Now, do you want to talk about it?" she asks in her slight Russian accent. What the fuck is this, some kind of intervention? Is she actually trying to be... motherly? Or is she pranking me? My father laughs from the door, but neither of us pays him any attention.

"No, Mother, I do not wish to talk about my cock with you."

She clicks her tongue. "Not that. Why you took it." She raises a perfect brow at me. "Is everything okay?"

I groan, putting the pillow over my face.

Why did I take it? Why do I do anything? It's just my fucking personality to try new things and not think about the consequences. But this time, I definitely should've thought about the consequences of my actions because my penis paid for it. Looking back now, I probably should've only taken one. I have no issues in the bedroom, but I felt like I needed to impress Ivy even more, so when she did actually come over, and thank fuck she did agree, I thought it would be fucking incredible. And it was... until it wasn't.

Why did I feel the need to impress her? Well, because she's a lot like me. And she knows what she wants and what she likes. It's one of the many reasons I'm enchanted by her, which isn't surprising once you get to know her. But I'm not sharing any of that with my parents.

"Because I wanted to have fun. Now, Mother, if you would kindly leave so I can go back to sleep, that would be amazing." She looks past me and to where River stands at the door.

"We didn't just come for that. We wanted to check up on you. We were advised you weren't partying as much, and you got messy on the last guy you killed in the hospital."

I stare at them. "Are you... *worried* about me?"

"Of course we are. We're your parents," my mother says as if it's obvious. "Besides, you're the one I worry about the most since you do things and then think after the fact. You've just been slightly different since the incident with your brother, so we wanted to make sure everything was okay."

I think I've been staring for too long. My mother does not have heart-to-heart conversations. I mean, I'm certain she has a heart, but only for my father. And I know she cares about me and Ford, but she has peculiar ways of showing it. Playing therapist isn't one of them.

"I'm okay," I finally say, still looking between them skeptically. "Really, I just did a stupid thing."

My mother perks up with that, taking it as answer enough to remove herself from what is most likely the most uncomfortable motherly role she's taken.

"Also, we'll be hosting an opening for one of your father's new restaurants. Make sure you're there. Oh, and I've invited Ivy Walker."

My jaw drops as I realize that's most likely the reason she's here. "Mom, that is so not cool, inviting her without me asking her directly!"

"Why? We've known the Walker family for years. Is there a particular reason I shouldn't have asked her?" she asks with a knowing smirk. I open my mouth and then close it. I swear this woman put a tracking device in our skin somewhere when we were teens. How she finds out everything is baffling. "Make sure you don't scare that one off. I'm rather fond of her," she says before stepping out of my room.

My father hovers at the door with a smirk, always impressed by how our mother puts us in our place.

"Call us if you need us, even if it's that issue..." he says, waving a hand toward my crotch. I nod, but I know deep down inside I would never have fucking called them for that. Who calls their mother to say their fucking cock is hard as a rock, and they can't get it down because they stupidly took Viagra? Not fucking me, that's for sure.

A text message appears on my screen, and I jump out of bed as Ford relays a time and place.

Looks like Ivy has herself a date.

CHAPTER 37

Ivy

I'm walking to the restaurant where I'm meeting Jared for, in his words, "our date." The guy seems to move on quickly for someone in mourning over his ex-girlfriend.

My phone buzzes, and my heels stop clicking against the pavement as I freeze in place at the name on my screen. I answer Anya Ivanov's call.

The only reason I have her number is because she called me once trying to find Hawke, who had later been found in a field after killing three men and lost his phone and car keys in the process. It's only because my father could track his car in the first place that they found him, and I heard about it all week as my father complained that he had to help the little shit at all.

I never understood why she called me then, and I sure as shit don't understand why she's calling me now.

But I certainly know better than not to answer when Anya Ivanov calls.

"Hello?" I answer.

"Hello, Ivy. I'm sending you details for a party River, and I will be hosting. We look forward to seeing you there." And then she hangs up.

"Hello?" I say, looking down at the phone. Okay, that was fucking weird.

As promised, details come through for a party being thrown a few days from now. My mind goes blank. Okay, I'm not even focusing on whatever the fuck that was about until after this. I'm sure Billie has all the details and will be going as well, so it'll be fine.

Except maybe it won't. If everyone in our circle knows that Hawke and I are sleeping together, I'm sure it hasn't taken long for his parents to hear about it. Which I know will eventually get back to my parents, and I'm not really sure how they will handle that kind of news. My mother loves Hawke. My father, however... will probably hunt him down to the ends of the earth, promising him immediate death.

Whatever. I'm not dealing with those spiraling thoughts right now.

I walk into the restaurant and give my name to the hostess, who then takes me to where Jared is waiting. I try to put on a sympathetic smile, playing the part of the grieving friend who's worried about his mourning, which is very fucking difficult when I know he's the one who slit her throat.

I'd gathered enough information to confirm it was him. All I need is the name of who he's working for but more importantly, why he did it.

He stands and gives me a hug, which I grudgingly return. "Sorry I couldn't come back sooner; I had some business to deal with," he says as he takes the seat across from me.

"No problem. I'm sure you're dealing with a lot." I lean across the table and lay my hand over his. His gaze dips straight to the contact, and his face softens as if falling into the role he's supposed to play. *Piece of shit.*

"I knew you'd eventually come around," he says, signaling to the waiter that he's ready for the food that he's pre-ordered for the table. This man does not waste any time, and the waiter places two plates in front of us. If this were a real date, I'd probably walk out the door at the fact that he ordered me a fucking salad. *Asshole.*

But I grit my teeth and smile as I ask, "What do you mean?"

He sighs as if he's reluctant to tell me, but it's all an act. For the first time, I can see the real Jared. I never had a reason to look deeper before. "I always liked you, you know that, right?"

A lump forms in my throat. Is this guy fucking serious? Then again, I'm pretty sure men who slit their girl-friends' throats don't exactly tread on the side of sanity.

"I don't know if it's appropriate, what with Makayla's death, you know. It'd be wrong to—"

"We were never that serious," he interrupts as he reaches across the table and takes my hand. I resist the urge to pull my hand away from his. This guy is out of his fucking mind, but if I can use that to my advantage, I will. Whether he confesses or not, everything else is in motion. I'm just the bait. But I want him to confess. I need him to admit to me what he did was *wrong* and all kinds of fucked-up. Makayla wasn't perfect, but she didn't deserve to be manipulated and murdered by this piece of shit.

I sigh contemplatively, playing the role I've given myself for this evening. "You're not around very much. You seem to jump around from place to place."

"You do, too." He's not wrong. "It doesn't have to be anything serious."

I shrug. "I'm starting to like Manhattan a little more lately. I'm taking more jobs here, so I think I'm after something stable."

His eyebrows dip as he licks his lips. "I've just got this new job that I can't really pull out of anytime soon. But I'm making a fuck-ton of money from it, so it'll be better for us. I can spoil you."

I try to hold back the vomit that wants to rise up my throat. As if a piece of shit like this could ever spoil *me*. I wonder when the crazy started for him or if it was something that was always beneath the surface, waiting to be exploited. I consider my next words carefully as I lean in, giving a clear view of my cleavage.

"I don't know if you can handle me. Besides, I've just started some new work too. I can't really go into much detail, but it pays well too."

"Really?" he purrs, staring at my tits.

"Yep." I smack my lips together, and his gaze goes straight to them as if hypnotized. I place my hand under the table on his knee. "You have me curious now. I want to hear more about your job."

His gaze snaps to my eyes, but I don't let it deter me. I'm a confident woman; getting men to respond to me has never been difficult. And I won't allow Jared to be an exception. Once he's in my trap, it's game over.

"I really shouldn't..."

I giggle. "Now I'm even more intrigued. I like a man with secrets. Someone who's doing mysterious things. Makes for a good time. But I do have high expectations of a man if he says he can look after me."

He licks his lips, and I know for a fact that Jared has never been with a woman like me, and it makes it easy to play on the fantasy.

"Uh, well... It's not exactly... legal," he stammers, and I slide my hand farther up his thigh, dragging my nails against his pants. I bet the pour guy is already rock hard. "I mean, I don't think it's that bad, though."

"What is it?" I encourage.

"Drugs," he blurts quietly as I squeeze as high as my hand can reach.

"Oooh," I purr. He's staring at my mouth and licking his lips. This guy couldn't be any easier to lure into a honeytrap. "What kind of drugs? The fun kind?" I arch an eyebrow.

Wherever this is leading, I hope it gives me an indication of his employer, or I'll thread it into a confession of Makayla's murder. I know I'll get the answers, but I want them for myself. I want to crack this man in two since I've been consumed with him for the last two weeks. I want the answers. I need them for my own peace.

"Just stuff. But my boss pays me a lot of money for it. But sometimes he's intense."

"Intense is good, isn't it?" I ask, pretending like I care.

"Not like this guy. He was unhappy with a recent mistake I made, and so I had to do a job I wasn't comfortable with," he admits.

Interesting.

"Everything okay? You can tell me, you know. It's not easy keeping things to yourself," I push.

He stares at the food between us, and I feel the shift before I see it in his gaze. Has the asshole actually snapped?

"No, it's not okay. I wouldn't have had to do it if the drugs just worked on you and shit didn't start going pear-shaped."

My entire body freezes. Did he just say what I think he did? No way, surely not. A manic smile slowly creeps onto his lips as I retract my hand and realize he might be cracking far more quickly than I thought he might. The thing with ordinary men is when they're introduced into this world, not all of them can handle its expectations or its repercussions.

"What do you mean?" I ask, leaning back in my chair now. The Jared who was sitting across from me a moment before is gone. The facade of who or what he might've once been vanished.

I didn't touch my food because I didn't trust his intention before, and I certainly don't trust it now. He studies me with curious eyes, and I wonder how I missed it. How I missed his interest in me. Because now when I look at him, I can see it clear as day written all over his face.

"If only it worked on you, and Lester didn't go missing because of it. You should've just gone home with him like a good girl. That was our plan. It was as simple as that. I wish I could've seen you then, and we could've talked about *us*."

"You were the one behind drugging me that night?" I ask quietly, realizing he's furious with me as if I'm the reason it all went wrong. It takes my breath away. I'd come to terms with what happened, but knowing it wasn't just Lester but him as well? It makes me feel sick. How many women...? I let the thought trail off.

I always assumed he and Makayla just had a weird relationship, and somehow they made it work. She never really shared many details with me about him, and I never really cared enough to ask. But this asshole has a few screws loose, and not in a fun way. In a way that's he nurtured himself to take advantage of women and then blame them for him having to face any kind of consequences.

He picks up his knife and fork, cuts into the steak, and puts a piece in his mouth, chewing furiously as if that will calm down his mood.

"I was just trying to create a time for us to speak privately. But every time we were at parties, you were always off with some other guy," he grits out.

"You were with Makayla," I remind him. *Remember the dead ex-girlfriend you killed?!*

"Fuck Makayla. She always got in the way," he bites back.

I'm gobsmacked by how deranged this guy is, and I wish I had never touched him, even if I was only trying to get answers from him. He's looking around the restaurant now as if we're being spied on, and I realize he's living in a state of paranoia, certain he's being watched or waiting for his fall when he makes another wrong move.

He's a desperate man.

And desperate men end up in deeper trouble, or worse, in this world.

His hair is styled back, and he's wearing a nice suit. I

thought at first it was because he was trying to impress me, but maybe this is him uncomfortably living in a world he was never cut out for. And it's very clear he wasn't meant for it because I know men who certainly don't squeal. Especially to impress a woman.

He makes me want to vomit. Not only would I never want him, I don't even find him attractive.

Without a doubt, he's the worst type of man.

"You're awfully quiet. You should eat," he says, pointing his knife at my salad.

"Did you do it?" I ask. Fuck this coy shit. He's going to pay for what he did anyway. Now I want him to see me for the real me. A powerful woman. One not enticed by his cheap cologne or rented suit. A woman who basks in the world he so desperately wanted to be involved with and so clearly can't handle.

He glances over his shoulder. This asshole's in too deep, and he doesn't know how to get out.

So I'll make sure he's taken out.

"Do what?"

"Makayla. Did you kill her?" I ask directly.

He stops cutting his steak and raises his gaze to mine. There's a twinkle of being recognized but also the erratic movement of a man who's about to crack.

"The possibility is there," he says, glancing down at my tits. "I never meant for it to happen. But I was punished for being sloppy here in Manhattan for selling the drugs. So I had to kill some politician's daughter.

Makayla wasn't supposed to be there that night, but when she heard I asked one of her friends on a date, she came anyway. Convinced the other girl to have a three-some with us. Maybe I should've fucked them both before I killed them." He's speaking so rapidly now it's like he's glorifying his actions. "I'm not a killer. I just had to show my boss I was dedicated, you know." Something changes in his expression, and he meets my eyes again. "But girls like a bad boy anyway, right? I'd never hurt you. You're different. You should eat."

"No," I say, crossing my arms over my chest.

He chuckles as if hearing no is a challenge, and he's completely in control of this situation. He reaches for his glass of wine and takes a sip. "That's what I've always liked about you. You have a little more bite. Before I dated Makayla, do you even remember me trying to get your number?" He's trying to romanticize the situation.

Wow, this asshole is a total manipulator, but he's fucking terrible at it. But I suppose if he's encouraged women around him to take drugs, they're more suscep-tible to it. I feel so stupid not having intervened with Makayla sooner. "It was you I wanted, but I settled for her to be closer to you."

I consider the fork to my right and how it might look in his eye but curl my nails into my palms instead. I might be boiling inside, fueled by rage, but a killer I'm not. Not for him. But it doesn't mean there aren't ways to hurt a man, just a little. *Because someone has to do it, right?* I think, shooting a quick glance at the steak knife on my right.

"But it's okay. That obstacle is gone now. I made it work for us," he says, deranged. "I even came back sooner than I thought I'd be able to, just so I could see you. Can't you see how much I love you?" I think I'm going to be sick. "Let's go back to my place after this and talk about it. We'll have more privacy there."

Nausea churns in my stomach. This guy actually believes what he's saying, and I don't know if this is before or after he killed Makayla and the other woman. I can't tell if he was sane or wasn't. But one thing's obvious—he killed them to save his own ass, and they never deserved that.

My nails are biting into the palm of my hand because I know I need to lead him somewhere secluded so the boys can grab him, but I don't want to be anywhere near him. Just as I'm about to agree and suggest we leave now, a voice booms over my shoulder, and all that nauseating tension curling in my stomach quickly dissipates. Even if it's not the plan, I feel safer knowing he's here.

"Sorry to interrupt, lover, but I heard there was a fuckhead trying to steal my girl."

But he's a little before his cue.

CHAPTER 38

Hawke

Ford rang me as soon as Billie filled him in on the details Ivy had shared with her. I'm proud of my little hacker for opening up to her best friend about what's happening. She's more than capable of dabbling in this life, which isn't a surprise considering who her father is. But I don't want it to harden her like it has most of us. Ivy seems like someone who needs the support of her friends.

I'm watching from outside the restaurant, as we previously discussed. Ivy might've thrown me off her case when we argued that night, and she found out about Eli's separate operation, but having them reach out to me is her way of saying she's sorry. Besides, even if I didn't have the time and location of this meetup, I would've found out pretty fucking fast because there's no way I'm letting some douchebag like that enjoy a date with my woman.

Ford and Billie are parked on a side street just across the way. And Ford is watching me, leaning against his car. I refuse to be *waiting* for her because I won't risk anything happening to her.

I watch as Ivy leans over the table, intentionally pushing her cleavage together. He's practically drooling at the sight. Fuck, it turns me on seeing her in action. Her confidence that can bend any man to her will. I'm no exception to that, but I know without a doubt I'm the only man who can handle Ivy Walker. Anyone else she'll eat alive, like the tool she's with right now. I adjust my cock as I watch her run her hands up his leg under the table.

It brings me great pleasure to know I'm going to be breaking that little man into tiny pieces. But watching her at work... is everything to me. The fucker never had a chance.

I can tell the moment the conversation turns. I've seen it all too often. There's a truth in our darkness, and not everyone can handle it. We've become attuned to the moment when the inner crazy comes out in others. Some people's sins eat them from the inside out. Grief devours others whole until they're a shell of the person they were, letting their demons run on autopilot.

A flash of the woman I killed comes to mind. She'd

become fixated on killing us after we killed her boyfriend. I can't blame her. I'd do the same. But I would walk away without so much as a second thought. It ate her alive. This schmuck seems like the same type.

Except I haven't walked away from that unscathed, I remind myself. Killing that woman will never be okay with me. It's the only code I've lived by to not entirely hate myself or what I do because I don't love every part of my job. But that? That makes men feel dirty.

I can lipread some of the bullshit he's saying. That it was always Ivy he wanted. Not her friend. This guy's fucking delusional if he thinks someone like Ivy will give him the time of day.

My temperament changes the moment I notice how her shoulders stiffen, and she becomes tense. Most people probably don't notice her subtle changes, but I notice everything about her. Ivy is a lover, not a fighter. It's something I find very interesting about her because, at the same time, while she might be classified as a lover, her intelligence is lethal. Especially now as she honeytraps this pinprick.

I see her nails curl into her palms, and I'm moving.

"Wait, Hawke, she needs to isolate him. Hawke!" Ford calls out after me, and I hear him growl his irritation.

I loom over her, my favorite position to be in, as my glare burns a hole in the douchebag sitting across from her. "Sorry to interrupt, lover, but I heard there was a fuckhead trying to steal my girl."

She turns in her seat to meet my gaze, and I see instant relief wash over her. Then it's quickly replaced with something else, and I know she's probably pissed because I came in a little earlier than planned. I don't give a fuck. Everyone says I'm impulsive anyway, so I have a reputation to maintain.

"A little early, don't you think?" she quietly whispers. There are a few couples at nearby tables, but I don't particularly care. Especially when my father owns this restaurant, and anything that happens can be covered up quickly.

"Stand up, lover. We're leaving," I tell her. Her job here is done. We'll handle the rest going forward. The moment she started to become uncomfortable was the moment I was always going to pull her out.

"What the fuck is this? You're the same asshole from the party. You fucking hurt my friend!" he snaps, standing up. "Ivy is going with me, so I suggest you leave."

"Oh, ho?" I growl as I size him up, and Ivy stands between us. "Did the little asshole grow some balls because he killed someone?" He pales as if realizing he's exposed himself. Fucking idiot. I lean in. "Let me tell you, from one killer to another, anyone who so much as touches a woman is a piece of shit. You're a coward, and I particularly enjoy torturing cowards."

"Hawke, you need to stop," Ivy says, and I don't know why I'm getting lectured. There are only a few onlookers. Besides, there's not a thing to see here. But when I glance down, I notice the steak knife she's holding, and my mind goes blank. "I want to hear what he says."

"Then come with me. Fuck this guy," Jared says, encouraging her into his arms so he can leave. I'm impressed that instead of comprehending he's been backed into a corner, his tiny ego thinks he's a king when a goddess is standing in front of him with a knife in her hand.

She does exactly as he says, stepping into his space, and I watch with fascination as she angles the knife and stabs it straight into his stomach. I'm already moving, shifting behind them as if we're in a big group hug, and I cover his mouth when he goes to scream.

"Makayla deserved better than you," she seethes under her breath. "I saw the whole thing, you piece of shit." Then her gaze slides to meet mine, and I can't remove the shit-eating grin from my face. I'm so fucking proud of her, and my cock is so fucking hard.

Is she a killer? No. Is she a scornful goddess? Yes.

His breath comes in short bursts as she removes her hand from the knife protruding from his stomach. She's shaking but holds the determination of a woman's wrath. Fuck, she couldn't be any hotter. I reach into my back pocket, pull out a wad of cash, and throw it on the table.

I'm already going to hear about this from my parents, so I better make sure the bill's paid, at the very least.

I maneuver him toward the door as Ivy grabs her purse and slides the strap over her shoulder, quickly following me out. The fucker can barely use his legs, so stunned by the knife hanging out of his stomach. I continue leading him to the car as Ivy walks in front of us, blocking the protruding knife from anyone's view. I stare at her back, knowing in that moment, I've undoubtedly just fallen in love.

Ford already has the back door open and is waiting expectantly. Ivy notices Billie in the passenger seat but says nothing as they offer each other a tense smile. Okay, maybe we're not good influences on them, but I haven't witnessed anything more perfect as my brother and I pushing a sad sack of shit into the back of his car.

Jared tries to struggle, but it's clearly his first time being stabbed because he doesn't seem to know what to do with his body. When his ass is on the seat, and Ford is blocking us from being seen, I pull the knife out of Jared's stomach, charmed by the blood glistening on the blade. It pisses me off how he holds his stomach, his breathing starting to go erratic as he panics. But I want his attention again. I wave the knife in front of his face.

"You thought she was a good girl," I say. "She's my very favorite bad girl." I wink and then stab the knife into his leg. The moment his mouth opens to scream, I punch him in the face hard enough to knock him out cold, and he falls onto the seat.

"I'll see you there," Ford says, nodding to me and walking around to the driver's seat.

Ivy leans into the passenger window and asks Billie, "Why are you here?"

"We're in this together," Billie replies with a small smile. "You didn't think I'd let you fight this on your own, did you?"

"You're looking more like a passenger princess to me, Billie Taylor," I say, coming up behind Ivy.

Billie pokes out her tongue, and then they drive off. When we're alone, Ivy finally turns around to face me. "Where is he going?"

"Somewhere where I can play later. But right now, what are you doing looking mighty fine dressed like that?" I pull her in by the hips so she can feel my hard-on. She seems almost confused as she places her hands on my chest.

"He was the one who tried to drug me." I stare at her momentarily, realizing he's worse than I gave him credit for. Maybe I won't hand him over to Braxton after all.

"I'll make sure he pays for that." I lean down and kiss her lips. She responds willingly. I want to take all of her worries away, and my cock jumps at the thought of her stabbing him again. I wasn't expecting that from her. Then again, Ivy has always been a wild card.

"Shouldn't we go now?" she asks breathlessly.

"No fucking way. I'm taking you first before I get blood on my hands. And let me tell you right now, Ivy, that says a lot. I love fucking you more than I do torturing a man."

"That's kind of fucked-up. Maybe we should focus on—"

I tilt her jaw so she's forced to look at me, making her understand there is no option. "I need you now. I don't like you touching other men, although watching you work turns me on more than it should."

Her eyebrows dip as she stares at my lips, and I know she's as hypnotized as I am. We always have been, it's why we naturally gravitate toward one another.

"Are you upset because I was on a fake date?" she asks as her lips brush against mine. I groan. Her scent and feather-light touch are enough to make me want to come, and that's a serious problem. I'll never have enough of this woman.

"Nope. Because I knew no matter what, it was my bed you'd end up in. So let's go home. Work can wait for another hour."

She chuckles. "You think you'll last that long unassisted?"

I grab her ass and squeeze hard as punishment. "You're never going to let me live that down, are you?"

She grins as she pulls me into her with a defiant "Nope." But I know as she kisses me. I can feel the shift in her body, the tension receding as I pull her into me and remind her through touch that, no matter what challenge she takes head-on, I'll always be there to back her up.

This is my place.

By her side.

It's never been more abundantly clear.

CHAPTER 39

Ivy

One thing about Hawke is he's very self-assured. He always knows what he wants and doesn't let anything get in his way. And if something does, it's just a roadblock he barrels through. Every time I'm with him, I know I'm wanted by him. And I've come to depend on his unwavering confidence. When I stabbed Jared, I was nervous, but the moment Hawke was standing behind me, I knew I could take on anything.

I'm not a killer, but someone like Jared definitely deserves a knife to the stomach for what he did to Makayla. I know what the guys will do to him will be much worse, but I had to do it for her. I'm now just as involved with this as she was, if not more.

Hawke kisses me all the way to his bedroom, carrying me up the stairs. My weight is never an obstacle for him.

He groans as I pepper him with desire. He walks straight into the bathroom and turns the shower on, most likely understanding that having blood on my hands and dress is not common for me.

He's so in tune with my needs, and it terrifies me as I further lean into depending on it. He places me on the counter, kicking out of his shoes and removing his clothes. I bite my bottom lip as I watch him, my pussy pounding. I don't think I'll ever have enough of this man.

"I'm going to wash every part of you he put his hands on," he promises with a growl, and his eyes turn to that stark black shade I love so much. When he steps between my legs, I place my hand on his chest.

"Do you get jealous when I'm with other men, Hawke?" I want him, but this is important. I need to know how he truly views me because it's become too difficult for me to compartmentalize him in the "just sex" category. As much as I've pushed it away, I need to know where we stand. Tonight, I need to know.

"I don't like men touching what's mine. So, yes, it turns me on when you stab them."

I try not to laugh at his misinterpretation, and I remember Billie giving advising me that I need to speak directly with Hawke. But does he even understand what he's saying when he says, "what's mine"?

"Maybe we should be a thing," I suggest, feeling all the air rush out of my lungs as I say it. I've never once worried about a guy rejecting me, but part of me wonders if I misunderstood all this. Maybe I really am just someone to fill his time with until the next person comes along.

"What do you mean? I thought we already were," he says, confused. A weird tension runs between us, and we pause, his very hard cock standing at attention between us.

"As in, we don't see any other people," I clarify, just to make sure we're on the same page because you never know with Hawke.

"Obviously. You were just on a date, weren't you? And I stabbed him. See, we're a thing." He smiles, and it's so big that it makes my heart beat faster. Why does he make my heart do that?

No man has ever done that.

"So, are we a thing?" I repeat with a stupid smile on my face.

"Of course, we're a fucking thing!" he crows just before he crushes his lips to mine, holding my face with one hand, his other sliding up my leg and pushing my dress up. I help him, raising it over my head, and let him grab me by the waist as he forces me straight onto his cock. It takes my breath as I adjust to his size, and he walks us over to the shower. I love how he carries me, how he pins me against the tile wall and pumps into me, kissing me and branding me as water washes away our sins of the day.

I whimper as he destroys me from the inside, always pushing me to the threshold of my limits with the size of his cock. But it's not just that. It's Hawke and all he embodies, and despite the circumstances, I feel like we're finally coming to an understanding that goes beyond sex.

I want Hawke. I dig my nails into his shoulder blades, feeling them shift beneath my hands as he pumps into me, water raining over us as blood washes down his back from my hands. It's a fucking mess, and my head feels all over the place as I try to work through everything that's happened today. But right now, I'm with Hawke, and he's always had this ability to pull me out of my fixations and focus only on him.

And so I fall into a steady rhythm, matching his thrusts and kisses as he fills me with confidence for whatever we have to tackle next. Because the storm isn't yet over, but I can depend on him to ground me.

CHAPTER 40

Hawke

"I'm a thing," I announce to Ford, Eli, and Dutton. Dutton shakes his head as if he thinks I'm crazy, which I kind of am, but I don't take judgment from them seriously since they're just as unhinged.

"Okay, is that supposed to mean something?" Eli asks as we enter one of his many warehouses. When we walk in, Jared is tied to a chair. I was in such a good mood, and seeing him there puts an even bigger perk in my step.

"I was wondering what took you so long," Dutton says under his breath. I was only an hour late, but there was no fucking way I was leaving Ivy by herself until I claimed her as mine all over again. I left her at my house, running her a hot bath before promising I'd be back. I swear to God, if she runs out on me, I'll be banging down her apartment door.

Jared begins to struggle against his restraints. The wound to his stomach has been somewhat bandaged, but he's sweating and looking an interesting shade of green.

"You know, like you and Jewel. We're a thing," I tell him proudly.

Ford starts laughing, and I smile big at Eli, who takes a moment to realize what I'm saying. "Is Ivy aware of this?"

"I'm also guessing it's *with* Ivy?" Ford says.

"Of course it is," I tell him. "Who else would it be?"

"Just wanted to check. You never really know with you," my brother replies.

"Yep, a thing." I nod in acknowledgment. Did I ever think Ivy would ask me to be a thing? No, but I had high fucking hopes, and now I'm not letting her go anywhere. "Yeah, we talk, you know, not just fuck. Although that's one of my favorite things to do with her, and–"

Dutton cuts me off. "Okay, so you're exclusive with Ivy; that's what you're saying," Dutton clarifies as if I wasn't making any sense. "I have somewhere to be, so if we can torture this fucker now, that'd be great."

"Way to rain on my parade." I sulk as I crack my knuckles and loom over the little man about to shit himself in the chair. "Listen here, you piece of shit. You're lucky. I'm in a very good mood at the moment. Make it easy for me. Give me the name of your employer, and instead of killing you, I'll beat you into a vegetable that will kindly be handed over to the police, with whom you might live another day. Behind bars."

He spits at my shoes, and my smile grows. "Excellent." I punch him in the face, and he falls over, skidding a little along the cement floor. He gasps in pain as I pull him back up and repeat the process. Hit after hit after hit. I'm not even using my gloves this time because I want to feel his blood running between my fingers.

He tried to hurt Ivy. Tried to drug her. As if I'd ever let some asshole like this live. I don't care what agreement Ivy made with Braxton. And I'm pretty sure Eli doesn't either. Sure, Ivy might be upset, but we don't need to hand him over. The moment we're given a name, that's all we need.

"Hawke," Eli says my name, and it's the only thing I need to hear to clip my raging thoughts and keep me from hitting Jared again. I sit him upright in the chair. He's missing a few teeth, and bruises begin to swell on his face.

He's gasping for breath.

"A name?" Eli repeats, adjusting his suit. "Or I hand you over to my cousin here, who enjoys writing messages into the chests of men like you."

Dutton smiles, and it's fucking terrifying when his mask slips as he comfortably flips a knife through the air. And I'm not in a particular mood to share.

"Waylon Striker," the man is quick to say.

"From the Boston Delinquents?" I skeptically ask as I turn to Eli.

Eli shakes his head. "That doesn't make any sense. We've reached a mutually beneficial agreement with them in the last year. I know Waylon; he's above petty shit like this and doesn't stand for hurting women."

"I don't ask questions," Jared gasps. "I was just told to start funneling it here. I'm not even a main guy. I'm nobody." He begins to cry. "I didn't want any of this. I didn't want to kill Makayla, but I had to, or they'd come after me. You understand, don't you?" The grimy fucker has the audacity to look into my eyes, begging for his life.

The door opens, and guns are pulled and aimed at the intruder. Braxton puts his hands up in the air.

"Boys," he says, looking directly at Eli, who makes no move to lower his gun.

"What's the meaning of this?" Eli asks. "I don't recall us handing you our location."

Braxton looks at Jared and whistles, impressed by his bloodied face. "No, you guys didn't. But Ivy did."

Eli looks at me unimpressed, and I shrug. "I didn't tell her we'd be here. But she is pretty good at tracking." Then I smile wide and add, "Oh, Braxton, Ivy, and I are a thing."

Eli rolls his eyes and pinches the bridge of his nose as he pockets his gun. Everyone follows his lead.

"Will you stop calling your situation a 'thing'? She's

your woman, girlfriend, many other terms," Ford suggests with a raised eyebrow.

"But I like 'thing,'" I reply, and Ford swears under his breath.

"You don't really care if you get to play hero with this, so why are you doing it?" Eli asks. "This asswipe won't last a week in prison."

Braxton smiles. "True. But you'd be surprised how much a politician is willing to pay for his only daughter's murderer."

Dutton's eyebrows perk. "You wouldn't have known any of that without the information Ivy provided."

Braxton casually shrugs. "I'm an opportunist when money is involved, and besides, I'm honoring the bargain I made with *her*. She wanted him to be put on the media, most likely as some way of offering their families peace."

"In other words, Hope is busting your balls to do as her friend says." I laugh at him. Fuck me, we're all pussy whipped.

"I'm somewhat impressed," Dutton says to Braxton as he stands to take his leave. "We're done here. He's given us all we need to know."

"Wait. So what now?" I ask. "You can't seriously believe Striker is behind this?" Sure, he's the president of a motorcycle club and does some shifty shit, but I like Waylon, and we haven't had any issues working with him this past year.

"We go ask Striker some questions," Eli growls,

clearly irritated by the only answers we were able to get. "At least we've found a thread to this recent problem. We'll see him tomorrow. I want this sorted."

"And if he's involved?" Ford asks, stuffing his hands into the pockets of his black jeans.

Eli's jaw tics, but he doesn't hesitate as he says, "Then we'll make the problem go away."

I'm not paid to use my brains like the others, but I have a gut feeling that Waylon has nothing to do with this. And I think Eli has the same feeling which is most likely why he's coming to address this head on instead of simply sending us instead.

"So, can I take him now?" Braxton asks, interrupting us. "Maybe pump him up with some drugs so I can say I found him overdosed?"

I turn to Eli, who nods his head. I walk over to one of the containers we have and find an old needle.

"Boss?" I say, holding it up.

Eli is watching Braxton. "It could kill him," he points out.

Braxton shrugs. "I don't think any of us care about that, do we? We're just making sure our women are all okay and feeling in charge."

"Seems like my wife is the only obedient one," Eli grits, and I throw my head back and laugh.

"I'd love to see you say that in front of Jewel." But when I see his lethal expression, I'm quick to clear my throat and apologize as I line the needle up with a vein in Jared's arm.

At the end of the day, he's just a pawn in a game.

He weakly tries to fight me, but I pin his arm easily to the chair before I stick the needle in. His eyes go wide as I inject him with the contents.

Too fucking bad.

This is far kinder than I've been with any asshole I've wanted to torture.

His mistake was coming for my woman.

Ivy

"Weren't going to stop, huh?" I growl at him as he sheepishly walks past me in the bedroom. I'm not that mad because I know Hawke well enough to know he had no intention of letting Jared make it out of whatever dungeon they were torturing him in, which is exactly why I put a tracker on his favorite boots a week ago. I can also track his phone, but this made it easier. The moment he stopped at the location, I sent it to Braxton and Hope.

He clears his throat. "I was just excited by the fact that we're a thing," he says, and I roll my eyes as he goes into the bathroom to shower off the blood he's covered in.

I'm not entirely mad at him. If anything, it makes me feel safe knowing he'd go to such lengths to protect me. But I want Jared's face to be on the news. I want Makayla's family to know it was him who killed her. Anything past that, I don't care, and I'm satisfied that he will be killed one way or another.

I'm under the blankets in Hawke's bed, wearing one of his shirts, as I flick through the channels. He reappears, totally naked, with a smug expression on his face. But instead of joining me, he leaves the bedroom and heads downstairs. I stare after him, curious as to what he's up to. A few minutes later, he returns with several takeout containers.

"I take it you haven't eaten today," he says as if it's the most casual thing in the world.

"One cookie," I say, shifting to make more room for him on the bed. My stomach growls as a reminder. I was so focused on everything that was happening that eating was the last thing on my mind. How this man kills and tortures and still has an appetite afterward will always impress me. It's past midnight, but I suppose it's as good a time as ever to have a few bites.

A random movie is playing in the background, but I watch him as he happily spreads the food out in front of us. I try to hide the smile as I think about our earlier conversation. Who would have ever thought that Hawke and I would discuss being exclusive? It was easy—maybe too easy—but that has always been our relationship. Maybe I thought it could never be more because I wasn't prepared to face my feelings for him.

"What?" he asks with a smile as he snaps the chopsticks apart and offers them to me. He got noodles—one of my favorites.

It's strange to think of what a future with him might look like, and to what extent? Is it still a *now* thing? Maybe in a year's time, we'll get bored of each other? Or could it be... a forever type of thing?

I can't help but think about how good of a father he would be. It's a strange feeling, considering I've never looked at a man that way.

"It's nothing," I say, opening the box.

"Spit it out, or I'll tickle it out of you," he warns, and I roll my eyes. But when I look at him, I see he's dead serious, and I'm not risking shit.

"I was just thinking you'd be a good dad. That's all."

His eyebrows arch in surprise. I feel stupid after I say it. My God, he probably thinks I've gone gaga after we've become exclusive, and I'm jumping into some happily ever after fantasy. I'm an idiot. I should've just taken the punishment of tickles.

He's quiet as he tries to hold the chopsticks the right way. I try not to laugh as I push through the awkward tension and show him how to use them again, which makes him uncomfortable.

"I'm sorry. I didn't mean to make it weird. I just meant—"

"It was nice," he says sheepishly, looking down at his food and then up at me. I can see the vulnerability there. "It's nice to be taken seriously for once."

My mouth opens and then closes.

"I think you'd be a cool mom, for what it's worth. Do you want kids?" he asks, unable to meet my gaze, and it's so strange to see this side of him.

"Yeah. I'd love to have kids. I had a really good relationship with my parents, and I think it'd be cool to have tiny humans running around. What about you?"

I never expected to have a conversation like this with Hawke. At least not so soon. I've been so used to being labeled as the party girl that I can share his sentiment of no one ever taking me seriously. But I was never ready for the conversation of marriage and kids. I find it ironic that I'm talking to Hawke about it.

He seems to think it over carefully. "I think it'd be really cool having kids. I love them, but we're never around them. But I didn't think it was something possible for me, you know? Considering what I do for work and all."

"Are you ashamed of what you do?" I ask carefully. I thought Hawke loved working for Eli, and his parents run the underworld auctions, so it's not like he's going to live a cookie-cutter type of life. That's just not Hawke.

"Fuck no. I love my job," he says with a cheesy grin. "But it's not exactly a mood setter with women. Not that I've ever found a woman I want to do that with." He looks at me and then quickly diverts his gaze, and I feel like I missed something important as he continues. "But

I've done things, awful things that I don't think make me a good person."

My eyebrows furrow in confusion as I place my untouched box of noodles down and place my hand on his knee. His cock twitches, and I try to remain serious because his body is far too responsive, but it's the hurt in his eyes that concerns me.

"You're a good person, Hawke." He tries to smile, but it's so weak it breaks my heart. "I'm a vault, remember? You can tell me anything."

His dark-brown eyes snap back to me again, and he seems to struggle with his words. It's the first time I've seen him shrouded in shame, and I want to shake it right off him because this is not the Hawke I know. "Talk to me. *Please*," I say, cupping his cheek.

He's staring through me now, into my soul, as if searching for something. For what, I'm not entirely sure.

"I killed a woman," he confesses. My heart stops. Not because he killed a woman but because of the pain that's loaded in that statement. Hawke kills people all the time. I wait for him to continue so I can fully understand. "Ford and I always had a rule that we would never hurt women or children. I know I'm not all that good because I kill people, but that was our absolute rule, so we didn't feel like complete monsters. When Billie was kidnapped, and Ford went after her, I asked you to track them for me, but I never told you what happened afterward."

I swallow as I watch him break apart, his tough

persona crumbling, and I see a side of this man I immediately know I have to protect.

"When I got there, she was running toward her car. I pulled up and saw that she was holding one of Ford's crowbars. I just *knew* in my gut she did something to him. I knew he was close by. I knew they were in trouble. And when she pulled out the gun..." He looks down, ashamed, but I lift his chin and force him to look at me. I will not let him be ashamed of whatever this is any longer. "I had to make a choice. And I chose my brother. I'll always choose my brother. So I shot her between her eyes." His voice breaks, and I can see he's fighting tears. "I see her every night when I try to sleep. I replay what I could've changed, but every time..."

"You listen to me," I say, digging my nails into his skin to bring him back to the present. "You did what you had to in order to save your brother and my best friend, for which I am so grateful to you. You're not a monster, Hawke. You could never be a monster, not in my eyes. What you did was *heroic.* Think about the lives you saved instead of the one you took. That woman knew exactly what she was doing. If anything, you probably set her free from her own demons."

His eyes widen, and I see something shift in him. Instead of letting me see him tear up, he pulls me in for a hug, his warmth immediately spreading through my chest. I pat the back of his head, stroking his dark, wet locks. I've learned many things about myself these last months, but I'm learning even more about Hawke. This great oaf, who has been hovering around in my life for almost a decade, has become such a beacon to my heart.

"How about instead of focusing on her and what you might've been able to do differently, you focus on me," I suggest. Hawke is a simple man in the way he expresses himself, the way he focuses, and the way he loves. "You can focus on protecting me now instead."

His hold on me tightens, and I feel when he releases his breath as I continue stroking the back of his head.

"It would be my honor, Ivy Walker, to protect you," he says earnestly. Before the situation with Jared, I never considered myself someone who needed protection. Although I can still stand on my own, it's nice to know I have someone like Hawke covering my back in instances that I might not be able to myself. It's nice to know that no matter what might happen between us in the future, I can also give him this peace. I can give him something else to focus on besides this thing that's clearly been eating him alive since the incident happened. I knew he'd been acting differently; we'd all noticed. And I wonder if this was part of the conversation Billie had overheard. I truly hope Hawke can heal from this because no matter what he does for a living, even if he gets sickening plea-sure from it, I can never see him as a bad person.

"Told you it wasn't a mood setter," he grumbles as he pulls back, pressing a kiss to my cheek. He then looks down at his noodles and pulls a face, and I can tell it's because of the vegetable in there he doesn't like.

"Eat your greens," I reprimand as I try to cover my laugh. "And you set plenty of moods."

"Yeah, well, none that will ever make a woman think, *Wow, he's the one!*" He rolls his eyes, and I jerk back, shocked.

"Hawke, did you just say *the one*?"

His eyebrows furrow. "Yeah. Don't you believe in that shit?"

I bite my bottom lip, always surprised by this brute of a man who sometimes has the heart of a sixteen-year-old girl who needs to be protected from the world.

"Do you want to watch a rom-com tonight?"

"Fuck no," he scoffs.

"Hawke, have you ever watched a rom-com?"

"No... isn't it girly shit?" he asks, and I try not to laugh at him. I don't want to dissuade him from watching my choice of movie.

I roll my eyes as I pick up the remote. It's no surprise he's never seen a rom-com, especially since I couldn't imagine Anya ever watching them.

"Let's start with a classic," I suggest as I press play on *Pretty Woman.*

I wake up with a sharp breath. It's dark, and Hawke is still asleep. Jared's eyes flash before me, and I can't seem to get my heart rate back down.

He did it. He killed her.

I already knew he had, but listening to his confession of the reasons behind it made it so much worse.

All because he wanted someone he couldn't have.

Why couldn't he just be normal and break it off with her? Why did he drag her into this abyss? She believed in him right until the very end. She was even willing, as drugged out as she was, to accept the fact that he killed one of her friends right in front of her.

It's all so fucked.

"Your thoughts are so loud." Strong arms wrap around me and pull me back before he starts kissing my shoulder. "Let me ease them." I fell asleep before we did anything; listening to him laugh was relaxing. And now I can feel how hard he is. I pull his hand from around my waist and down to the top of my thighs. I slide his hand up underneath the shirt I'm wearing and let him take control. I love it when he takes control. So many men I'd been with did better when I controlled them, but not Hawke. Though, he'll let me when I demand it.

He knows exactly how to please a woman, and I fucking love it. His hand slips between my legs, and I know he can feel how wet I am as he starts massaging my clit. "You like that, don't you?" he whispers in my ear as his lips find my earlobe, and he takes it in his mouth. He pushes his cock harder against my ass, and I spread my legs a little wider, giving him more access.

At this point, I'm pretty certain I'll give him everything he demands of me because I'm weak to not only the pleasure he can give me but all the fractured pieces of himself he's slowly revealing to me as well. Waking up in his arms, knowing that he'll protect me no matter what.

I moan and wriggle against him as he rubs his cock against my pussy, trying to force myself down on him.

Hawke is the greatest distraction for my overactive thoughts. But he's also the best thing that could've happened to me. My body has always understood that. It's just taken my heart longer to catch up.

CHAPTER 42

Hawke

I'm woken by the sound of someone honking outside my house. When I reach for Ivy, she isn't there. When I open my eyes, I see her standing across the room, still wearing my shirt that hangs past her knees, holding a travel cup.

I rub my hand through my hair. It's dark in the room, but that's because I have blackout curtains. I pick up my phone, and my jaw drops when I notice the time. "Why is it so late?" I say, hopping out of bed and grabbing my jeans and the first shirt I can find.

The honking continues, and I curse, knowing it's Ford and Eli. Fuck, I'm late.

"You clearly needed sleep, so I turned your alarm off," Ivy replies.

I lean back into my walk-in closet to grab my boots. "Eli's going to fucking kill me."

She pops a hand on her hip. "If Eli has a problem with it, you tell him to take it up with me. You tell him I said that," she says defiantly. I growl, agitated that my cock jumps at her sassy mouth. I loom over her, squeezing her cheeks.

"You're so lucky I love punishing this smart little mouth of yours."

"I think you're the lucky one here," she bites back before I crush my lips to hers. Because for all I know, it might be the last time I ever see her. Eli is not a patient man. I go to run out the door but come to a halt as she calls me back and hands me the travel cup.

"It's a protein shake I made for you. Good luck today."

Fuck me. I could get used to this. I kiss her again before running out the door, still trying to do up my jeans.

"You're late," Eli growls from the back seat as I practically throw myself into Ford's passenger seat.

"Sorry, boss," I say, licking my lips and glancing around awkwardly, unsure where to put the travel cup. He arches an eyebrow, and I avert my gaze out the window as I try to get my bearings. I yawn, patting down my shirt and pants, making sure I'm wearing both.

It's a fucking miracle. I slept peacefully all night. Aside from when Ivy woke up and, I eased her back to sleep the most natural way I know how—in every position I can possibly bend her into.

I didn't plan to open up to her about murdering that woman; a small part of me expected to be judged for it. To be shamed. To be hated. I didn't realize Ivy's opinion was the one I cared for the most. But she held me, consoled me. Told me I was heroic.

I don't know how or why hearing that shifted a weight in me, but it's as if I've been waiting to hear her say that to set me free. To give me something or someone to look forward to when I feel lost.

We arrive at the private landing strip and prepare ourselves for the hour flight to Boston. The atmosphere in the car is tense, as we're all most likely thinking the same thing. We don't want Waylon to be a part of this underhanded drug distribution in our area. But if he is... He'll meet the same fate as anyone else who's tried to cross Eli Monti.

But to lighten the mood on the plane, I ask them, "Have you guys watched *Pretty Woman*?" And then I begin to explain to them why they should watch it.

CHAPTER 43

Hawke

"Shut the fuck up about *Pretty Woman*, or I'll shoot you myself," Eli growls, irritated, as we park outside a bar on the outskirts of Boston.

Outside, two men are standing near the entrance, and a long row of motorcycles lines the curb. I almost drool at the sight of them. Dutton is the only one who has a bike himself. I was strictly warned off owning one because, well, as my mother says, I'm reckless. So when she found out I'd bought one when I was twenty, she set it on fire. I didn't bother buying another one because nothing stays secret from her.

The two men size us up as we stride toward them. Ford pockets the keys, and I'm so up Eli's ass that if anything were to happen, I can push him out of the way.

"Boys," Eli says, and I can tell the way he's addressed them has already pissed them off. Under normal circumstances, it would make me very excited and have me grabbing for my gloves that are half hanging out of my back pocket. But we don't want to go to war with Waylon Striker's motorcycle gang. "We're here to see Waylon."

"Pretty boys from New York finally make an appearance, eh?" one of them says.

"Thank you for noticing our good looks," I can't help but reply, and their attention snaps to me.

"Oh fuck off, Clint. Let them in," a woman with long brunette hair says as she appears from around the side of the bar. She has the same brown eyes as Waylon and is almost as intimidating as the club president.

"I'm Hayley, Waylon's sister." She introduces herself to Eli, holding out her hand. He takes it.

I vaguely remember Dutton mentioning that Waylon had two sisters. And apparently, Hayley is as crazy as her brother and rules with a fair but iron fist. The youngest sister, Lola, however, is known to be more eccentric in her methods.

Hayley adjusts her leather jacket, pushing back her hair as she looks me up and down with a smirk. Eli glances at me with a strict don't-you-fucking-go-there expression. Which he's done in the past, but I'm a kept man now. I'm not even tempted in the slightest when I have the most beautiful woman waiting for me at home.

She leads us inside. My understanding is that this is one of many bars the Boston Delinquents own, but Waylon's most likely brought us to this one—basically in the middle of nowhere—just in case this meeting goes bad. Especially considering he has quite a delicious round-up of rough-looking men and women in here.

Two men are playing pool toward the back of the room, one breaking the balls as we walk in. Women stand from their men's laps, and some of them even go into another room.

But the person who grabs our attention is the man himself, sitting at a table on his own like a king overseeing his empire.

Waylon is young for being the club president, and from what I've heard, he's had to make examples of some men who weren't happy about following him after he killed their previous leader.

I don't give a shit; it's above my pay grade.

If the jackass weren't in leathers and wearing a stern expression, he'd probably break many women's hearts. Fuck, he probably does that anyway.

"That's it?" a woman asks from across the bar. We all turn in her direction. She has light brown eyes and pink hair rolled into two buns on top of her head. "You three think you can take all of us on?"

"No one is taking anyone on, Lola," Hayley says as she moves to stand by Waylon's side.

"Excuse my sister," Waylon says, glaring at Lola. "She doesn't seem to understand that this meeting is under friendly circumstances. Right, boys?"

I look around the room at the men who show the

guns at their waists and the chains dangling from their hands. Ford is doing the same, quickly measuring how many we'd have to take out. Eli looks at none of these things; he's probably already figured out his next three moves. He's here for answers.

"Good to see you're doing well," Eli says, and he and Waylon both smile like the devils they are. My blood hums with anticipation.

"We've recently had an influx of date rape drugs and the like in our area. It's not something we tend to circulate ourselves, let alone allow someone else to do so, specifically not under my management."

Waylon's eyebrows knit together. "We have a good working relationship, but if the issue isn't on my turf, I have no interest in dragging my boys into something that doesn't concern them."

Eli nods as if agreeing. He'd say the same thing if the situation were reversed. If anything, Waylon sounds slightly more diplomatic. "There was a murder in Springfield committed by one of the supplier's men. The murderer is only a pawn, but as we... dealt with him, it was your name he spoke as the supplier," Eli says.

The tension in the room shifts.

"You believe him?" Striker asks, his gaze turning deadly. His men straighten up, the closest one playing pool walking over with a cue stick, proud of the knife in his other hand. I try to push away the excitable chills running along my skin, reminding myself I'm not here to kill anyone today. *These are our friends.*

"If I did, do you think I would have so politely knocked on your door instead of busting it down?"

Striker smirks. "It's what I like about you, Eli. You get straight to the point. But I have no need to drag my men into it. Sure, let's say, theoretically, the distributor is in Springfield, but I won't act until it's on my turf. No offense, but this has nothing to do with our current business."

"What if I asked for a favor?" I speak up, and Eli frowns. Ford warily watches me. I don't often speak over Eli, but I have no intention of going around in circles here when I know that on the other side of this could be a direct answer or name. I need to bring down the assholes who put everything into place to drug Ivy that night. They're nothing but vermin that need to be exterminated.

I'm not above begging or pleading when it comes to protecting my woman.

Striker's eyebrow raises as he looks between me and Eli.

"A word, Hawke," Eli says, calling Ford and me both out for a moment.

"Want to tell me why you're throwing out favors for information now?" Eli asks, not at all impressed.

I swallow hard as Eli and my brother stare at me. And then I look at my feet, trying to figure out what to do.

Lying always feels icky for me. But when it's Ivy's secret, it's different. I can't stand to know that those fuckers might get away with this again and again.

"It's personal," I finally say.

"Be more specific," Eli growls, and I'm torn between giving my boss the answer he needs to hear and not betraying Ivy's trust.

"Ivy was drugged and targeted by Jared," Ford blurts. I whip my head in his direction, but he just looks straight ahead, not meeting my gaze. I want to throttle him for telling her secret, but I realize he's protecting me from breaking my word to Ivy. Billie most likely told him.

"He did what?" Eli barks, his silvery gaze snapping at me. "Why didn't you tell me this? She's one of our own."

"Not everyone wants their wounds on display," Ford says on my behalf. I want to punch him as much as I want to hug him. Eli looks at him then and seems to understand.

"Had I known about this earlier, it might've changed things." Eli sighs. "Jewel likes Ivy."

"Everyone likes Ivy," I say, pointing out the obvious and realizing I have to come back to the point. "Just please let me talk to Striker."

"I don't like you making deals with other devils," Eli carefully says, glancing back at the bar. "But if you think it's the most effective way to get answers, I'll give you five minutes. We don't mention this again."

"Agreed," Ford says, and a wave of relief passes

through me, knowing they mean to bury this information with them. I look at my brother with a silent nod of appreciation. Ford has always saved me from saying the wrong thing. This time, he saved me from holding my tongue.

When I walk back into the bar, Striker is waiting. He lights a cigarette and tells his men to stand down. His youngest sister watches me curiously. Perhaps a few months back, I would've made it my goal to fuck her before I leave, but I find myself at the mercy of someone I consider a colleague. And I'll continue throwing myself on my knees for my woman. If I can burn down the nest of fuckers who did this to her, I will.

"We're not asking for your help. You don't have to bring your men into the situation; we can handle it ourselves. I'm just asking for a name if you have it. For whatever reason, that pinprick asshole knew yours. Which means that his higher-ups are also aware of you. I just need a name. A starting point. *Please.*"

"Begging doesn't suit you, Hawke," Waylon says.

"Anything suits me if it protects the people I love," I reply quickly.

His fingers hover in front of his lips, the cigarette pinched between them. "This is personal for you?"

"Yes."

"Hmm." He considers me as his sister leans over and whispers something into his ear. He nods but says nothing. She looks over to the youngest sister, whose arms are crossed over her chest, and she stares from the corner like she's in detention or something.

"Give me access to your tracker to help me with something, and I'll see what I can find out," he states.

"Will Walker won't do me any favors."

"Then it looks like you're shit out of luck," Waylon says with a fake smile.

"You give me a name, and we'll take them out before they become a problem for you, and I'll give you access to a better tracker." I don't like the idea of bringing my girl into the deal without her permission, but I'm happy to pay whatever price she charges. Hell, I'll even buy her a new apartment or wardrobe as a reward on top of her price.

Waylon laughs. "You realize you've just downgraded your offer."

"Not at all. I'm showing you how quickly I need that name, and I don't want to banter much longer, knowing those assholes are out there. I'll give you my left fucking testicle as well. Whatever I need to finalize this shit so I can go back to my woman at a reasonable time tonight."

Hayley chuckles, and Waylon turns to her as if receiving a silent instruction. I wonder if the two work closely together. Maybe she's the same to Waylon that Ford and I are to Eli. It's hard to tell.

Waylon is smirking when he meets my gaze again. "It just so happens I have a left testicle myself and have no need for yours."

"Scared yours will feel inadequate?"

Waylon's smile grows wider. "How's the Viagra treating your left nut?"

My smile drops. "How the fuck did that shit get here?"

Waylon laughs as he stands and holds out his hand to me. I shake it as he says, "I might have a source, but let me verify that information and name before I give it to you. I'll be in touch. Being monogamous looks good on you."

"You should try it sometime," I say with a grin.

"You guys might be suckers, but that is not for me." I shake my head as I walk back through the doors, knowing I once thought the same thing. But when it happens—when *she* happens—there's not a thing in the world that will stop it.

But I'm sure he'll learn that in his own way.

"She's a very lucky lady," the youngest sister purrs from her corner as I walk out. "Let me know if it doesn't work out." She winks.

"You'll be waiting a long time, sweetheart. She's literally the best," I reply as I take my leave.

CHAPTER 44

Ivy

I saw it on the news that afternoon. Jared had been taken into custody and publicly announced as a murderer. Billie and I watch in a bar, and a sense of satisfaction and justice rushes through me. I hope it gives Makayla's family a bit of peace. I still haven't come to terms with it all, but at least I've done this much.

Now, we wait patiently for Ford and Hawke to return from Boston. He told me last night that he shouldn't share anything with me, but because it might be tied to what happened to me, he'll tell me. I don't like the idea of knowing there's been such a massive push of this drug reaching the streets I live on, but it's not surprising, either.

I know Hawke sees himself as a killer, but to me, trying to hunt down a drug ring sounds like something a hero would do. I'll never get it twisted; I know he's not a hero, but sometimes it takes the bad to deal with a greater evil. He made it very clear that ordinarily they wouldn't deal with things like this outside the city, and they only get involved if it directly impacts Eli's power.

The news switches to another breaking story, and I take a sip of my water as I spot Hawke strutting in, Ford closely behind him. He walks straight up to me, throwing his arms around my shoulders, and pulls me in to press a kiss at the top of my head.

Ford rolls his eyes as he scoots in beside Billie and kisses her on the lips.

"So, you two are officially a thing now?" Billie asks, raising her eyebrows.

"Yes! See, you get it," Hawke says as he smacks Ford on the shoulder.

"Do not get him started on the 'thing' part again, please," Ford grumbles, looking at the menu, his gaze immediately falling to the desserts. Billie smirks as she casually pulls out a lollipop and passes it to him.

"What are you guys talking about?" I ask, confused. From the way they walked in, I'm assuming it went well today, but I'm not sure if I'm allowed to talk about these things in front of Ford.

"We're a thing, and it seems some people have issues with that," Hawke explains, and Ford shakes his head.

"No one has an issue with you two being together. If

anything, it's not even surprising. It's more you using the word 'thing' to describe it. Just stop saying it," Ford tries to tell him.

"We could be a thing, but we're brothers, and I'm sure it's illegal in many states," Hawke jokes.

"You're disgusting and have screws loose, you know that, right?" Ford quips back. I tap Hawke's arm around my shoulder, and before I can say anything, he picks me up and takes my seat before he places me on his lap.

"Better." He sighs. I should've expected this from him. The moment I give him an inch, he'll run a mile with it. But I'm certainly not someone against PDA. In fact, I like it.

I've never really been in a relationship, so I'm not sure exactly what emotions to feel, and I'm not used to people staring at me with someone who is so publicly affectionate. Hawke really doesn't care who sees what he does.

I feel his lips just below my ear as he kisses me and, at the same time, holds a conversation with Ford about a new tattoo idea. He only has a few open spaces to insert a tattoo, so I'm curious where he'll choose, but I don't comment because it's his body, and he can do whatever he wants with it. Whatever he's been doing with it so far has been fucking magnificent.

From the first moment I kissed him to now, it's like it's come full circle. We shared our first kiss as teens. I don't know if he remembers, but I do because it was my first. I dared him to do it, and he smacked it right on me when I was fifteen. It wasn't until I was twenty-one that we slept together for the first time. And that situation was a little dare mixed with curiosity.

Maybe that's one of the reasons I kept going on dates and sleeping with strangers. I was missing something I knew was already there with Hawke, but I didn't understand it. Not that he gave me any indication that he wanted something more than what we had. Yes, he's always been playful, but he's playful with everyone, especially women. And I can't say that his affection for other women turned me off because I was much the same with him. I thought I'd feel insecure because of that, but I'm not. If anything, Hawke makes me feel confident in where we stand together, and although our being together is new, I know I can ask him anything. And if we get into an argument? Well, I'll just take my top off, knowing the moment I do, I'll win.

I smirk at the thought, but then I tune back into the conversation as everyone finishes their meal. Hawke ordered burgers and fries and polished them off within two minutes.

Billie and Ford get ready to leave, but before they take off, Billie leans in and kisses my cheek as she whispers, "I like this for you."

Hawke laughs, and I know he heard her. Once

they're gone, I go to stand and take the seat she vacated, but he pulls me back between his legs and holds me there.

"I want to talk about us being a thing. I need some ground rules." It feels silly having this conversation now, but last night didn't seem like the right time since what we'd talked about was so much deeper.

"Oh God, you want to talk. Can't we just go to one of the bathrooms and fuck instead?" When I look back at him, he waggles his brows.

"No." I push his hands away, and he lets me sit on the stool next to his. I cross my legs, and he watches the movement with a smirk. I'm down for heading to the bathroom with him. Make no mistake about that, but first I want to talk to him about the things swirling around in my mind.

"What do you want to know? Do I want you?" He looks down at his jeans. "That answer will always be yes," he says with pride. "Will I share you? That answer is no." He smirks at me as if he answered all my questions.

"What about you seeing other people?" I ask.

"That's a no. Why would I need to when I have you?"

"What if I'm away? I like to travel a lot," I remind him.

He leans in with a mischievous smile.

"Well, you can send me a naughty photo like the ones I took on your phone, and I can play with myself to them," he suggests, and I notice I'm biting my bottom lip. Fuck, it's so unfair how this man knows how to speak to my most primal needs.

"What if you get bored being in a relationship?" I ask, and he shakes his head in disbelief.

"Why are you even thinking that? You are more than enough for me. You're everything I compare anyone to. You're literally on my fucking brain twenty-four-seven. I'm never going to tire of you, lover."

He lifts his big hands and puts them on either side of my face as he leans in so our lips are almost touching. Then he whispers, "And I sure as fuck know I'm not going to let you get bored of me."

"Yes, you seem to be awfully cocky about the fact." I try not to laugh because Hawke has this effect on me. He makes everything light again, bringing me back to the right now instead of what our future might look like. And maybe it's only because I'm worried we've never been in a relationship. I don't know what kind of exit strategy I might have, but even when I think about it, I don't think I'll ever need one with Hawke. And maybe that's what terrifies me the most. I didn't expect him to agree so easily to be exclusive. And I don't know why I thought that at all since it seems so obvious now.

"I guess time will tell." He winks, but I can tell he's uncomfortable with something. The thing with Hawke is he's easy to read. He wears his heart on his sleeve, perhaps more than I ever gave him credit for.

"What's wrong?" I ask.

"I'm scared you'll be mad, and I don't want to do anything to make you mad," he says honestly. Great, that's never a good start.

"Our meeting today was intense." He swallows as he reaches for my hand as if I might run away at what he's going to tell me next. "It makes me feel icky not telling you this, so I'm going to say it and hope you don't hate me for it."

"Okay. Spit it out, Hawke." A sinking feeling starts in my stomach.

"Eli and Ford know about what happened that night. So does Braxton." His dark-brown eyes snap to mine, and I can clearly see the dread in his expression. "The night that you were drugged, I called Braxton over to watch you while I dealt with that Lester asshole."

I'm so confused. "Why Braxton?" I know I should be more concerned about him telling my secret, but surprisingly it doesn't hurt as much as I thought it would. Maybe it's because I already concluded the worst of him weeks ago when I overheard him discussing it with Eli. But Braxton? Why him, of all people? The two of them don't even get along.

He licks his lips. "I didn't want to call Ford because I knew he would've told Billie, and you asked me not to tell anyone, but I couldn't let hours go by knowing that fucker who tried to hurt you was still alive." My heart swells. "So I asked Braxton to watch you and help me clear some things up around that night for a favor. To get the name of the supplier today, I also offered Waylon Striker a favor, and I might need your help in the future when he calls it in."

"Me?"

"He needed someone who can hack and track, and well, you know your father hates me and won't help me. And I might be biased, but I think you're better than him anyway."

A small smile blooms on my lips, and his eyes widen in shock. "You don't hate me?"

I place my hand on his jaw, stroking the shadow of his scruff. I probably should be mad, but I feel so much of that is wasted on Hawke. He has a good heart. And I know Hawke is doing this to protect me. He would never have told them my secret in a casual conversation, so if he felt it was necessary to share it, I have to trust his reasoning.

"I'm not mad," I tell him, thinking about the world of difference from weeks ago and how I reacted when I overheard him speaking with Eli. Or maybe it's because I've had the time to process it myself, open up to Billie, and to be free of its shameful weight. And Hawke has told me secrets that I feel far more scarring. Not that I intend to tell anyone those, but we're in a completely different place now. "Thank you for doing all of this. I know you have to because of your work, but thank you for including me in this."

He grabs my hand. "I'm doing this for you, lover. No

one gets to touch you. They're nothing but rats that I'll get rid of. Even if it wasn't their hand directly that touched you, I'll follow this to the end so it never troubles you again."

I smile. "You'll chase away all of my monsters, huh?" I purr, quite enticed by Hawke's protective nature. It's fucking hot. *He's* hot.

"Your fight is my fight. Always."

My heart skips a beat at that declaration. I don't even know if Hawke understands what those words and the intentions behind them mean to me. I knew he was smooth, but my God. This man knows how to put a woman at ease. He waggles his brows. "Now, how about a really quick visit to the bathroom?"

I throw my head back and laugh, and as quickly as he puts me at ease, he puts me on my back to fuck me.

"Really quick?" I ask as he stands. His hand slides from my face and down my arm until he grips my hand. He pulls me off the stool and then leads me straight back to where the bathrooms are, shutting us inside one. He locks the door behind us and then immediately pulls his stiff cock out. He reaches for me, sliding his hand up my dress and straight into my panties. He pulls his hand back out, licks his fingers, then goes back again. I keep eye contact with him the whole time. He leans in and bites my lip before he drags his teeth down my neck. I tilt my head, giving him better access.

"Fuck me," I whisper. I want him inside me, not

playing with me. He nods his head and removes his fingers from between my legs. Then he lifts me effortlessly and then lowers me straight onto his cock. A gasp leaves me, and I wonder if I will ever get sick of him, sick of the way he makes me feel or the way he touches me. I doubt it. I think he will be my favorite chapter yet.

CHAPTER 45

Ivy

When you get a message from the one and only Anya Ivanov inviting you to her husband's restaurant, you can't turn it down. So I do what any good woman would do—I put on my best dress. It's gray with rhinestones all over it, and the bottom hem sits just above my knees. One thing I admire about Anya is her style. She's as fashionable as they come, and she puts her money where her mouth is with all the jewels she wears.

So even if I don't know what type of function it is, I know to wear my best since that woman always dresses like she's walking off a runway. Strangely, I find some nerves skittering in my lower stomach. I wonder if they know about me and Hawke yet. Gossip circulates quickly amongst our families, and I certainly know that Hawke hasn't been able to keep his mouth shut. So perhaps displaying her son like this isn't the best for first impressions, but also, a bet is a bet.

I lead Hawke through the room by a leash attached to a collar fastened around his throat. He proudly walks as if there isn't anything peculiar to see.

"You didn't even get me off, so I don't know why I still have to wear this," he grumbles under his breath as everyone stares at us. However, I quite enjoy the dynamic play in front of our family and friends.

"I was still an active participant. It's not my fault you thought taking *three* Viagra pills was smart," I chastise.

The restaurant is closed to the public for tonight's party. I don't recognize everyone here, but many of our family and friends are in attendance.

The moment Anya spots us, she pauses her conversation, glaring at her son, and makes her way over to us. Suddenly, I'm not so sure about walking him around with a collar and leash.

I'm surprised when she places a kiss on either side of my cheek and then stares at Hawke. "What bet did you lose?" she asks him in her Russian accent. A wave of relief washes over me. Of course, she knows her son well enough.

He mumbles something, and all either of us can catch is the word "Viagra."

She shakes her head as she looks me up and down approvingly. "I'm glad you came. I've recently heard you two are a *thing*."

I glance at Hawke, who's wearing a shit-eating grin. His arm wraps around my waist, and he pulls me in close, proud as shit. Anya doesn't miss a thing, and I can never read what she's thinking. But finally, she says. "Keep him in check. He often likes to be reckless."

"You make it sound like she's not as reckless as me," Hawke scoffs, and I elbow him in the ribs.

The corner of Anya's lips curve as she notices a waitress walk by and she's clearly furious about something the girl is doing wrong. "Enjoy your evening. Congratulate your father on his new restaurant opening."

I always find it ironic that although these powerful men and women run deadly underground businesses, they also use legitimate businesses to mask their true fortune. Her husband, River Bently, owns most of the high-end restaurants in Manhattan.

I spot Billie, who's sitting down, waving at me. She's wearing a beautiful honey-colored dress, and Ford can't peel his gaze from her as he sits beside her.

We wind our way through the crowd to get to their table, and she pulls out the chair next to her, indicating I take it. Ford is staring at his brother, but it's Billie who speaks on both of their behalf.

"I don't even think I want to ask what the collar and leash are about." She takes my hand and squeezes it. "I'll settle for, 'I'm glad you came.'"

"That's what she said," Hawke jokes, and I nudge him in the ribs again. He chuckles and then notices Eli and Jewel standing across the room. "Be right back," he says and goes into business mode, which is rather comical when he's wearing a collar and leash. But I'll be fucked if I'm removing them anytime soon. I quite like everyone knowing whose bitch he is.

I'm searching the table for a glass of water when someone suddenly takes the seat on the other side of me. "Ivy Walker," River says. Wow, I'm really getting the full treatment tonight. When he greets the other two, Billie smiles, and Ford watches him with amusement.

"Congratulations on the opening of your restaurant," I say to him.

"Thank you. I hear there's plenty of things to celebrate as of late," he replies. "I hope it's not too presumptuous to say, but welcome to the family. You too, Billie." He makes a point to include her.

Goose bumps rise all over my skin because it feels strange how quickly everything is moving. It feels right, but it also feels like we're all in from the start, and there's no way to backpedal. Not that I want to backpedal, but it's like there's no safety net. And I still haven't told my parents. I know they're back in town, and I should speak with them soon, but I've been so preoccupied with everything else that updating my relationship status hasn't seemed like a priority. It has to Hawke, though. I look over at him as Eli frowns at something he says when it makes Jewel laugh. She's wearing a black dress with a long slit that ends at her upper thigh. She's hot as fuck, and the way Eli possessively holds her, he lets everyone know she's off-limits, as if the ring that can be spotted across the room isn't indication enough.

"You don't want a glass of wine?" River asks, furrowing his brows when he realizes I'm the only one without a drink.

"No, thank you. Water is fine," I tell him with a polite smile. The problem is that people get suspicious when you go from a party girl who likes to celebrate getting a pedicure with a mimosa to someone who just drinks water. But I don't give a fuck what people think.

River nods as he says, "My wife doesn't drink either; she has never drunk alcohol from the day I met her." He then looks at Ford, who has a drink in front of him. It's known within our inner circle that Ford doesn't drink and only uses the glass as a prop. I've never asked about the reason behind it. But it makes me feel better that River tries to normalize not drinking. I look at him appreciatively. If he didn't have a psycho wife, and I wasn't besotted with his son, I'd say River Bently is a catch.

That's when someone reaches between River and me with a glass of water, cutting off how closely we're sitting beside one another. I'd recognize those inked fingers anywhere because they've been marking my body for months now.

"Thank you," I say to Hawke, who puts his hand on my shoulder possessively and looks at his father.

"You're in my seat," he says to River, who smirks and blinks once, then twice, noticing the collar and leash. He keels over, laughing. And I nibble on my bottom lip, so proud of myself that they love it just as much as I do. Hawke is fucking huge, so to see him walk around like it's an accessory is hilarious.

"Is this foreplay, or did you lose a bet?" River tries to ask diplomatically.

"Foreplay, I hope," Hawke replies, and I tug on the leash in warning. But it only seems to turn him on. I can tell by the way his eyes darken. Reading the tension, River stands. Then he leans in and whispers something to Hawke, whose gaze drops to mine before he takes the seat. He lifts me and pulls me into his lap, as if it's the most natural thing in the world.

"Enjoy your evening, kids. Don't get up to any mischief your mother wouldn't approve of," River teases, bringing a glass of amber liquid to his lips.

"Are you still sore from this morning?" Hawke asks, low enough he thinks no one can hear, but I know Billie does by the way she smirks and starts talking to Ford.

"No," I mischievously lie as I take a sip of my water.

"Good. Then you're coming home with me again."

"You're so sure of yourself, aren't you? I might have to make you work for it tonight because you've been a very bad boy," I playfully chide, slapping him twice across the cheek. I feel his cock twitch beneath me, and I laugh. I love how responsive he is to me. It makes me feel like the most desirable woman in the world. I've always had confidence, but having this man's undying attention fills me to new heights.

I try to partake in Billie and Ford's conversations, but my focus is on Hawke's hand that slides around my waist. I'm aware some people might be watching us, but that's their fucking problem. I love how clear Hawke makes it that he wants me, that he's mine as much as I am his. If people don't like it, they should divert their gazes before I threaten to do it for them.

He leans in and whispers into my ear, "I can take you here, in the bathroom."

"No." His hands tighten around me. I look over my shoulder, our lips close as I smirk. "Patience is a virtue, *lover*."

He kisses me, his callused hand cupping my jaw.

It's not until Ford clears his throat that we realize we're still in a room full of people, and if I stand, everyone is going to see how very hard Hawke is. But Hawke doesn't look at them or anyone else as he says, "You know patience is not my strong suit."

"But all dogs can learn new tricks," I say, tugging on his leash and kissing the tip of his nose before turning back to Billie with a grin. I can feel his smile on my back, and then he nuzzles into my neck, pressing kisses along my skin. *Fuck*. Patience isn't one of my strengths either.

CHAPTER 46

Hawke

"Will you stop fucking moving?" Ford grumbles as he adds another tattoo to my chest.

"What? I'm not moving; you just suck today." I curse him in his own tattoo room.

He punches me in the stomach hard, and I roll my eyes and put my hands behind my head as I let him get back to work. I've always loved letting him tattoo me, but I'm not a patient fucker, and I can't sit for long periods of time, which only annoys my brother. Lucky, the son of a bitch loves me.

"Mother asked me about you and Ivy last night," Ford says as he dabs more ink.

"Did she?" I reply with a shit-eating grin. I'm glad my mother has become so interested in the woman who was so perfectly carved for me. My mother has always had good taste.

"Yes. She wanted to know if it's serious between you two."

"It's a thing," I tell him, waggling my brows.

"Fucking hell, you annoy me."

"Love you too." I blow him a kiss.

"Do you love her?" he asks, glancing up at me as he pauses the tattoo.

"Yep," I say without a doubt.

His brow furrows as if he's surprised to hear me say that. I suppose I've never said that about a woman before. No one was like her.

"How do you even know that? Are you sure?"

"Oh yes, I'm sure." I nod my head.

"How?" he asks, running his gaze over the design he's inking onto me. "You've never been in a relationship, let alone been curious about monogamy."

I only think about that for a few seconds because I know my truth. It's not rocket science to figure out how I feel about her. "I think I've always loved her in some way, but now that I have her, I know I'll never let her go. She's it for me. I look at other women now, and it does nothing for me. I just want to see her. I wake up, and I want to see her. I go to sleep, and I want to hold her. And I get this weird feeling in my chest and stomach when she's near, like I have to touch her. I can't contain myself."

"Hmmm," Ford hums as he concentrates on my tat.

"What? You think it's fascination?" I ask, twisting to see him, and he glares at me. *Fuck*. I go back into my original spot.

"No. I always thought you two might end up together. You both are just slow as fuck." He laughs then as he wipes excess ink and blood from my skin.

Ford always made comments when I was with a woman, saying it wouldn't last, and I never really questioned it or cared about it. Hell, I didn't want any of them to last. But now, when I think back, it's like he always knew who I was going to end up with. I guess to end up with the right person, you have to go through the trenches first. Though I'm not going to lie and say it wasn't fun. I always have fun, no matter what. The only time I'm not having a good time is when it involves Ivy getting hurt or upset with me.

I hate having her mad at me.

"Hello!" Ivy calls out as she enters Ford's house.

His eyebrows knit together, and I quickly explain, "I gave her a key and told her I'd be here."

"Jesus. You just letting all the strays in my house now. Billie could've let her in."

"In here!" I shout as Ford shakes his head and continues the finishing touches of my tattoo. I hear her heels click down the hallway. Then she opens the door and peeks in.

"I found a location on that guy, Dallas Rigger, your

biker friend told us about. He actually lives in Springfield and—" Her words cut off when she looks up, and it takes her a second to figure out what's happening. "What are you...? Oh, a tattoo?" She approaches and looks down at my chest. "Is that...?"

"Ivy," I say, glancing down at the plant he's tattooing on me.

"You're crazy, you know that, right?" She shakes her head and takes a seat across from us.

"Billie is in the shower. Continue telling us what you've got on this guy," Ford says, all business and it snaps me to attention as well.

"Right," she murmurs, unable to stop staring at the tattoo. I catch a small smile as she glances down at her phone. "I've sent the information to Eli as well. I dug up some interesting stuff about this guy. He's used to cleaning up after his messes; it's just too bad that flying under the radar doesn't work when he crossed me."

My chest puffs up proudly as she says that. This asshole might've never been caught, or not anytime soon, at least if he hadn't been unlucky enough to cross paths with my fierce goddess. She's the brains behind the operation, and I'll happily dole out the dirty punishments needed to bury them.

"I've narrowed it down to two locations where he most likely produces and filters his drugs, both in Springfield. He doesn't move around much himself. He sends his little minions like Lester and Jared out. When I looked further into it, I suspect he might be starting a sex ring, too.”

Ford and I look at one another. We're not good men, but we draw the line when it comes to women and children. These assholes are the worst kind. Ford and I both receive a text at the same time. We lift our phones in unison, and my smile curves as I'm guaranteed a blood bath tomorrow.

“Looks like we'll be dealing with it tomorrow, lover,” I inform her.

“Eli doesn't fuck around, does he?” she comments.

Ford continues with my tattoo, so I challenge Ivy, “Why don't you get one, lover?”

She rolls her eyes. “I am not getting matching tattoos with you.”

“Come on. When have you ever backed down from a challenge?” I antagonize her, and she bites her bottom lip, shaking her head. I know she can't resist it. I enjoy the subtle burn of the new tattoo of ivy all over my chest, gratified at the way she can't keep her gaze from roaming my bare chest and stomach.

“Fine,” she chirps, then asks Ford, “Do you have time for me?”

“You two are fucking crazy,” he grumbles. “Where do you want it?”

She looks over her body thoughtfully, then lowers her pants slightly to expose her hip, and I'm out of my seat in a shot, blocking Ford's view.

"Hey! You're lucky you didn't fuck up that line, asshole," Ford curses at the same time she says, "Maybe on my hip?"

"No," I immediately tell her removing her hand and pulling her pants back into place so he can't see any more skin. "Nothing below the waist or near the tits." I glare at my brother. "I don't want you looking at my woman."

Ivy laughs, then shoves me back toward the chair. "You have a screw loose, you know that?"

"It's why you love me." I wink as I sit back down. I can tell when her body locks up, and she shifts uncomfortably. Ah, the big L word. Whatever. I don't care. I'll wait. I've waited this long already.

Ford rolls his eyes as he continues tattooing my chest. "He loves you, just so you're aware."

"Hey!" I shout, slapping him because it clearly makes my woman uncomfortable.

"I know," Ivy quietly says, and I whip my gaze over to her, surprised.

"You do?"

"I do. You say it to me every night when you think I'm sleeping," she says matter-of-factly. *Shit.* I've been saying that for almost a month now. I thought she had no fucking idea, but I couldn't keep it to myself.

"Okay, that's good and all, but, woman, you gotta tell me you love me too. We're a thing after all," I tell her. This woman really knows how to bust my balls.

Ford groans at my words, and I swear he pushes the

needle even deeper into my skin as if irritated by our passionate love. *Jealous much?* I think while I smirk at him. And I'm certain he knows. We've always understood one another in ways we can't entirely explain.

"Just tell him and put us all out of our misery," Ford grouses, focusing on the tattoo. "We're broken, we need words. It's why he always uses his," he explains, and it feels nice being acknowledged by him. Everyone gives me so much shit for having such a big mouth, but at least they know where they stand with me. He, Eli, and Dutton are all ice cubes who like to play "Guess what mood I'm in." Even if they are in a good mood, they look like they've just bitten into a sour lemon.

"I'm falling for you. Does that count?" Ivy says, tucking a piece of her hair behind her ear, and I swear my fucking heart stops. I don't know what could make her any more perfect.

"Damn right, it does. I knew you couldn't resist my good looks and charm. I'm a catch." I wink at her.

"Damn, now his ego is going to be bigger than his fucking house," Ford says, wiping at the tattoo and checking his handiwork.

"Too late," I grumble as he pulls away, finally finished.

"I'm checking up on Billie. I have no interest in watching you two fuck or listening to your fucked-up words. You have ten minutes before I start on your tattoo, Ivy, so think about what you want. And don't break my shit," Ford says.

"So, seems like I have your family's approval?" she asks when he leaves, and I inwardly die as I realize she's not going to attend to Hawke Junior's needs. I guess so easily telling her that I love her might be shocking for her if she's not on the same page. Even though I know she is. But I'm happy to wait.

"Why wouldn't you?" I ask as I pull her to me.

"We haven't told my parents yet," she says quietly, and I know how close she is to her family and how much they mean to her. The obstacle is her father. That asshole has been cock blocking me from his daughter for years. And we both know that by now, they're most likely aware of our relationship. Getting Will Walker's approval is going to be difficult, but I've made it my life's mission to have him call me son. It's going to fucking happen.

"Then we'll organize a meal with them after tomorrow," I state, sensing the tension bundled in her.

She slides her fingernails over my chest, careful when she gets to the new tattoo, and I see her lips twitch with the start of a smile before she lifts her head and admits, "I like it."

"Good. I like you."

"My mother likes you."

"That, I already knew," I reply smugly.

"*I* like you," she says.

"Yeah? Well, how about I show you how much I like you?"

"Hawke, be serious for a moment," she chides, her blue eyes pinned to mine. "Thinking about tomorrow is scary for me. Do you guys just go in, kick down doors, and kill them? Is there something I can do to help?"

I press a kiss to her lips to silence her worrying thoughts. I curl her fingers above my heart, right where the new tattoo is. "Kicking down doors is fun. But killing is my favorite part. But you don't ever have to worry about me not coming back to you."

"You can't promise that," she says quietly. It's strange to see this powerful woman lose her confidence, and I realize it's up to me to fill her with that reassurance.

"I can promise you that I love you. And you don't have to say it back right now. I've waited long enough for you; I can wait more. But what I can tell you is that no one's kicked my ass yet. Except Ford on the odd occasion when I felt bad for him. But I will come back to you. This is a part of me you'll have to accept. My spiked gloves, and I can literally take on the world. It might be drenched in blood afterward, but that's who I am. But if that's not what you want..." I think about what I might have to change about myself to appease her. For her to understand this part of me.

Her hand cups my jaw. "I don't want you to change, Hawke. I know you enjoy killing. Just be safe. Please. And don't leave me waiting for long."

I kiss the inside of her wrist. A silent promise. "Move in with me?"

She chuckles, shaking her head. "You are such an opportunist."

I squeeze her hand and kiss her lips. "I'm very persistent as well," I growl. "And stop avoiding the question."

"Ask me when you come back in one piece. Every scratch, bruise, or wound on you equals one day without sex."

I stare at her in disbelief. "What? You can't be serious."

"Deadly serious." She nods.

I'm so fucked. I always come back battered and bruised, but that's because I live for the thrill. But I also love sex. With her. *Fuck*.

She's laughing at my inner turmoil, and I dive in to tickle her, the only form of attack I can torture this woman with. Ivy kicks and screams, trying to wriggle out of my grip.

Who would've thought that I, playboy of the year, would settle down with the hottie of the year? I guess it was always meant to be. Luckily for her, she likes my sense of humor. But I think she likes what's between my legs even more, and I can't say I blame her. I have a very beautiful cock. That likes to do very beautiful things to her very beautiful pussy. And I'm always starving, parched, and needing my fill of her.

I don't give a fuck what my brother says.

Ten minutes, my ass. I won't be timed making love to my woman.

Even when I always feel like we don't have enough time.

The thought of kidnapping her and never letting her escape comes to mind.

I'd never be able to clip her wings, though. I can only bask in what she's willing to give me.

CHAPTER 47

Ivy

The inside of my bicep itches from the tattoo I got yesterday. I decided on a pair of spiked gloves, and I swear Hawke almost cried, complaining about some dust in his eyes.

Telling him that I love him scares me. Hawke so easily wears his heart on his sleeve, but I feel like there should be some kind of resistance or a timeline for relationships. But as I look at the women sitting in my apartment—all of them in the same boat as me—as our men are out taking care of business, I realize none of their timelines are the same.

I've never been in a relationship, but I can't fault any of what Hawke says. When he says he loves me, he means it. I've felt it in his words since he started saying it to me in the dead of night.

But it feels like it's the final thing to keep me from

356

going all in because I know the moment I say it to him, I'll fall so deeply I won't be able to turn back. Maybe I already have. No, I know I have. If not, I wouldn't have gotten the tattoo of his gloves on my arm to go along with the ivy on his chest.

I wanted the gloves specifically to represent my acceptance of that part of him. I never want to change him. I know beneath the larger-than-life energy is an unquenchable hunger for violence. But also amongst that is something so sweet that I'm privileged to cherish.

Hope is enjoying a cup of tea at my kitchen counter. Billie stopped pacing back and forth a few moments ago and is now sitting down with popcorn as she flicks through the channels. It must be hardest on her since she almost lost Ford once already. Although I heard Hope's dad shot Braxton in the chest, so that could be scary, too, I suppose. But Hope is as calm as they come. Posie stayed home to look after her son, Bentley. And Jewel, being the badass she is, went with Eli, Dutton, Ford, Braxton, and Hawke to Springfield.

We've been talking about things idly since they left, but the nerves are obviously starting to filter through the room. But I don't want to normalize not being able to talk about these things. I want us to support one another, no matter what, and since we all seem to have screws loose loving men who are all killers, we might as well have the discussion.

"I'm surprised they asked Braxton to join," I say to

Hope, and Billie whips her head toward Hope expectantly.

"Oh no, they didn't. I told him to go because it would be a good bonding experience for them," she replies matter-of-factly. "I'm not worried about him coming back. He knows the only one who can kill him is me, so he'll return."

Billie chuckles. "I still have to get used to you saying things like that."

"The last thing I said to Hawke was to kick their ass, but it doesn't mean I can't worry," I admit. "But I know he'll return. It just feels different now. I can't remember how many times I saw my father walk out and return with blood all over him. My mother always seemed so calm about it, but I think deep down maybe she was worried."

"It's only natural to have those thoughts, isn't it?" Billie says, and I'd wanted to start this conversation primarily for her. Because I know this hits her the hardest. "I told Ford to come back home in one piece, and he said with a deadpan expression"—her face changes and she tries to mimic her boyfriend—"'Why wouldn't I? I just want to come back home to Netflix and chill with you as soon as possible.'" She laughs at herself. And I must admit it's a good impression. "But I trust him."

I sigh thoughtfully. Despite it all, these last few months of uncovering the secrets behind this operation have been exciting. I wonder if maybe I was cut out for this—finding locations of those who are hurting and abusing women. With a boyfriend who's practically carved out of stone, I can't help but think of what a good team we make. It might've started as personal, but this is making me realize there are so many things I can do with my skills besides just making money.

I can help women. I don't need the credit for it; if anything, I prefer to work in the background. It's an idea I've been playing around with lately, but I'm certain all this happened to point me in a new direction.

"How's Posie doing?" I ask Billie. She was at her house before she came over here.

"She's fine. Apparently, Dutton said he'd make sure he's back home at a reasonable time so he can read *Star Wars* to Bentley. He's really into *Star Wars* now."

My nose scrunches up. "I don't recall Dutton ever being into *Star Wars*."

"He wasn't," Billie says with a smile. "He'd literally do anything for that kid."

I'm smiling as I go to the kitchen to make a coffee.

Who would've thought we'd all be in relationships at this point in our lives?

I pull out my phone to check the trackers I put on Hawke. I've placed several on him, including his boots, car, jacket, and even his gym bag. I haven't checked my phone for two hours, knowing I'd be going crazy if I kept checking it. Besides, I know deep in my heart my man is going to return covered in blood with a grin on his face.

The door bursts open, and I almost drop the mug I'm holding because I'm so startled.

As if materializing from my thoughts, Hawke is standing there with a big-ass smile. *He's okay.* I scan my gaze over his chest, quickly counting the cuts and flesh wounds, but he scoops me up in a hug and spins me.

He's still on a high from the kill, and his hard cock pressing against my stomach expresses that this asshole only has one outlet.

"I said no sex for the number of days equal to the cuts and bruises—"

He grabs the back of my neck, pulling me in for a kiss, devouring my mouth. I don't even notice what state Braxton and Ford are in as they walk in because Hawke has already lifted me up by the ass, wrapped my legs around his waist, and is carrying me into the bedroom.

"I told you I'd come back at a good time like a good boy," he says, biting my lower lip and tugging. It pulls at my core, my pussy immediately pounding as he slams the bathroom door behind us.

My last thread of control snaps, and I run my hands through his hair as he begins undressing us both through broken kisses. "Fuck, I had so much fun today." His energy is buzzing as he walks us over to the shower and turns it on. He kisses me again. There's still blood on his ear, and I think he must've tried to clean his face before coming up to my apartment.

"There were big explosions, and I killed eleven guys,

and..." He kisses me again, but it shifts as I direct it into something softer. I'm just grateful he's back in one piece. That he came back home as promised. Someone like Hawke needs a reward system to ensure he's not reckless, not that I think I can or want to ever change that about him. But I want him to always come back like this, and the way we've been able to best communicate is through touch.

He follows my lead as he lifts me and hovers me over his cock. He leans back to scan my eyes. "Did you miss me, lover?" he purrs with a cocky grin.

I line his cock up with my greedy, wet pussy, needing to remind him of what home feels like, as I say, "You took your fucking time."

He chuckles as he slams me down onto his cock and begins thrusting into me against the tiled wall as hot water runs between us, rinsing away his adventures of the day. I never thought I'd love this man so irrevocably, but the truth is, it's hard not to.

He continues pounding into me, dispersing all of that jittery, excitable energy he walked in with. I let him use my body, abusing me so he can expel his carnal urges. He sucks, bites, and curses as he jerks into me, filling me with his cum. I sigh, relieved, the moment I feel it hitting inside of me. My own body crumbles as I break into pieces, my pussy squeezing around his cock and milking him for every last drop.

Home.

Hawke.

Peace.

Our breaths are shaky as he continues to lazily kiss me like we have all the time in the world. I cup his jaw as I look up at him, realizing I'm a sucker for him.

"I love you too, Hawke," I tell him, and he breaks out in a shit-eating grin as he spins me, almost slipping on the wet tiles as if forgetting where we are.

Images of him being in this very shower, slipping in oil, come to mind, and I throw my head back laughing. I'll never not love this man because he's entertaining, at the very least.

"You better not be thinking about the oil incident," he growls as he places me gently on my tippy-toes and I wrap my arms around his neck, looking up at him sweetly. It's answer enough, and he rolls his eyes, trying to hide his smirk.

He leans down to press a kiss on my lips and he says, "It took you long enough, lover. I love you, too. More than you'll ever know."

CHAPTER 48

Ivy

"You're dating who?" my father demands the next day as he storms into my apartment, acting as if he's been betrayed. The object of his anger is currently asleep in my bed, but I don't think my father is ready to hear that news.

"Who told you?" I ask, letting out a huff as my mother comes in and presses a kiss to my cheek. My father is acting like a diva, throwing his hands up in the air.

"Word gets around, Ivy. You kids suck at keeping secrets. Especially when you're sitting on that ape of a man's lap every chance you get." I roll my eyes, and my mother seems to find it amusing. "So, were you planning on telling me?" he asks as my mother places down the plate of food she brought in. I can see bacon, pancakes, and bread, and there are more than likely other options as well. My parents often drop by with food when they're in town. It's finally registered that almost everyone around me has been supplying me with food. Even Hawke's gotten into the habit. I don't notice it myself in the moment, but when I get hyper - ixated on something, I lose my appetite and sense of time.

Not that I don't eat; I love to eat.

"I was planning on telling you when I saw you next," I tell him, helping my mother with the food. The corner of her mouth turns up when she notices I grab four plates instead of three.

"So, what are you?" he demands.

"A thing," I say cryptically, just to mess with him. I chuckle, as the term has the same effect on him as it did when Hawke kept saying it to Ford.

My father licks his lips and runs his hands through his hair as if in panic. I get he never liked Hawke, but this is dramatic even for him. But I guess there's something in it when they say Daddy's little girl.

"Okay. Is it serious?" he asks at the same time Hawke walks out of my bedroom without a shirt on, his chest on full display, including all the cuts and bruises from yesterday.

"It's serious," Hawke says with a smirk, and my father swings around to face him, gobsmacked that the devil should appear when summoned. I'm just thankful he has pants on.

My mother goes to Hawke, and he pulls her in for a hug before she says, "I brought food. It's on the table."

"Alina, we are having a serious discussion here. Don't distract the man with food," Dad says, self-imploding, but we all work around him, ignoring his dramatics.

My mother can't hide her smile, and I almost feel bad for my father as we all take a seat, trying not to snort and laugh at his reaction.

"Okay, let's eat," Mom announces, and Hawke wastes no time loading his plate full of food. I'm certain my mother brought over extra today because she's well aware of how much he likes to eat. I'm not surprised that she assumed he'd be here. My father might be the tracker, but my mother has always had this... sense of knowing that I've never quite understood. It's probably what my father gravitates toward because she's the only one who can keep him in check.

My father grumbles his displeasure as he takes a seat at the table, piercing a piece of bacon as he glares at Hawke, who comfortably threads his fingers through mine and places our joined hands on the table as if to make a point. A vein in my father's temple pulses as he glares at our hands, and I know Hawke is purposely grating on his nerves. They've always been like this. Maybe it was my father's intuition that I'd always end up with Hawke.

"So it's serious, then. Has he also moved in?" Dad asks as Hawke puts a piece of bacon into his mouth.

"No, of course not. He just stayed the night," I say, trying ever so slightly to bring my father back from the imaginary ledge.

"I did ask you again last night to move in with me, though," Hawke reminds me casually. My father's eyes widen, and my mother '*oobs*' at his words.

"I said no," I tell my father. I don't want him to have a heart attack.

"It's okay. I'll keep working on her." Hawke stuffs his face with some bread and smiles. "She knows I'm the one for her, and I'm not letting her go."

"Do I?" I ask, raising a brow at his cocky arrogance.

"It's love, what can I say?" He chuckles, and I shake my head as I look away, trying to remind myself that my parents are in the room.

"I'm happy for you both," Mom finally says as she grabs my father's hand and squeezes it. "We both are."

"Like fuck I am," Dad mumbles sulkily.

Mom shakes her head, whispering, "He'll come around."

I'm not entirely sure if that's true. But one thing I'm willing to bet on is if anyone is capable of wearing down my father, it's Hawke.

CHAPTER 49

Hawke

I'm holding Ivy in my lap as we look out at the rain pouring down. I've never once used my back patio, and it wasn't until she moved in a month ago that we made it a regular thing. When I'm not at work, and she's not in what I like to call her "death dungeon," which is basically the dark little room with an ungodly number of snacks where she works on her free-lancing gigs, this is where you can find us.

I couldn't be prouder of my woman. She works fucking hard, and I wonder how many people might've been thrown off by her party-girl persona. She still enjoys partying, but without drinking now. I've followed suit because I don't need the buzz or thrill, not while I have her by my side. And I have no intention of letting her go.

I press a kiss to her temple. Those short little shorts she's got on killing me. I swear she has a matching set in every color, and she uses them to keep me in a continuous state of needing to fuck her. And I just fucked her thirty minutes ago.

"What?" Ivy asks, looking at me skeptically. I don't know how I'm looking at her right now, but it's probably like I'm a big, smitten asshole.

I raise my gaze back to the rain, having a new appreciation for it. I never cared for this kind of shit before. When I was a kid and it rained, it was bad because Ford and I had to find shelter for the night. But with Ivy, it's a beautiful thing.

"I was just thinking about how nice it is that you've moved in without me having to throw you over my shoulder, kicking and screaming."

She scoffs. "Well, living in a five-bedroom home by yourself is a little excessive. And I can go back to my apartment any time I want, so don't give me a good enough reason to leave."

I chuckle as I tickle her ribs, and she flails back and forth. I receive an elbow to the nose, which, to be fair, I should've been expecting. I laugh, swearing I taste blood.

"I warned you," she growls, grabbing a tissue to hold to my nose. I do it to her all the time now, and I haven't admitted that I'm fucking into it. I like it when she fights me and puts me in my place. I most definitely have some screws loose, but for this woman, I'm completely okay with that.

I'm looking past my nose as she holds the tissue to it.

"You're going to be a good mom," I say with a nasal voice, and her body locks up on me.

"You really believe that?" she asks quietly.

I remove the tissue so I can look her dead in the eyes.

"Are you kidding me? The best! You're so cool! Our kids will be so lucky to have you as their mom and me as their awesome-as-fuck dad."

She chuckles at that. "You think you're awesome-as-fuck, do you?"

I'm affronted. "Obviously."

Ivy angles herself so she can keep dabbing at the blood. Her blue eyes flick to mine and then back to my nose.

I know when she's struggling to say something, so I squeeze her ribs and coax, "Out with it."

"Stop! Unless you really want it broken," she chides, trying to treat my nose again. I know it isn't as bad as she's making it out to be, which means she's just avoiding voicing whatever is on her mind. "Would you really be okay if we had children together?" she asks nervously, and my heart stops.

"Are you crazy, Ivy Walker? It'd be my honor to trap you and make you my wife. We have five bedrooms here. We can have a bucketload of kids. If we need a bigger house, we can get a bigger house. Or we can build an addition to this one. Or maybe we can have twins and give them bunk beds and—"

She squeezes my nose to shut me up. "God, you're

something, aren't you?" She shakes her head, wrapping her arms around my neck and staring at me lovingly. She dips her lips to mine and kisses me softly. "That's nice to hear. Because I have a secret for you, but you can't tell anyone."

I lean back so I can look into her eyes. And I see it then–the twinkle of mischief. Before, she was wary, but now she's... she's...

I glance down at her stomach, and my hand goes straight to it. "Pregnant?"

She bites her bottom lip, and I jump out of my seat, bringing her with me. I jump up and down, screaming as she wraps her legs around me, laughing.

"Are you fucking kidding me, Ivy Walker?" I cup her cheek, unable to contain my excitement. "Are you fucking serious? Are you going to be a mom?! Am I going to be a *dad*?" My voice wobbles on the last word, and she brushes back my hair. I follow the sweet, endearing touch as she strokes me as if petting me.

"The best and awesomest dad on the block," she says as tears prick her eyes. "I've only known for a few days. I didn't know how to tell you. I'm sorry."

I pepper kisses all over her face. This beautiful fucking woman. All mine. Every bit of her. I'll give her everything, knowing that she chose me. This beautiful goddess of a woman who can literally bring any man to their knees, and she's chosen me.

"Promise me you won't tell anyone yet," she says, holding her pinkie up.

I groan as I throw back my head. "That's torture, lover." But when I look at her again, she's smiling.

"Trust me, it'll be worth it."

I wrap my thick pinkie around her delicate one because no matter what, it always feels like it's us against the world —mischievously getting up to no good.

"Then I guess this is a good time to bring this out," I say, setting her back on the chair so I can drop to one knee. I fish out the ring from my back pocket, my heart falling for a moment when I think I've lost it. But it's still there, thank fuck.

Her hands go to her mouth.

I pull out the yellow diamond engagement ring, and tears begin to spill down her cheeks. My smile wavers as I can't help but notice that dust has somehow found its way into my eyes as well.

"Ivy Walker, will you do me the honor of first and foremost becoming my wife, then being the mother of my children?"

"How long have you been carrying that around?" she squeaks as she stares at the ring in disbelief.

"I've been carrying it around since the day I told you I loved you," I confess. I knew then that Ivy was definitely the one for me, and I wasn't going to let her slip through my fingers. Up until now, I'd just been waiting for the right moment. But every ordinary moment felt perfect, then I'd accidentally fuck her instead, and it began this fabulous cycle of not getting down on one knee. "You kind of haven't said yes," I nervously remind her.

She bursts out into laughter. "Yes, you big oaf," she says against my lips, and I feel the wave of relief pass through me as I take her breath as my own. Finally, she's mine.

Not that she ever had much of a choice in the matter.

Her hand is shaking as I slide the ring onto her finger. I can't stop kissing her. Can't stop breathing in her scent and that of the fresh rain that seeps through.

I never imagined this for myself, only offering myself brief daydreams of someone accepting me so completely. But I should've known from the start that Ivy was that woman. I had, but I wasn't ready to admit it then. Wasn't ready to be the man she needed. But I've since grown to meet her expectations.

A mischievous twinkle dances in her eyes as she says, "Why don't we have one more prank together?"

CHAPTER 50

Ivy

"Shotgun!" Hawke and I yell together as we gather with our family and friends in our backyard, where an officiant waits underneath a beautiful white arch. Seats with lovely bows tied to them are arranged on the lawn, and an excessive number of flowers are on display.

"Come here," Anya grits out as she tugs Hawke by the ear and then whispers not so quietly, "I don't care that you've done this, but you didn't think to tell me first so I could wear better jewelry on the day?"

"Let me have a word with him," my father is quick to say, and I cringe as Alek Ivanov places his hand on his chest to stop him. He simply shakes his head no. My father looks like he's going to cry.

"Wow, this is unexpected. But it's very you, I

suppose," Billie says, giving me a hug and congratulating me.

Ford is with River, the two of them trying to figure out what the fuck is happening. I catch Hawke's eyes, and he's grinning like a complete dick. I bite my bottom lip, silently congratulating us on our mischievous lie.

We'd told everyone we were having a barbeque, and everyone was expected to attend. What they weren't expecting was me to be wearing a wedding dress and Hawke wearing a suit. Which, might I add, he looks ridiculously handsome in.

"I thought you were going to elope," Hope says, giving me a hug. I love my friends dearly, but the person I need to creep over to is my father, whose blue eyes are scanning the area, most likely for the closest weapon.

My mother tries to reassure him by patting him on the chest as she whispers to him. Neither of them has noticed I'm behind them, and I catch their conversation.

"He didn't even ask for my permission," Dad growls in complaint.

"You gave him your permission when you bet a sixteen-year-old he couldn't steal your daughter's heart," Mom reminds him.

My heart falters. Did I hear that right?

"Little shit," Dad grumbles as he spots me.

"What did you just say?" I ask quietly. My mother turns to me and pulls me in for a hug. At that moment, Hawke stops at my side, and I look at him.

"Did you two have a bet about me?" I ask, unsure how I should feel about it or what it was even for.

My father curses as he looks at the sky, the muscle in his neck bulging.

"Fuck yeah, we did. And he lost," Hawke says proudly.

"Okay, I didn't so much as lose…" Dad begins.

"Outright lost. I told you I'd marry your daughter one day. Welcome to the wedding, Pops," Hawke says, bringing him in for a bear hug that he's clearly not excited about. My eyebrows pinch together, and my mother shakes her head.

Hawke then turns to me, grabbing my hands with a shit-eating grin. "The first time I saw you, we were at Uncle Alek's house. I was only sixteen then. I didn't know who Will was, but when you walked in, I knew immediately you were the girl I was going to marry."

"Little shit had the nerve to say it right beside me. Couldn't even keep it to himself," Dad adds, recalling events. "I told him a girl like you would be too good for him."

"So I said, 'Wanna make a bet?'" Hawke smirks.

My father is shaking his head.

"This is why you never liked Hawke," I say, finally getting it, and then look at my mother, who is smirking. "And you always loved him."

"I always had a feeling about you two," she says smugly. "But I wanted you to have some fun before you settled down, of course. Nobody wants to settle for the same old dick unless it's exceptional."

My father clears his throat and shoots her a pointed look as he says, "Way to kick a man while he's already down." She just laughs.

"Wait. So what do you lose?" I ask my father, and he turns a shade paler as he glares at Hawke again, who can't wipe the smirk off his face. It's so strange to see my father back out of any kind of bet.

"Go on," Hawke encourages, which seems to only piss my father off.

"Have I mentioned how much of an asshole this guy is?" Dad says to my mother, pointing a finger at Hawke.

She smirks. "Takes one to know one, dear. Now, tell her. You made the bet."

He sighs and looks me dead in the eyes as he says, "I have to streak at your wedding in front of everyone, and at least one photo must be taken as evidence."

I snort and glance at Hawke, who seems impressed by himself. I throw my head back and laugh, folding into Hawke's chest as I try to keep my makeup from running with the tears of amusement welling in my eyes.

"I thought it was good too," Hawke says, laughing.

And even with all the people here who we love, it still just feels like us. I don't feel an ounce of ill will at this bet. In fact, it reassures me that from the very start, Hawke had always noticed me. Even amidst all the games and taunting, we were always going to end up right here. It's also hilarious because I can just imagine my smug father being challenged by a cocky sixteen-year-old Hawke.

"Wait. If it's a shotgun wedding, isn't that supposed to mean Ivy's pregnant?" Ford asks, and everyone falls silent. It's like the other shoe has finally dropped, and the energy in the crowd shifts.

"Yep!" Hawke says proudly, lifting me into his arms to parade me around.

"We're having a baby!" I yell out excitedly, and my father drops to his knees, staring at the ground. My mother laughs as she drops to his side, most likely whispering encouraging words.

"You can't be upset. Remember, we weren't expecting Ivy either," I hear her say.

But I know he can't hear anything right now. We might actually give my father a stroke today.

I notice Alek still standing beside him, looking down at him. When he raises his head, there's a slight smirk on his lips. His wife, Lena, nudges him as she pulls Hope in for a hug.

"Are you kidding me?!" Eli growls. Hawke shifts to turn and face the lake where the sun is setting. Eli is holding Jewel by the waist. "I've been trying to impregnate my wife for over a year now."

"Yeah, well, we're on birth control," Jewel says, tapping his shoulder.

"No, we're not because I've been tampering with it," he admits.

"You what?" she screeches, and when he looks at her, I'm certain she's going to destroy him when they get home. But the glint in his eyes indicates he's well aware and can't wait for his punishment.

Hawke turns us back around, and I look at all my family and friends, how they celebrate amongst one another, cheering us on, and it couldn't be any more perfect.

Hawke slides me down his body and places me gently on my feet. He grabs me by both sides of my face and kisses me, and I can't help but giggle as I wrap my arms around his waist, and he bends me backward.

"Come on, you two, you're meant to do that in front of the officiant," Posie says, shooing everyone into order. I can't help but continue staring into Hawke's eyes, knowing without a doubt I've found my partner in crime.

"Ready to take on the world together, lover?" he growls, and I can feel it all the way down my throat.

"As long as you promise to be on your best behavior," I reply, wiping the lipstick that's smudged on his lips.

He smirks. "Then wouldn't that be a mischievous lie?"

Also by T.L. Smith

Black (Black #1)

Red (Black #2)

White (Black #3)

Green (Black #4)

Kandiland

Pure Punishment (Standalone)

Antagonize Me (Standalone)

Degrade (Flawed #1)

Twisted (Flawed #2)

Distrust (Smirnov Bratva #1) FREE

Disbelief (Smirnov Bratva #2)

Defiance (Smirnov Bratva #3)

Dismissed (Smirnov Bratva #4)

Lovesick (Standalone)

Lotus (Standalone)

Savage Collision (A Savage Love Duet book 1)

Savage Reckoning (A Savage Love Duet book 2)

Buried in Lies

Distorted Love (Dark Intentions Duet 1)

Sinister Love (Dark Intentions Duet 2)

Cavalier (Crimson Elite #1)

Anguished (Crimson Elite #2)

Conceited (Crimson Elite #3)

Insolent (Crimson Elite #4)

Playette

Love Drunk

Hate Sober

Heartbreak Me (Duet #1)

Heartbreak You (Duet #2)

My Beautiful Poison

My Wicked Heart

My Cruel Lover

Chained Hands

Locked Hearts

Sinful Hands

Shackled Hearts

Reckless Hands

Arranged Hearts

Unlikely Queen

A Villain's Kiss

A Villain's Lies

Moments of Malevolence

Moments of Madness

Moments of Mayhem

When He Read To Me

Lethal Vows

Virtuous Vows

Cunning Vows

Deranged Vows

Misguided Vows

Connect with T.L Smith by tlsmithauthor.com

Also by Kia Carrington Russell

Insidious Obsession

Fractured Obsession

Mine for the Night, New York Nights Book 1

Us for the Night, New York Nights Book 2

Stranded for the Night, New York Nights Book 3

Token Huntress, Token Huntress Book 1

Token Vampire, Token Huntress Book 2

Token Wolf, Token Huntress Book 3

Token Phantom, Token Huntress Book 4

Token Darkness, Token Huntress Book 5

Token Kingdom, Token Huntress Book 6

The Shadow Minds Journal

Lethal Vows

Virtuous Vows

Cunning Vows

Deranged Vows

Misguided Vows

T.L. Smith

USA Today Best Selling Author T.L. Smith loves to write her characters with flaws so beautiful and dark you can't turn away. Her books have been translated into several languages. If you don't catch up with her in her home state of Queensland, Australia you can usually find her travelling the world, either sitting on a beach in Bali or exploring Alcatraz in San Francisco or walking the streets of New York.

Connect with me tlsmithauthor.com

Kia Carrington-Russell

Australian Author, Kia Carrington-Russell is known for her recognizable style of kick a$$ heroines, fast-paced action, enemies to lovers and romance that dances from light to dark in multiple genres including Fantasy, Dark and Contemporary Romance.

Obsessed with all things coffee, food and travel, Kia is always seeking out her next adventure internationally. Now back in her home country of Australia, she takes her Cavoodle, Sia along morning walks on beautiful coastline beaches, building worlds in the sea breezes and contemplating which deliciously haunting story to write next.